A CENTURY OF JAPANESE PHOTOGRAPHY

A CENTURY OF JAPANESE PHOTOGRAPHY

JAPAN PHOTOGRAPHERS ASSOCIATION

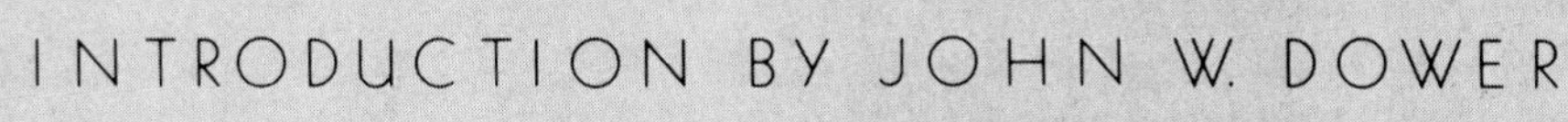

INTRODUCTION BY JOHN W. DOWER

PANTHEON BOOKS NEW YORK

First American Edition 1980

Published in the United States by Pantheon Books, a division of Random House, Inc., New York, and simultaneously in Canada by Random House of Canada Limited, Toronto. Originally published in Japan as *Nihon Shashin Shi, 1840–1945* by Heibonsha.

Library of Congress Cataloging in Publication Data
Main entry under title:
A century of Japanese photography.
Translation of Nihon shashin shi, 1840–1945.
Bibliography: p.
1. Photography—Japan—History. I. Nihon Shashinka Kyokai.
TR105.N5413 770'.952 80-7710
ISBN 0-394-51232-4

Manufactured in the United States of America

Typography and binding design by Elissa Ichiyasu

CONTENTS

EDITOR'S NOTE

■ *A Century of Japanese Photography* is based on the Japanese volume compiled by the Japan Photographers Association and published in 1971 by Heibonsha under the title *Nihon Shashin Shi, 1840–1945* [A History of Japanese Photography, 1840–1945]. The organization and layout of the photographs follow the Japanese edition exactly. Captions are adapted from the Japanese and presented here in two forms: briefly under the plates, and in fuller detail at the end of the book. The introduction is original, but draws upon the textual material in the Japanese edition.

Japanese names are rendered throughout in Japanese order: family name followed by given name. Dating requires special comment. It is impossible to date many of the earliest photographs precisely, and consequently they are now simply assigned to slices of time peculiar to Japanese history. The Bakumatsu period embraces the years 1853 to 1867, but refers primarily to the 1860s where photography is concerned. The Meiji period, coinciding with the reign of the Meiji emperor, extended from 1868 to 1912, and it is conventional to speak of early, middle, and late Meiji. Keeping in mind the fact that historical middles never really begin or end precisely, "early Meiji period" thus refers to roughly 1868–1882; "middle Meiji period" to 1883–1897; and "late Meiji period" to 1898–1912. Under the plates, the dates that coincide with this Japanese scheme have been used. In the list of captions at the end of the book, the Japanese era names are reproduced as they appear in the Japanese edition.

J.W.D.

A CENTURY OF JAPANESE PHOTOGRAPHY

WAYS OF SEEING ■ WAYS OF REMEMBERING

THE PHOTOGRAPHY OF PREWAR JAPAN

John W. Dower

■ The photographer both reflects and creates reality, invents a past while capturing a fragment of the present, and this of course is a potent but subtle contribution. It is certainly more ambiguous than what the earliest photographers thought they were up to, which is nicely suggested by the two ideographs used to denote "photograph" in Japanese: *shashin* 寫眞 literally means to copy truth, reproduce reality.

This rendering probably became established in the mid-1860s, some two decades after photography was introduced from the West. The traditional date of the first photograph taken in Japan was long held to be June 1, 1841, a scant two years after Louis Jacques Mandé Daguerre and William Henry Fox Talbot formally presented their parallel inventions in Paris and London respectively. Although the anecdote on which the 1841 date is based has been shown to be spurious, photography clearly did enter feudal Japan through Dutchmen in Nagasaki prior to Commodore Matthew Perry's exercises in gunboat diplomacy in 1853–1854. Japanese writings in the late 1840s render the daguerreotype (which Oliver Wendell Holmes called "the mirror with a memory") as "mirror that stamps images" or "mirror that stamps reflections" *(inshō-kagami; inkei-kagami),* and confirm that native scholars of "Dutch learning" were struggling to master the process at least as early as 1848, albeit with uncertain success. The earliest extant daguerreotypes in Japan date from 1854 and were taken by a member of the Perry expedition. There exists today but a single daguerreotype that can be attributed to a Japanese photographer, a portrait of the feudal lord Shimazu Nariakira that dates from 1857 and was only discovered in 1975. Japanese photography really began to flourish in the late 1850s, with the introduction of the "instantaneous" wet-plate collodion process (which was invented in England in 1851 and soon supplanted both the daguerreotype and the talbotype) and the appearance of Japan's first two professional photographers, Ueno Hikoma and Shimooka Renjō, each of whom proceeded to establish a studio in 1862.

Although the legacy of Japanese photography differs from that of the West in offering no treasure trove of early daguerreotypes and talbotypes, the timing of photography's introduction to Japan does have special resonance for students of the country. It preceded by over a decade the signal event in Japan's transition from feudal to capitalist society: the Meiji Restoration of 1868. The camera thus was present to capture the faces of a people under feudalism and the final moments of a warrior class that had ruled for seven centuries. It was a small product of Western genius that arrived early enough to record the subsequent massive onslaught of Western culture and technology. It was available from the start to bear witness to the traumatic course of the modern Japanese state: the swift innovations; the emergence of cosmopolitanism, industrialization, and bourgeois culture amidst persistent backwardness and exploitation; the succession of imperialist wars; the devastated landscape of 1945.

Among Westerners, the historians of photography have neglected Japan, and the historians of modern Japan have neglected photography and indeed much of the whole Japanese visual record, including paintings, posters, prints, and cartoons. As the selection in this volume reveals, the photographs taken by Japanese prior to 1945 are diverse and evocative. As a contribution to photography, they are impressive. As a witness to history, they are a compelling complement, supplement, and corrective to the orthodox written record on which most historians rely. They are also potentially deceptive witnesses that the general historian must use carefully.

This caution deserves brief explanation. The camera can convey what scribes ignore or are simply incapable of expressing: details, sensations, worlds outside the realm of words. It is the mirror with a memory of things that otherwise might have been neglected or remembered differently; but as a record of the past, it can also become a distorting mirror. Most obviously, what the camera remembers is what the photographer selects, and capable photographers usually find what they seek, whether it be order or disorder, sun or shadow, freaks or the family of man. More subtly, the photograph can confer a kind of arbitrary immortality upon those images and events that happen to be captured; and what is a compelling way of remembering can simultaneously operate as a way of forgetting, as later generations literally lose sight of what for one reason or another was not preserved, or not memorably preserved, on film. The frozen moment of the photograph in itself contradicts the essence of history, which is flow and interaction; and terrible violence can be done to the past as the camera turns poses into personalities, fragments into wholes, transience into permanence, minute splinters of time into eternities—or gives a romantic patina to what actually may have been experienced as routine, mundane, miserable, painful, heartbreaking. As Susan Sontag has observed so persuasively, the camera can not only beautify the commonplace but also trivialize the extraordinary. It can harden or inure one to brutality, to which modern Japan has contributed its full share. It can democratize perception in a manner that is illusory and perhaps even immoral—for all subjects are not equal, not equivalent.

This said, the photograph remains a powerful and penetrating way of seeing and remembering, and as the decades accumulate and prints proliferate, the historical-minded aficionado has greater and greater opportunity to exercise his or her own discretion and to use old photographs in new ways. One such opportunity lies in juxtaposition, and the photography of Japan prior to 1945 illustrates how this can operate on various levels. One can set photograph against photograph in a manner that graphically illustrates not merely change over time but also social contradictions and historical ironies: the clan portrait of young men in samurai garb and the team portrait of their descendants in baseball uniforms; the capitalists behind their neckties and workers behind their machines; the wholesome young ladies touting crackers, dry goods, or beer and their male contemporaries killing and burning abroad. One can juxtapose the generally austere black-and-white photographs of the nineteenth century and the brilliantly colored prints or "brocade pictures" *(nishiki-e)* that remained in vogue until the turn of the century. One can quite devastatingly place photographs alongside the conventional homilies and rhetoric of Imperial Japan: photos of strikes, riots, and demonstrations with captions describing the innate "harmony" of Japanese social relations; photos of miners or poor tenant farmers or slum dwellers with quotations praising the traditional "beautiful customs" of Japan; photos of aggression and atrocity abroad with captions about "coexistence and coprosperity." At the same time, many Westerners may find their own stereotypes of prewar Japan eroded by a photographic record that reveals women workers in the front ranks of the May Day parades, or surrealist influences in the period of mounting militarism.

■ The initial impact of photography in Japan was part of a larger Western impact upon both scientific and aesthetic ways of seeing, and the earliest photographic inquiries were expensive, particularly where they entailed importing basic materials. Among the first patrons of such investigations here as in other areas of Western studies were the daimyō, or feudal lords, of a few of the several hundred fiefs into which land was divided. Satsuma in the southern island of Kyūshū took the lead in this, and inquiries were also sponsored by the lords of Mito, Chikuzen, Fukui, Tendō, Matsumae, and Tosa. After the opening of the country in the 1850s, would-be Japanese photographers were assisted directly by a number of foreigners, with the intensified Western influence emanating most strongly from three points of contact: Nagasaki in Kyūshū, Yokohama in the Kantō region of the main island of Honshū, and Hakodate in the southwest corner of the northern island of Hokkaidō. Both Nagasaki and Yokohama had been opened to foreign trade and residence as designated "treaty ports" in 1858, while Hakodate was opened in 1854. The three great meccas of pioneer photography in Japan became Kyūshū (plates 25–47), the Kantō area (plates 77–122), and Hokkaidō (plates 48–76), and thus coincided loosely with the geographic accommodations conceded to the imperialists.

As a new style of perceptual and aesthetic "realism," photography reinforced the portrayal of shadow and perspective the Japanese discovered in Western paintings and engravings, and offered a fidelity to the subject depicted that was conspicuously lacking in such dominant native traditions of visual representation as the Yamato pictures *(Yamato-e),* ink paintings *(sumi-e),* or woodblock prints *(hanga)* and demimonde "pictures of the floating world" *(ukiyo-e).* Where human subjects were concerned, the faces recorded by the camera were vastly different from those depicted in the highly stylized conventions of Japanese portrait art. Yet there is a puzzle here, as well as a danger of exaggerating the contribution of photography to a more "realistic" way of perceiving and depicting the physical world. During their so-called "Christian century," beginning in the mid-1500s, the Japanese had already encountered Western ways of seeing, and with a few notable exceptions deliberately turned their back on them. The camera obscura had been introduced to China by the West in the seventeenth century, and to Japan by China in 1718. It was used by the woodblock artist Maruyama Ōkyo in the mid-eighteenth century, and later by the Western-style artist Shiba Kōkan. In the 1730s, Okumura Masanobu experimented with "perspective pictures" *(uki-e)* influenced by European art, while several decades later Maruyama Ōkyo enjoyed considerable popularity producing works in this vein known as "eyeglass pictures" *(megane-e)*. The Japanese aesthetic tradition, moreover, did include styles of great literal exactitude. From an early date, there was a powerful realistic strain in Buddhist sculpture, for example, while in the later feudal period there flourished a genre of colored depictions of flora and fauna that were detailed and accurate enough to serve as guides for the serious naturalist. Indeed, the new machines that copied reality had a linguistic and conceptual predecessor of sorts in the "pictures that copy life" *(shaseiga)*, a school of painting that entered Japan through Nagasaki from Ming and Ch'ing China. Photography thus did not teach the Japanese to render the external world less stylistically or impressionistically, but rather further encouraged them to do so.

Actually, the more interesting question may be: What if anything did traditional art contribute to early photography in Japan? In the West, it seems possible to detect the influence of engravings upon the composition of certain early photographs of landscapes or architecture (as well as the later reciprocal influence of photos on engravings); and the inspiration of the grand painterly tradition of the West is dramatically evident in photographs such as the famous series of talbotype portraits done by David Octavius Hill and Robert Adamson in the 1840s. In Japan, one might have expected the photographer's eye to be influenced by the dynamic sense of composition and line that distinguished woodblock prints—and even more, by the disciplined use of form and emptiness in the great tradition of *sumi-e*, or ink painting, which could indeed be regarded as a long and brilliant tutelage in the aesthetics of black and white. In practice, however, the earliest Japanese photographers appear to have been uninfluenced by these traditional ways of seeing. The photographs of nineteenth-century Japan have many strengths, but they are not distinguished by any distinctive sense of line and balance, any remarkable use of space. It was not until the vogue of "art photography" began around the turn of the century that Japanese photographers found inspiration in paintings, and even then such inspiration often came from contemporary Western painting rather than from traditional Japanese art.

At a less esoteric level, the subject matter of early photography did pick up certain themes already popularized in the native arts of the late feudal period. These included scenes of famous places, depictions of evocative women, portraits of actors, and impressions of artisans and the laboring classes. The presentation of these subjects, however, was greatly influenced not just by the technology of the camera but also by treaty-port tourism and the tastes of the Westerners. Although the foreigners' tastes were often aesthetically trite, their curiosity was buoyant and their pocketbooks were frequently full. This was a major factor behind the creation of the intimate pictorial record of mid-nineteenth-century Japan that exists today. Both as purchasers of photographs and as photographers themselves, Westerners showed an interest in subjects that Japanese photographers on their own would in all likelihood have ignored. Customs commonplace to the Japanese were exotic to the foreigners. Furthermore, the foreigners were interested in a fairly comprehensive photographic record of occupational types and lower-class persons who in other circumstances almost certainly would never have found themselves posed before the camera. Although craftsmen and commoners of every sort had been depicted in Japanese genre art ever since the illustrated scrolls of the twelfth century, in the mid-nineteenth century the costliness of photographic equipment and the relatively high sitting fees for portrait photography would have made the poor unlikely subjects indeed had there not been a Western market for their likenesses.

One result has been that some of the more interesting photographs of Japan and the Japanese dating from the 1850s through the Meiji period were taken by foreigners, or at least acquired by foreigners, and are now preserved outside Japan in the archives or rare books of the West.

They depict a broad spectrum of people in addition to the men, women, and children of the ruling samurai caste—prostitutes, rikisha pullers, palanquin bearers, artisans, shopkeepers, vendors, farmers, doctors with patients, priests, children in a temple school, orphans under a bridge—and the effectiveness of these photos derives partly from the very fact that although their subjects paused to pose, they left no names.

The full range of these materials is fare for a different sort of pictorial history of Japan, but their flavor emerges in some of the selections in this present volume. Japanese catered to the treaty-port clientele of foreign residents and visiting sailors both by taking their portraits (if desired, in Japanese garb or with a young Japanese woman) and by selling them pictorial Japanalia. This was an especially lively trade in the Yokohama-Tokyo hub of the Kantō area. When Shimooka Renjō opened a new two-story shop in Yokohama in 1868, it sported a huge sign in the shape of Mount Fuji, with the English word "Photographer" running up the left side and again down the right side of the sacred mountain. "Renjio's Branch House" (using the old-style Romanization of the name) wriggled under this, and a separate large sign declared "Pictures Up Stairs." Photographs prepared with foreign customers in mind occasionally bore captions in English, and some are simply conventional scenic postcards. Others are plain kitsch: a handsome Gilbert-and-Sullivan couple selling a child (they appear about to burst into song about their pretty baby in a basket); a warrior performing "Harakiri" in an appropriately tinted print, with red blood and green complexion (plate 114); "Eating Macaroni"; "Girls in Bed Room" (plate 116); "Home Bathing" (plate 113); and so on. This tourist-oriented tradition continued into the twentieth century, and was well exemplified by the prolific Ogawa Kazumasa (plates 110, 152; possibly also 114–116), who contributed illustrations to several score of books published in English during the Meiji period.

The early treaty-port photos of anonymous persons by usually anonymous photographers included numerous poses by nude or seminude women, many of whom were prostitutes or "teahouse maids" in Yokohama and Nagasaki. The crudest of these photographs, which are not included here, made minimal pretense to art. Poses were stiff, and although pubic hair was brushed out, the groin was frequently exposed and apparently never coyly covered. Again, foreigners appear to have been among the major customers for such items, and in this respect the early nudes can serve as slight reminders of the whorehouse dimension of the treaty ports and the sexual exploitation that commonly accompanies imperialism. At the same time, Japanese art itself boasted a tradition of graphic eroticism, ranging from the woodblock prints of prostitutes, maids, and low-ranking geisha in dishabille to the exuberant pornography of the "spring pictures" *(shunga)*. Bawdiness, pictorial titillation, and sexual exploitation did not need to be imported into Japan, and the depiction of nakedness was not taboo, although never a part of high art as in the West.

The early photographs of nudes or seminudes thus can be seen not only as another form of catering to treaty-port tastes but also as a rather predictable development: poor daughters of the erotic tradition in Japanese culture (and poor sisters to the *carte érotique* of the West). While certain of these compositions such as "Home Bathing" make some pretense to artistry and convey an air of naïveté, the overall impression left by this mild early erotica is that it does indeed "transcribe reality," but in a manner different from that intended and experienced at the time. Certainly the reality transcribed is worlds apart from the lubricous and often hilarious sensuality depicted in the *shunga* and other *ukiyo-e* from the pleasure quarters. Occasional photographs such as the unsmiling post-town prostitute applying cosmetics (plate 84) survive as unintentionally effective pieces of realism. In the cruder poses, the models are usually very young, often stiff and vacant-looking, sometimes physically unattractive. They are clearly sexual objects rather than participants. For some contemporary Japanese commentators, their stumpy bodies, slightly bent backs, and general facial features provoke images not of eroticism but of the wretchedly poor farm families in the Tōhoku region and other deprived parts of Japan from which many of the young women in the treaty ports and urban centers were recruited. Depiction of the nude in painting, sculpture, and photography was subjected to government restrictions beginning in the late 1890s, and in some instances even involved placing cloth "underskirts" over the portions of exhibited works deemed morally offensive by the authorities. Restraints were not eased until 1918, and serious nude photography did not appear in Japan until the 1920s.

In contrast to the early treaty-port nudes, there also emerged a more decorous and enduring genre of photographic pinups in the form of portraits of famous beauties. Here the continuity with the more dignified woodblock prints of famous geisha was notable. The Meiji beauties upon whom the camera doted were also mainly geisha; and in contrast to the pathetic and anonymous nudes, they were or quickly became celebrities. The face was virtually all that mattered, and the standard of beauty was usually a somewhat softer version of features that had been glorified by such masters of woodblock art as Harunobu, Utamaro, and Kunisada: oval face, white complexion, high-bridged nose, sensuous mouth, almond eyes, fairly strong eyebrows. Poise, intelligence, and taste emanated from these perfectly regular countenances, and although some of the geisha were photographed in fashionable Western dress, the majority wore kimono.

In the early 1870s, after the introduction of albumen paper made reproduction easier, photos of these beauties as well as other traditional woodblock subjects such as actors and famous places were pasted on thick paper and sold in special shops, in the manner of woodblock prints. By the time of the Russo-Japanese War (1904–1905), when printing processes were more sophisticated, standardized postcards of beauties had become available throughout the country and were often carried to the front by enlisted men, who in official propaganda were concentrating on the emperor. Subsequently, stage and screen actresses merged with these geisha idols, and more "exotic" (that is, Westernized) ideals of beauty, albeit still primarily beauty of countenance, saturated the country in the form of pinup cards known as "bromides" *(buromaido)*. In the realm of highly idealized feminine beauty, it has been said, the Japanese were not "liberated from the face" until after 1945.

Alongside kitsch, souvenir photography, and the general pandering to foreign and popular tastes that characterized much early work, especially in the Kantō area, the pioneers of Japanese photography also moved in more sober directions. One such direction, a mainstream in Japan as elsewhere, was portrait photography. Initially, again as elsewhere, various superstitions arose concerning the occult powers of the camera. "Once photographed, your shadow will fade; twice photographed, your life will shorten," went one. Another held that if three persons were photographed together, the one in the middle would die early. Like comparable fears concerning the telegraph and other Western technologies, these fears were soon dispelled, and Japanese who could scrape up the fee began to flock to photographers' studios. Foremost among them were the samurai, for as Shimooka Renjō recalled, "The warriors of various fiefs, being resolved to fight and prepared to die, asked to be photographed as a memento." Indeed, instead of losing one's shadow, one could now hope to leave it to posterity.

Thus, from before the overthrow of the *ancien régime* in 1868 until the last futile agony of samurai resistance in 1877, the warriors sat for the camera. They posed singly or with their comrades, retainers, families, women of pleasure. They sat with pistols as well as the traditional two swords, in lounging postures as well as stiffly, sometimes looking straight at the lens and sometimes to the side. They left images of status, pride, and also unpredictable explosiveness, particularly the portraits of the younger men—effective "mementos" of the youthful, determined, radical, but ambiguous nature of the personal forces behind Japan's transition to "modernity." The photographic record from before the overthrow of the old feudal regime in 1868 includes portraits of several of the more famous "men of spirit" *(shishi)* who were cut down before their plots succeeded, as well as portraits of other conspirators who survived to don frock coats and be rephotographed as pillars of the new establishment. It is these later images as doyens of the status quo by which the latter figures chose to be, and commonly are, remembered.

The acknowledged master of portrait photography in mid-nineteenth-century Japan was Ueno Hikoma (plates 25, 26, 28, 29, 31–47), who was only twenty-five in 1862 when he opened his first studio in Nagasaki. Prior to 1868, his subjects included many of the activists associated with the Restoration cause, both the well known and the unheralded, as well as a gamut of non-samurai and non-Japanese denizens of the treaty ports. The sharp lighting and bare settings of the unretouched portraits by Ueno and his contemporaries, which place them so obviously before the advent of artistic and soft-focus influences, probably have a special appeal to the sated eyes of today: their very lack of sentimentality and finesse seems a closer approximation to the "truth" of lives and years that were hard.

Despite these promising beginnings—and despite the elite tradition of portrait painting, the inclination toward personalized history, the near mania for compiling "definitive" collections in Japan, and the overweening egos of most of Meiji Japan's leaders—Japanese photographers somewhat surprisingly did not proceed to produce a systematic and coherent gallery of their eminent countrymen. The sheer volume of individual, family, and group portraits that has accumulated in Japan since the time of Ueno and Shimooka is probably as great as or greater than anywhere else in the world, but there is no counterpart to Mathew Brady's *The Gallery of Illustrious Americans* (1850) or the multivolume French *Galerie contemporaine* (1876–1884). Among photographers, there were no personal counterparts to such nineteenth-century masters of portraiture as the Frenchman Nadar (Gaspard Félix Tournachon), the Englishwoman Julia Margaret Cameron, or the Scotsmen Hill and Adamson.

From a broader perspective, it can be argued that documentary photography in general developed slowly in Japan. Ueno Hikoma did not restrict his activities to the studio, and some of his outside work was distinguished. His panorama of the harbor at Nagasaki nicely captures the physical landscape of the treaty ports (plate 25), while his famous shot of a white man being pulled in a jinrikisha followed by an endless procession of ox-borne luggage can be read as an effective evocation of the psychological landscape of the ports (plate 26). He turned his camera upon subjects like the huge, ugly Takashima coal mine that had been gouged out of the hills near Nagasaki, and he contributed perhaps the most famous war photograph of mid-nineteenth-century Japan: the scene of the empty battlements at Kagoshima in 1877 (plate 47), a shot worthy of both a haiku by Bashō and a place alongside some of the scenes of still battlefields from the American Civil War.

The greater significance of this photograph, however, is that it stands virtually alone. Although the Japanese had the technology, however cumbersome, photographers did not cover the military struggles both before and after the Restoration of 1868 in any depth, and the failure to do so is especially conspicuous because of the striking coverage given around the same time to the Crimean War and the American Civil War. There was no counterpart to the "Brady boys" in Japan even in 1877, when the more reactionary samurai waged war for seven months against the new government. Ueno actually was commissioned by the government to cover this insurrection, and took eight assistants with him; their total output was sixty-nine photographs, in contrast to the thousands taken by Brady and his colleagues. Thus, Ueno's record of the deserted Kagoshima stronghold is impressive not only as a good photograph but also because it is a rather solitary photograph. For a pictorial record of the two decades of domestic strife and struggle surrounding the Restoration, it is necessary to rely on the highly dramatic but unreliable "brocade pictures" of the old woodblock process. Documentary photography of a sustained nature did not develop seriously in Japan until the Sino-Japanese War at the turn of the century, although the genesis of a powerful documentary style can be seen among the third group of pioneer Japanese photographers, the so-called Hokkaidō group.

That a high point in the development of Japanese photography was attained in the least developed part of Japan is not as surprising as may appear at first glance. To a certain degree, Hokkaidō was the Japanese equivalent of the American West. It was a rough frontier region that attracted a tough breed of settlers. In the Ainu it had its own vanishing race, a counterpart to the American Indian. The initial development of Hokkaidō was even guided by foreign technicians, most of whom (46 out of 63) were Americans who were knowledgeable about the pioneer work in frontier photography being done by their own countrymen such as Timothy O'Sullivan and Alexander Gardner under the sponsorship of the United States government. Interest in photography in Hokkaidō had quickened prior to the Meiji Restoration, with the support of the local daimyō Matsumae Takahiro (plate 5) and the tutelage of certain Russians in Hakodate. The two greatest pioneer cameramen in Hokkaidō, Tamoto Kenzō and Kizu Kōkichi, were both assisted by Russians in their early studies, and Kizu established Hokkaidō's first photo studio in Hakodate in 1864. The most intense period of accomplishment for these men and their colleagues, however, was the decade following 1871—the year the new government announced its ten-year plan for development of the northern island and began hiring foreign advisers. The general budget allotted for this frontier task included generous sums for photographs, which were used both to record progress in reclamation and construction and to publicize the undertaking among prospective settlers. For the two years 1879–1880 alone, the allotment for photographic materials was a handsome 210,029 yen.

Although the names of many of the Hokkaidō photographers are well known, their work, as in the case of the Kantō group, has tended to survive in good part as a collective contribution. Some photographs, such as Takebayashi Seiichi's portraits of prisoners (plates 63–65) are clearly identified as the work of a specific individual, and a large percentage of the early photos are believed to be by Tamoto (plate 131 is definitely by him; plates 49, 51, 53, 54, 56, and 60 may be). In most cases, however, the identity of the photographer is uncertain. As with some of the sod-hut and frontier-town photography of the American West, the great impact of many of the Hokkaidō photographs lies in their evocation of a harsh life amidst blasted landscapes and shabby buildings. On occasion, as in the depiction of men wandering on a grey plain of tree stumps taller than themselves (plate 55), the impression is almost surrealistic, and the fact that many of the Hokkaidō photographs were used to publicize the frontier can only deepen the awe of the contemporary observer. The relatively late date of this photograph, like that of the extraordinary "Cat of Sakhalin" (plate 69), is testimony to the fact that the severe environment of the north continued to inspire striking creativity with the camera even after the especially intense and coordinated activity of the 1870s.

Photographs of the racially and culturally distinct Ainu who lived in Hokkaidō (and Sakhalin) constituted a separate category that also received encouragement from the foreigners, as suggested by Kajima Seizaburō's choice of an English title, *The Ainu of Japan,* for an 1895 album (plate 76). Most of the Ainu studies were carefully arranged photographs of customary activities or straight-on portraits reminiscent of some of the American portraits of Indian chiefs. (Unlike the Ainu, however, the Indians usually had their names recorded.) When the camera wavered momentarily from this posed record to see the stupefied Ainu in beggar's rags sprawled in the dirt (plate 66), the result was a lasting vision of the demoralization and degradation of a people on the verge of extinction.

■ The first generation of professional photographers were men of high talent and high prices. Those who learned their craft in the 1850s and 1860s usually had been compelled to master the English and Dutch languages as well as the rudiments of Western science, and most of them were esteemed as genuine experts. A popular saying of 1872 included photographs as one of seven items in the "standard paraphernalia of civilization and enlightenment" *(bunmei kaika nanatsu dōgu)*—along with newspapers, the postal system, gaslights, steam engines, exhibitions, and dirigible balloons—while the photographers themselves were mentioned in limericks, songs, novels, and plays and even portrayed in the "brocade pictures" that their own craft would eventually supplant. By the 1870s, there were over one hundred professional photographers working throughout Japan, and several were listed in the various "Who's Who" publications of that decade. They worked exclusively in the wet-plate collodion process and almost entirely with equipment and materials imported from the West through Western treaty-port intermediaries.

As photography became more popular, however, photographers became less esteemed. In Japanese, this change was reflected in a new word for photographer that suggested an ordinary small tradesman rather than a professional with truly exceptional skills. Whereas the cameramen of the pioneer generation were (and still are) known as *shashinshi,* "masters of the photograph," most of their commercial successors from the 1880s on were simply associated with the workplace where photography was done. They were identified as *shashinya* (literally, "photograph room") or *shashinya-san,* that is, "photo-shop persons." In place of languages and science they marshaled an array of props and painted backgrounds that flattered their subjects and prettified their craft. This shift coincided with technological innovations, especially the dry-plate process, which was first imported in 1883 and made photography simpler, faster, and cheaper. A broader spectrum of the populace now could afford to sit for the camera on special occasions, while at the same time a new class of socially privileged amateurs could aspire to pursue photography as a serious avocation.

These developments also were interwoven with Japan's industrial revolution and the diversification of native entrepreneurship, as capitalists led by the Asanuma and Konishi companies slowly but steadily began to expand their involvement in both domestic manufacture and direct importation from Western suppliers. At the same time, advances in printing technology paved the way for wider dissemination of photographs in books, magazines, and newspapers. From the latter part of the 1870s, photographs were occasionally pasted onto printed pages; and a milestone in Japanese journalism occurred in 1890, when the newspaper *Tōkyo Nichinichi Shimbun* included photographs of the members of the newly created parliament as a separate insert. It was not until 1904, however, that it became possible to print photographs and type on the same page, and consequently photojournalism and the flowering of books and magazines containing photographs was largely a twentieth-century phenomenon. Until almost the very end of the Meiji period in 1912, the public's visualization of the great events and trends of the day remained highly colored by the imaginative "reporting" of woodblock prints and drawings.

There was subtle reciprocity in these developments. While technological and industrial change made possible the popularization and (more slowly) material domesticization of photography in Japan, photographs themselves—in the form of the family portrait, group portrait, or "commemorative photograph" *(kinen shashin)*—could offer a mild sort of ideological antidote to the ravages of technology and industrialization. Thus, the period beginning around the 1880s, when family albums became an almost obsessive part of popular culture, was the same period in which it became clear that traditional family relationships were being eroded by urbanization and modernization. Similarly, the popularization of formal portraits of the homogenized work group or social group coincided with fears, clearly expressed by Japan's leaders in the latter part of the Meiji period, that Japanese workers would jump their jobs if the opportunity arose and that egoism and individualism, or even socialism and anarchism, threatened to tear the social fabric to shreds.

The positive accomplishments and amiable associations conveyed by the "commemorative photographs"—the happy odysseys of birth, childhood, graduation, employment, recreation, marriage, and parenthood—were ritualized for the masses by the commercial photographers of Meiji Japan during the same period that other sources suggest was a time of uncertainty, pessimism, and "anguish" *(hanmon)*. The photo-shop men lived practical lives by portraying life ideally. They offered comforting scrapbook evidence that everyone had a place and everything was proceeding well—and in the same gesture they offered seductive models of harmony to emulate. In this respect their work was propaganda, the visual and generally unwitting counterpart to ruling-class rhetoric about the traditional "beautiful customs" and "harmonious" social relationships of Japan. The family album in Japan as in most other places is a classic example of the manner in which photographs function both as a way of remembering and as a way of forgetting, playing, in the process, an ideological role.

Occasionally, romanticization failed: the camera was gracious to the Meiji emperor (plate 128), who is known to have been surly and carnal, but no commercial photographer and no amount of plumage and braid ever succeeded in removing the dullness from the eyes of Meiji's son, the mentally infirm Taishō emperor (plate 129). Romanticization also could be iconoclastic: Ogawa Kazumasa's 1892 portrait of his aged parents, the mother resting her head upon the father's shoulder, was for its time an astonishing declaration of warmth and affection in a fiercely patriarchal society (plate 156). On rare occasions, the portrait business was even capable of contributing to wry and slightly manic humor, as in Ezaki

Reiji's 1893 collage of the faces of 1,700 babies (plate 111), looking at first glance like a bumpy shell midden (cf. plate 282). From late Meiji on, however, the mainstream of commercial photography consisted of portrait work of a solid and stolid nature, creating and perpetuating small myths by preserving touching, optimistic moments.

Like other forms of fiction, whether songs, novels, graphics, political pronouncements, or historical essays, these romanticizations produced with chemicals and glass are part of the reality of their times. Moreover, like any other meaningful way of seeing, photography itself simultaneously offered both refutations and elaborations of its own myths. The posed world of the photo-shop men was offset by the emergence of photojournalism and the maturing of documentary photography, represented in this present collection under war photography and "the camera's eye." At the same time, the more aesthetic inclinations of the studio photographers were isolated and nurtured and played with in a manner that ultimately proved extremely creative. This emerged as "art photography" at the end of the Meiji period, and was carried to an entirely new level of modern and modernistic visions in the 1930s. As revealed in the organization of this volume, contemporary Japanese photographers look back upon the decade prior to 1940 as the true "epoch of development" upon which postwar Japanese photography was constructed.

Beginning with the Sino-Japanese War of 1894-1895, Japanese photographers were given ample opportunity to develop the art of war photography. As recorded by the camera, the military stepping stones in Japan's emergence as a modern state now seem appalling to most observers, but this was not always so, and it still does not hold true for everyone. Some of the images captured by the Japanese photographers would seem to be wordless cries for peace as horrific and eloquent as any ever made: the helmet and skull in a stagnant pool (plate 479), the charred mother and child (plate 505). Sometimes it is words that make the difference. The mind becomes numb, the eye literally and figuratively films over, as images of death and suffering follow one upon the other and begin to seem nothing more than photographic clichés. At such times, a caption can make a photograph suddenly sear the mind's eye by offering an unexpected explanation and returning the observer to a sharp realization of the intimacy and individuality of the war experience. Thus, Yanagida Fumio's macabre photograph of a corpse with a blade protruding from his throat (plate 499) may change some people's way of remembering Japanese militarism when the caption sinks in: "An intellectual soldier from the Shizuoka Regiment who committed suicide with a bayonet during training." The war photography of Imperial Japan also enables the latter-day observer, if so inclined, to make Biblical points by juxtaposition: the carnage abroad and carnage come home, the sowing and the reaping. Or for Americans, confronted with the photographic record of 1944 and 1945: the shared guilt and the inability ever to cast the first stone.

In pre-1945 Japan, however, war photography did not conspicuously carry such antiwar messages. The problem of censorship is a complicating factor here. It is not clear how complete the photographic war record is, and it is difficult to ascertain how much of what is available at present was actually seen at the time by the Japanese public. From the Sino-Japanese War of 1894–1895 on, many war photographers were directly attached to the Japanese army, and controls were placed on permissible subjects. Some of the photographs now available, especially from the 1931–1945 period, are stamped "censored" *(fukyoka)* and were declassified only in recent years (cf. plates 487, 491). Other censored photographs are known to have been among the heaps of incriminating material that the Japanese frantically destroyed at the time of the surrender in 1945. Military censorship was abetted by self-censorship (as well as by rationing and simple scarcity of materials in the early 1940s), and for various reasons there are aspects of Japan's wars that are barely covered in the extant record. There appears to be but a single Japanese photograph of the Rape of Nanking (plate 482), for example, and coverage of Japanese involvement with White Russians and the White Terror in Siberia between 1918 and 1922 is thin (plates 186–192). Apart from Yanagida's suicide of the intellectual recruit, very little in the photographic record conveys the brutality of the officer corps or the despair or utter exhaustion of conscripts. Propaganda holds that most Japanese soldiers died with the words "Long Live the Emperor" on their lips, but those who survived have indicated that more commonly their comrades died calling for their mothers. The camera sheds no light here, for it records only the living face or the dead face, but not the face between.

However incomplete the visual record may have been, it is clear that Japanese in the prewar period were exposed to many sobering war photographs, and that in general they found them stirring and inspirational. Photography has been integral to the war propaganda of all countries in the twentieth century, and it was Japan that gave the world its first great, and greatly photographed, modern war with the undeclared attack on Russia in 1904. In the 1930s, the Nazis in Germany carried the art of photographic propaganda to an entirely new level of slick manipulation, and the Japanese militarists attempted to follow suit by establishing new publicity sections in both the Cabinet Information Bureau and the Imperial Military Headquarters in 1937. By 1940, one finds an article in *Fuoto Taimusu* [Photo Times], one of Japan's most reputable photography magazines, quoting with approval Goebbels on the obligation of the artist to the state. By 1943, photographic propaganda for domestic consumption was overtly fanatical and palpably lunatic (as witness the posed maniacs in plate 478). More interesting than such blatant and overt propaganda, however, is the very subtle, innate propagandistic potential of war photography, which in the Japanese case emerges with great vividness in the photography of the Russo-Japanese War of 1904–1905.

The Russo-Japanese War was covered by photographers from many countries, and the photography as a whole is stunning. From just the small Japanese sample included here (plates 172–183), one can begin to imagine the impact these photographs must have had at the time. Even at that late date, elaborate woodblock prints were still a major medium through which the war was presented to the Japanese public. But it is at this juncture that the photograph can be seen coming into its own as the more potent medium—partly because of its ability to convey a sense of immense space, partly because it held a mirror to the "real" faces of war in a way not possible with the slower lenses and processes of prior years, and partly because the journalistic breakthrough in reproducing photographs occurred at precisely this time.

The camera, like the Japanese soldiers themselves, captured Manchurian space in a breathtaking manner. To the Japanese then and for decades thereafter, there was an epic symbolism in these panoramic vistas and far horizons: images of space became intimations of destiny. That this new frontier was militarily and economically essential to Japan was rarely questioned by a vigorous people in a crowded place, especially when the other powers were also busy dismembering China. What the photographs of 1904–1905 etched in the Japanese popular consciousness was the vision of a Russian enemy, a virgin land, a sparse and backward native population, and a triumph of Japanese will over nature's forces as well as the tsar's. Photography went further, moreover, by assisting in the wedding of destiny to obligation, for the mounds of corpses recorded by the camera were an unforgettable memorial to the 120,000 Japanese who died to establish Japan's foothold on the continent. It was inconceivable that such sacrifice should ever be betrayed, and the more the corpses accumulated on later battlefields, the more impossible it became to abandon the imperialist quest. In such a context, photographs of patriotic gore could never serve as effective inducements to antimilitarism, for they were constant reminders to the Japanese of their blood debt to the dead.

Looked at now, these records naturally carry different messages. The same photographs of vast terrain and tiny figures seem symbols of Japanese fatuity rather than Japan's destiny. It is far easier now to perceive the blood lust rather than the blood debt, and the image of Japanese soldiers snickering over the decapitation of a prisoner (plate 182) emerges as a more accurate symbol of the course of empire that the Russo-Japanese War foreshadowed. There is scant honor to be found through such a reading of these war photographs, but rather a troubling reminder that today's pitiful Japanese corpse may have been yesterday's perpetrator of atrocities... all the while carrying sentimental family portraits, and possibly pinups of soft beauties, in his pocket. To begin to comprehend how all this could fit together, it is necessary to place the battlefield against the domestic scene, the war photographs against the camera's eye at home.

When the camera was taken outside the studio in prewar Japan, and used without deliberate artifice or sentimentality, the record that resulted bore striking parallels to the record made abroad by the war photographers. Here again are devastated landscapes, oppressed people, people in conflict—even severed Japanese heads (plates 379, 380), although after the 1870s the beheadings and public display of corpses were reserved for non-Japanese (plate 416). Prior to 1944, the devastation came from natural disasters which repeatedly wracked the country, and the corpses were often strewn as on battlefields (plates 382–389); the toll in the 1923 Kantō earthquake was over 100,000 dead or missing and over 500,000 injured. Oppression was structured by class rather than race or nation (plates 390–399); and conflict, so vigorously denied in ruling-class homilies of harmony and group loyalty, was not only class-based but also increasingly organized and articulate in the years following World War I (plates 401–402, 404–406, 408–412). The camera records intimations of the most ominous ideological threat the ruling groups could imagine: lese majesty (plate 413). This record of internal strife even embraces the Japanese military, but this time in arms against the Japanese government itself, in the abortive *coup d'état* of February 26, 1936 (plates 417–421). Viewed from this vantage point, Japan's military debaucheries can be seen as a kind of grotesque transposition abroad of dislocations, hatreds, and upheavals at home. Scholars of this period sometimes refer to diversion of resentment, explosions of pent-up rage, the transfer of oppression. Photography insinuates such propositions more intimately.

■ The social landscape of deprivation at home, however, was complemented by a landscape of relative privilege that became increasingly conspicuous as Japan entered the twentieth century. Here scholars attempt to impose abstract order through vocabularies of paradox, dichotomy, dualism, or contradiction. The camera's contribution to the perception and recollection of this experience is twofold. Photographs *show* many of the contradictions (in ways that often become complex, as when one sees here the oppressed and there the oppressor, and then recognizes that the same person may be both; or when one sets the pleasure-loving cosmopolitan against the poor farmer or worker on the one hand, but against the fanatic militarist on the other hand). Photographs also *exemplify* some of the contradictions, for the most creative developments in twentieth-century Japanese photography were rooted in the uneven but highly dynamic emergence of middle-class culture, bourgeois values, and a broader range of cosmopolitan interests—were, briefly put, an integral part of the landscape of relative privilege.

Because the memory of war-crazed and war-torn Japan is so vivid and the image of matchbox cities and dirt-poor farms so compelling, it is easy to forget that prewar Japan enjoyed a blighted flowering of politics and culture comparable in numerous respects to developments in Europe and the United States prior to World War II. Loosely referred to as the era of "Taishō democracy," a reference to the reign of the Emperor Taishō (1912–1926), this period actually extended from around the turn of the century to the very early 1930s. Like a pale version of the politics and art of Weimar Germany, it is an epoch that now raises ambiguous images of what might have been.

The economic base of the era of Taishō democracy was dynamic but unstable, as stimulation from the Russo-Japanese War and World War I helped promote the emergence of thousands of small and medium-sized enterprises, the swelling of the ranks of city workers, the appearance of flamboyant *nouveaux riches,* and the fattening of the great zaibatsu conglomerates. The political scene witnessed both energetic electoral politics and radical left-wing activities. The literary world saw articulate espousal of such schools as naturalism, romanticism, idealism, humanism, and aestheticism. In painting, Japanese and Western styles flourished side by side. The passionate "Orientalism" of Ernest Fenollosa and Okakura Tenshin had coalesced with Meiji nationalism in the 1880s to inspire the regeneration of highly idealistic traditional styles; and Western-style painting was revitalized by the introduction of impressionism in the 1890s and postimpressionist trends such as fauvism and cubism in the 1910s. Cinema and the modern-theater movement appeared on the scene in the early 1900s, and in the 1920s the gaudy cabaret and flapper culture was imported into Japan in a vogue of *ero-guro-nansensu* (eroticism, grotesqueries, and nonsense), as espoused by the *moga* and *mobo* (linguistic grotesqueries for *modan garu* and *modan boi,* that is, "modern girl" and "modern boy").

In this milieu, Japanese photography developed in several directions. Commercial photographers expanded into advertising and propaganda, for example, initially relying mostly on kimono-clad beauties to sell soap, cosmetics, and endless bottles of beer (plates 430–441). The peak of the coy soft sell was attained in 1922 in the warm sepia-toned poster of a kimono-less young woman gazing up at the viewer over a sparkling glass of red wine; this invitation to sample "delicious, nutritious" Akadama port wine, featuring an eighteen-year-old actress, was a sensation in its day and remains perhaps the most famous single piece of commercial art produced in prewar Japan (plate 423).

While some photographers were perfecting the art of commercial seduction, many more were discovering the seduction of Art. As in the West, the perception of photography as an art turned the medium in new directions, and in its initial stages "art photography" tended to mimic the fine arts closely. Much of the early impetus for this trend came from amateurs, with support from the photo industry and enterprising professionals such as Kajima Seibe-e. Kajima's clever late-Meiji photograph of men wearing mantles (plate 135) suggests a bridge between the studio-portrait genre and the new aestheticism, while his flamboyant activities personify the exuberant entrepreneurship that helped usher in the age of the amateur. Some of the photo excursions organized by Kajima in the final years of the Meiji period involved hundreds of upper-class participants rolling through the countryside in rented trains accompanied by geisha and musicians, singing and drinking and presumedly even taking an occasional picture.

The popularization of photography led to a blossoming of clubs, exhibitions, publications, educational courses, and domestically produced equipment and materials. The first photography association was formed in 1889, its membership including both commercial and amateur photographers. The first technical handbook for amateurs was published in 1900. The clarion call to "art photography" is generally dated from 1904, when the Yūbuzutsusha association was formed and Katō Seiichi published a landmark essay titled "On Photographic Art." The staging of photographic exhibitions on a major and regular basis began in 1907. The first photo club for young people was organized in 1913.

Several photography journals were published in the 1890s, one of which—*Shashin Geppō* [Photography Monthly]—remained in circulation from 1893 to 1940. Beginning in 1921, specialty magazines began to appear like mushrooms after rain, and several survived to become mainstays in the field; the most famous were *Kamera* [Camera], 1921–1956, with a break during World War II; *Fuoto Taimusu* [Photo Times], 1924–1941; and *Asahi Kamera* [Asahi Camera], 1926–1941. A magazine titled simply *Amachua* [Amateur] that was founded in 1922 is said to have sold around 10,000 copies of each issue before being wiped out in the 1923 Kantō earthquake. The 1920s saw a flood of mass-circulation weekly and monthly magazines with high photographic content, and the major newspapers emerged not only as promoters of photojournalism but also as publishers of photography books and sponsors of exhibitions. At this time, publishing houses such as Ars (the Latin word for art) also came on the scene as patrons of fine photography.

The economic boom from World War I stimulated Japanese photography in numerous ways. The number of amateur photographers ballooned, and imports of photographic materials increased almost eight times by value between 1916 and 1922. At the same time, a shift toward greater professionalism in camera work became discernable, and Japanese industry began to make more rapid progress toward the goal of relative self-sufficiency in the production of cameras, film, plates, papers, and the like. Educational courses in photography were offered from 1900, and the Tokyo Academy of Fine Arts included photography in its curriculum from 1915 to 1926, at which time the program was transferred to the Tokyo Higher Technology School. In 1923, the fully accredited Tokyo College of Photography was established, backed by the Konishi Company and offering a full three-year program. Foreign cameras were greatly prized by the affluent amateur as well as by the professional, with English models in special favor prior to the importation of the vest-pocket Kodak beginning around 1915; the Kodak remained in vogue until the appearance of the Leica in the mid-1920s. From the turn of the century, however, manufacturers led by Konishi began to produce a steady stream of domestic models, usually with Anglicized names: Champion, Paris, Noble, Pearl, Idea, Lily, Minimum Idea Camera, Idea Flex, and so forth. As one commentator has observed, the cameras of prewar Japan sound like the cigarettes of post-1945 Japan.

Art photography in Japan lagged somewhat behind its counterpart in the West, where Peter Henry Emerson's revolutionary theories and photographs first appeared in the latter half of the 1880s. The pioneer exhibitions of photographs as art (as opposed to heavy allegory in the Henry Peach Robinson mode) took place in Europe between 1891 and 1893. In the United States, Alfred Stieglitz returned from Germany in 1890, announced the Photo-Secession in 1902, and published *Camera Work* with his distinguished colleagues from 1902 to 1917. In Japan, as has been seen, photography was not effectively presented as an art until around 1904, and many of the techniques as well as ideals of the new movement were indebted to Western precedent. Akiyama Tetsusuke introduced the gum-bichromate process and other "pigment prints" between 1904 and 1909. Rough paper was used to further enhance the impression of a drawing rather than a straight photograph, and artistic effect was sought through soft focus, distortion (plates 212–215, 218, 219, 243), and outright abstraction (plates 224, 229, 230). Despite such an obvious relationship to trends in the West, it is nonetheless misleading to assume that the Japanese devotees of art photography were merely responding to outside stimuli.

"Influence" is an illusive beast, and the plain facts of contact between Japanese photographers and Western photographs in the early twentieth century are hazy. Emerson was introduced at an early date, and a photographic exhibition from London was shown in Japan as early as 1892. Alvin Langdon Coburn's discovery of abstract patterns through the camera was admired, and the Japanese were especially impressed by the writings and photographs of E. O. Hoppé, an individual neglected in current Western histories of photography. Paul Gauguin's paintings clearly fixed the photographic eye of Nojima Kōzō (plates 195 and 233), and many of the Japanese prints in the art-photography mode surely would have pleased the European impressionists (cf. plates 205, 206, 207, 220). But the impressionists at the outset had been inspired by traditional Japanese prints that arrived in their countries wrapped around chinaware, making the question who-is-fertilizing-whom, if not moot, certainly intricate.

The question of influence is further complicated by the fact that at the time Japanese photographers decided they were artists, a large portion of Japanese society was embracing Ernest Fenollosa, Okakura Tenshin, and National Essence. Photographers suddenly discovered the unsurpassed chiaroscuro of the traditional brush-and-ink tradition (plates 201, 202, 203). Or, more obliquely, they emulated this tradition by admiring and copying virtuoso contemporary painters in the classical mode such as Yokoyama Taikan (cf. plate 199). Or, more obliquely yet, photographers came to impressionism through their own literary tradition, in which suggestiveness had been reduced to the quick moment of the seventeen-syllable haiku. Nothing is more impressionistic—or painterly—than the haiku, and one of the most famous Japanese photographers said to exemplify the haiku spirit on film is Fukuhara Shinzō (plates 221, 222), who was also inclined to give haiku-esque advice to fellow photographers ("Find life's whole history in a stone, life's intricate relations in a tree, and life's inner movements in a leaf"). By the mid-1920s, Fukuhara felt that the photographic art of Japan had begun to reflect the "national character" *(kokumin-sei)* in a distinctive manner comparable to that of the great woodblock prints themselves. But Fukuhara also, as it happens, had studied in France and clearly imbibed the impressionist influence there (plate 220). In practice, if not so easily in theory, it was possible to reach simultaneously for the Japanese spirit and a cosmopolitan identity.

By the 1920s, there was a current of anticipation among Japanese photographers in the art-photography mode that they were about to become a respected part of the international world of photography. Photography journals attempted to attract the non-Japanese audience by including English captions and prefaces in their publications, and Japanese sponsorship of the First International Photographic Salon in Tokyo in 1927 sparked great hopes of an epoch of cosmopolitan relationships. Japanese entries began to be solicited more frequently for exhibitions abroad. An advertisement published in English in 1928 for one of the Japanese magazines captures this sense of excitement:

> There [is] something else in Japan besides the proverbial cherry blossoms and woodcut colour prints! It is no other than ...pictorial photography. In the past few years, not only have the flowers of the Japanese Photographic art blossomed, but their sweet fragrance and beautiful light have shone throughout the world.
>
> Today, no camera workers and enthusiasts in the world can do without taking heed [of] the progress of Japanese photography.

As it turned out, Japanese photography did have a decade of dynamic growth ahead of it, but in directions different from those suggested in this sugary paean to "pictorial photography." Although art photography at its best produced elegant works such as those selected for this present volume, the genre as a whole fell easily into a redundancy of misty scenes and blurry figures. A critic commenting on a major exhibition in 1928 concluded that Japanese photographers preferred nature over daily life, and what is quiescent in nature over what is active. They were, by and large, uncreative, indifferent to humanity, abstruse, and aristocratic. Such critical feelings were echoed by many Japanese photographers, who began to feel by the mid-1920s that art photography had become mere artifice, a romanticization as sentimental and divorced from reality as were the posed and tidy portraits of the conventional photo-shop men.

■ While the decline of art photography coincided with the demise of "Taishō democracy," for the historian there is a fascinating twist to this: the demise of "Taishō democracy" in turn coincided with the beginning of a decade of intense diversity and innovation in Japanese photography. To the present-day observer, this may seem quite astonishing, for it means that photography flourished as never before during a period popularly associated with the "dark valley" of mounting militarism and repression. This "epoch of development" continued through the 1930s and was not effectively throttled by the state until around 1940.

Upon closer analysis, and with the benefit of hindsight, it is clear that this was not an anomaly, not a solitary freak bloom in a cultural and social wasteland. Many sectors of Japanese society underwent immense transformations in the 1930s. Certain fields in the arts and sciences continued to play out the momentum, or the logic, of developments set in motion during the era of "Taishō democracy." In other areas, politically and morally onerous aspects of the period proved conducive to photographic creativity. Some of the most brilliant—even "humanistic"—documentary photography of prewar Japan, for example, was taken in the 1930s in the new puppet state of Manchukuo (plates 313–327, 337–338, 340–342), calling to mind the role played by the new frontier of Hokkaidō in Japanese photography a half-century earlier.

The photography of this "epoch of development" embraced a number of styles and labels—New Photography, News Photography, Vanguard Photography, the Real Photo, the Surreal—and reflected the way massive influences from the West meshed with the domestic influences and pressures of a wobbly but advanced capitalism. The most immediately obvious Western influence was the Leica and the new world of 35-millimeter work this permitted. A magazine titled *Geppan Raika* [Monthly Leica] was actually established in 1934, and it was altogether fitting that one of the most esteemed of Japanese photographers, Kimura Ihe-e, should publish a volume in 1938 titled (in English in the original) *Japan through a Leica*.

Beginning in the latter half of the 1920s, the Japanese also suddenly acquired almost unrestricted access to the latest trends in Western photography through a steady stream of articles, translations, exhibitions, and systematic photographic reproductions (including yearbooks of international photography). They were especially receptive to the avant-garde developments in the country from which the Leica had come—the *Neue Sachlichkeit* (New Objectivity) and visions of the Bauhaus group, as expressed by such innovators as László Moholy-Nagy and first introduced to Japan around 1926.

This attraction to the Germany the Nazis devoured is instructive when one recalls the Bauhaus ideal of a new unity of art and technology. For the receptivity of Japanese photographers to such theories derived from the fact that Japan itself now confronted the challenges and seductions of modernity—or at least (keeping in mind the contradictions) the attraction of modern forms. In addition to its war boom (and bust) and technology boom and communications boom, post–World War I Japan also had experienced "booms" in construction, urbanization, industrialization, consumerism—the list is virtually unending. The metropolitan heart of the country had been leveled in the 1923 Kantō earthquake, and rebuilt in part on more modern lines. The plunge into crass, go-it-alone imperialism beginning in 1931 was also the impetus for a "second industrial revolution" in heavy and chemical industry. Japan, racked by the strains of unbalanced capitalism and second-string imperialism, was now also confronted as never before with the nice geometries of modern buildings and orderly, functional machines. The aesthetic, psychological, political, and symbolic options in such a situation were diverse, and Japanese photographers explored many of them.

These options were not necessarily avant-garde, but however different their styles, the major photographers of the early 1930s shared the articulate consciousness of being engaged in the creation of "new photographs" or a "new photography" *(shinkō shashin)*. The popular phrase actually was adopted in the names of an association and a magazine founded in 1930 (the Shinkō Shashin Kenkyū Kai and its journal, *Shinkō Shashin Kenkyū)*, which is not only tidy for the historian of photography but also suggestive to the social and political historian. The vocabulary of new photography dovetails with the renovationist (and ideologically ambidextrous) ideals and labels that were being trumpeted throughout Japan in the 1930s: the "new haiku," "new bureaucrats," "new zaibatsu," and ultimately the "new structure" at home and the "new order" abroad. In embracing the new, moreover, many of these photographers made it explicit that they were casting off the "old" fashions of art photography. The tone of their iconoclasm is suggested by the following lines from an often-quoted manifesto on behalf of the "real photo" published by Ina Nobuo in 1932 in an essay titled "Return to Photography":

> Sever all connections with "art photography." Destroy every conception of established "art." Break down the idols! Keenly recognize the "mechanistic nature" unique to photography! The aesthetics of photography as a new art—the study of photographic art—must be established on these two premises.

Like most prose on the subject, this is somewhat ambiguous; but the product of verbal ambiguity was photographic diversity of a very creative sort. Whereas art photography had found its model in painting and its mood in an indulgent and romantic subjectivity, the avant-garde of the "new photography" looked to the modern and mechanistic world for models, and assumed a pose of unsentimental objectivity that emphasized the "real," the "factual," the impersonal. Such photography often focused on architecture and machines, the modern world of concrete and metal, and turned the very stuff of relentless, bewildering, chaotic change into photographic statements of form, order, and clarity (cf. plates 251, 259, 260, 262, 325, 327). Whether this was indeed objective and unsentimental is another matter.

It was also possible, on the other hand, to present the material forms of contemporary society in a manner that carried a stronger sense of disenchantment and implicit criticism. This is the mood, for example, that emerges from several photomontages by Horino Masao titled "The Character of Great Tokyo," which were published in 1931 in the well-known journal of opinion *Chūō Kōron* (plates 367–369). Photomontage was another of the techniques that had attracted European innovators, and Horino acknowledged his debt here to certain layouts by Moholy-Nagy. In its most dynamic form, the montage or photo spread or composite photograph can convey a graphic sense of dialectics, of both linkage and disequilibrium, and the character of modern Tokyo that emerged from Horino's juxtapositions and angles of vision was harsh and unstable. Yet the following year Horino himself presented a famous series of photographs of modern ships under the collective title "Camera: Eye × Steel • Composition" that seems to reflect the more naïve infatuation with modern forms that generally characterized the so-called functional aesthetics (plate 260).

As Ina Nobuo's manifesto reveals, the emphasis on "mechanism" also reminded photographers that in addition to the machines in their neighborhood, they had a machine in their hand. The camera too was a mechanical device—not a paintbrush, not a simple mirror, not a human eye—and exploitation of its "mechanical nature" could offer a unique perception of reality. To present-day observers this may seem obvious, but it was a genuine discovery for photographers of this generation, and a discovery that truly did alter ways of seeing. Through multiple exposure, manipulation of shutter speed, manipulation of lens, and other techniques, the photographer could draw a variety of unique impressions from the external world. Perhaps of greater significance in shaping the cast of the contemporary eye, photographers now exploited the camera's capacity for close-up work and unconventional angles of perspective, uncovering a new world of sensory impression through the isolated detail and unexpected vantage point (cf. plates 250, 252, 253, 255–258, 261–264, 278, 282, 283). Where the camera originally had been prized for its ability to "capture reality" in full detail and proper perspective, it now was cherished as a mechanism that could isolate fragments and transcend conventional perspective to reveal a new reality of patterns and spacial relationships.

As photographers emphasized the close-up or exploited the mechanical nature of the camera in other ways, the hard lines associated with the cult of functional modernity softened. The "real" became increasingly difficult to identify; the rational gave way to the unpredictable; the fact gave way to the suggestion. Thus, another dimension of the new photography was the semi-abstract or abstract composition, a trend already apparent in the art-photography mode but now carried further (cf. plates 252, 254, 256, 261, 265, 276, 277, 280). In this case, the product of the new objectivity became nonobjective imagery. In yet another direction, avant-garde photographers attempted to transcend materialist realism by introducing the human element as well as elements of dream and unreality. Their absurdly rational creations drew upon the conventions of another modernistic school that had emerged in Europe in the 1920s: surrealism (plates 245–247, 270–274). Many photographs naturally blurred the lines between the close-up and the abstraction, or the abstract and the surreal. The Japanese also incorporated Western techniques such as the "lensless photography" of the photogram (plate 279) and the solarization process pioneered by Man Ray (plates 269, 297).

What the mechanists excluded and surrealists dismembered, other contributors to the new photography attempted to present whole and even with reverence, and this of course was humankind. Such turning away from machines and modern geometries also could be undertaken in the name of "the real," and the vanguard photography of the 1930s included a variety of impressions of the human subject that were technically more sophisticated than those of the past. As had been the case ever since the introduction of photography in the mid-nineteenth century, the individuals depicted included both the famous and the nameless. They were now caught on film, however, in soft focus or by snapshot or from unusual angles or in more "natural" poses. Nojima Kōzō, whose work bridged the art-photography and new-photography modes (plates 195, 200, 233, 244, 291–295, 306, 308), produced many of his most striking and creative studies of women and nudes in the early 1930s, when he was over forty. Kojima Ihe-e, who was born in 1901, burst on the scene in the 1930s as a master of both the portrait and the street shot (plates 285, 286, 309, 310, 341, 353–356, 375, 452). With deliberate avoidance of finesse, Watanabe Yoshio caught the hurlyburly backstage jumble of a musical review (plates 363–366), while Hamaya Hiroshi cast a slow, loving, uncritical eye on rural customs (plates 370–374). The most distinguished amateur photographer of this period, Yasui Nakaji, abandoned the painterly tradition of art photography to produce powerful works of social realism before his death in 1942 at the age of thirty-nine (plates 328–330, 344, 348, 352). The versatile Horino Masao turned his camera on the lower classes (plates 345, 349, 362) at the same time as he was achieving recognition for his photomontages and images of the world of steel.

Had there been a counterpart to Roy Stryker and the United States Farm Security Administration in Japan in the mid-1930s, these photographic glimpses of the powerless and the poor might have been carried to the level of a truly sustained documentary vision. As it was, the closest approximation to a coherent documentary statement was created outside Japan proper and was inspired by imperialist romanticizations. This was the photography by Japanese in China's Three Eastern Provinces—the new photography in the "New Manchuria," to borrow from the title of a photo collection from this decade. Like the photographic record of the Russo-Japanese War three decades earlier, these were indeed powerful images of space, toughness, and destiny. They were by no means condescending to the peoples of the new imperium. Many of the best-known Japanese cameramen visited Manchukuo at one time or another during the 1930s (cf. plates 337, 338, 340, 341), but much of the finest work came from photographers, amateurs as well as professionals, who settled there. They were encouraged by the Japanese government, the Japanese Kwantung Army, which controlled Manchuria, and the South Manchurian Railway Company; they had an effective leader in the photographer Fuchigami Hakuyō (plates 313, 314); they had several magazines of their own through which to publish photographs in the neocolony; and they appear to have absorbed some of the genuinely idealistic dreams of a new order in Asia.

Photographers of the human condition in the 1930s worked within a variety of overlapping schools associated with photojournalism, "news photography" as redefined to include the pictorial chronicle of daily life, the proletarian-art movement, and the like. In addition, it is clear that they drew not only upon the abiding interest in portraiture but also upon the ostensibly outmoded aesthetics of the epoch of art photography, refreshened and revitalized by theories and examples from the West. Of notable influence here from the mid-1930s on were the teachings and photographs of Paul Wolff, the German master of miniature-camera photography who retained an appreciation of more traditional photographic aesthetics as well. Two well-attended exhibitions of Wolff's photographs in Japan in 1935 elicited the critical accolade "this is the art photography of a new era, and it can be concluded that both the old 'art photography' and the new 'new photography' have by and large completed their missions."

On one side, work associated with these new trends shades off into the photography previously discussed here under war photography and "the camera's eye." On the other side, the shading is toward overt propaganda, first for the company, then for the state. The modern photographic visions and techniques that had been solemnly advanced in the name of new perceptions of Truth or Reality were perfectly adaptable to selling soap, and it was but a small step from touting consumer goods to touting the country, the expanding empire, and finally war itself. Many of the most famous photographers turned their talents to advertising and propaganda work, always with two clear audiences in mind: domestic and foreign.

Western influences were at play here as elsewhere; as early as 1928, one volume in a multivolume series on contemporary commercial art had been devoted to European advertising, and the Bauhaus influence in this as in other artistic fields is widely acknowledged. The real takeoff in Japanese advertising photography, however, is dated from 1930, when the first association of advertising photographers was formed and Japanese won the first and third prizes in the First International Advertising Photography Exhibition (plates 442, 444), which was held in Tokyo. The following year, a team centering on Kimura Ihe-e made a dramatic departure from the traditional soft pitch by using a photograph of the slums in an ad for "99.4% pure" Kao soap (plate 452). This striking composition was a breakthrough in several respects: it moved some of the most promising trends in documentary photography into the hucksters' camp; it was addressed to a mass audience; it included a lengthy text; and it was presented as a large front-page ad in the daily press.

These trends suggest both a new domestic market and a new type of commercial professionalism, which is not what most observers would expect given the date: 1931 was the year of the Manchurian Incident, and Japan was still by all general indices in the depths of the Great Depression. Yet it was at this time that free-lance photographers and graduates from the new photography courses joined a variety of designers, journalists, and ad men to push luxury products on the masses and to cater very conspicuously to the "modern girl" (cf. plates 424, 425, 441; also, in the "new photography" mode, plates 300–303). There was a 1930s magazine for women titled *Shinkō Fujin* [New Woman], a title consistent with the pervasive vocabulary of renovation, and in 1937 some of these new women of leisure even formed their own photography group with the English name "Ladies' Camera Club." At the same time, a polished advertising campaign was directed toward the English-speaking market. Where in 1928 Japanese had dreamed of exporting the fragrant blossoms of their art photography to the West, by the mid-1930s they were using slick photography to sell the Westerners autos, textiles, light bulbs, and mandarin oranges (plates 427, 453–456).

Beginning in 1933, the hub of such commercial photography was the Japan Atelier (Nihon Kōbō; reorganized in 1939 as the Kokusai Hōdō Kōgei Kabushiki Kaisha), established under the guiding hand of Natori Yōnosuke, who had been a student and photojournalist in Germany prior to the Nazi regime. The Japan Atelier handled a large portion of the commercial advertising directed toward foreigners (plates 427, 453–456, 458), and in 1934 moved into the business of selling Japan itself to the West. The chosen vehicle was the English-language illustrated magazine *Nippon*. In Manchukuo, a bilingual counterpart already had appeared a year earlier under the title *Manshū Gurafu* (subtitled in English "Pictorial Manchuria," or later, "Manchuria-Graph"). In 1938, following the Marco Polo Bridge Incident and the undeclared "war of annihilation" against China, the Natori group began publication of the English-language graphic *Shanghai,* followed by three siblings the next year: *Commerce Japan, Manchukuo,* and *Kanton*. In 1939, the Japan Photo Service sent a book titled *Girls of Japan* into the battle for Western affections. Other glossy magazines were subsequently directed to European and Southeast Asian audiences, including *Van* (from 1940) and *Front* (from 1942; plates 428, 429, 463, 476).

In the process of selling their services, photographers associated with the Japan Atelier or its counterparts quickly revealed the conservative uses to which the "modern" or "avant-garde" could be put. The montage or composite photograph, for instance, could become a vehicle of pure propaganda, devoid of tension or contradiction and devoted simply and deliberately to reinforcing the orthodoxies of the ruling groups. In a sophisticated 1934 presentation prepared by the Japan Atelier this took the form of photomontages incorporating sharp and sparkling images of order, progress, and taste (plate 458). A different tone was ventured four years later in a composite photo six feet high and fourteen feet wide that the Japanese displayed at the Chicago Trade Fair. Made up of shots by Kimura Ihe-e and Koishi Kiyoshi, as orchestrated by Hara Hiromu, this impressive piece of wallpaper contained every soft cliché known to have titillated Japanophiles in the twentieth century: cherry blossoms, Mount Fuji, a geisha with trailing sleeves, the classic symbols of quietist culture (Shintō torii, pagoda, the Kamakura Buddha), an ancient castle, the Diet building, a few modern edifices, and a modern ship (plate 457). By 1943, such camera work for the state had ballooned out of control. The famous poster of fanatic soldiers and a trampled American flag (plate 478) was composed of photographs by Kanamaru Shigene and was first displayed as a giant billboard covering 1,800 square feet on the front of the Nichigeki Music Hall in downtown Tokyo. Subsequently this technical tour de force was widely reproduced with, as its caption, an archaic slogan that had been pried from the ancient classics: *Uchiteshi yamamu*—roughly, "Fight to the Bitter End."

As the camera was also present to record, without art or artifice, the end was closer, more bitter, more terrifying than anyone standing by the music hall in 1943 really imagined.

ONE ■ DAWN

1. Tsurumaru Castle in Kagoshima. Shimazu Nariakira. 1854–1860.

2. Self-portrait (?). Ōno Benkichi. 1853–1867.

3. Young man. 1860s or early 1870s.

lf-portrait. Kawamoto Kōmin. 1861.

5. Matsumae Takahiro, lord of Matsumae fief. 1853–1867.

6. Five samurai. 1853–1867.

7. Tetsuko, wife of Nakahama (John) Manjirō. Nakahama Manjirō. 1860.

8. Samurai and attendant. 1853–1867.

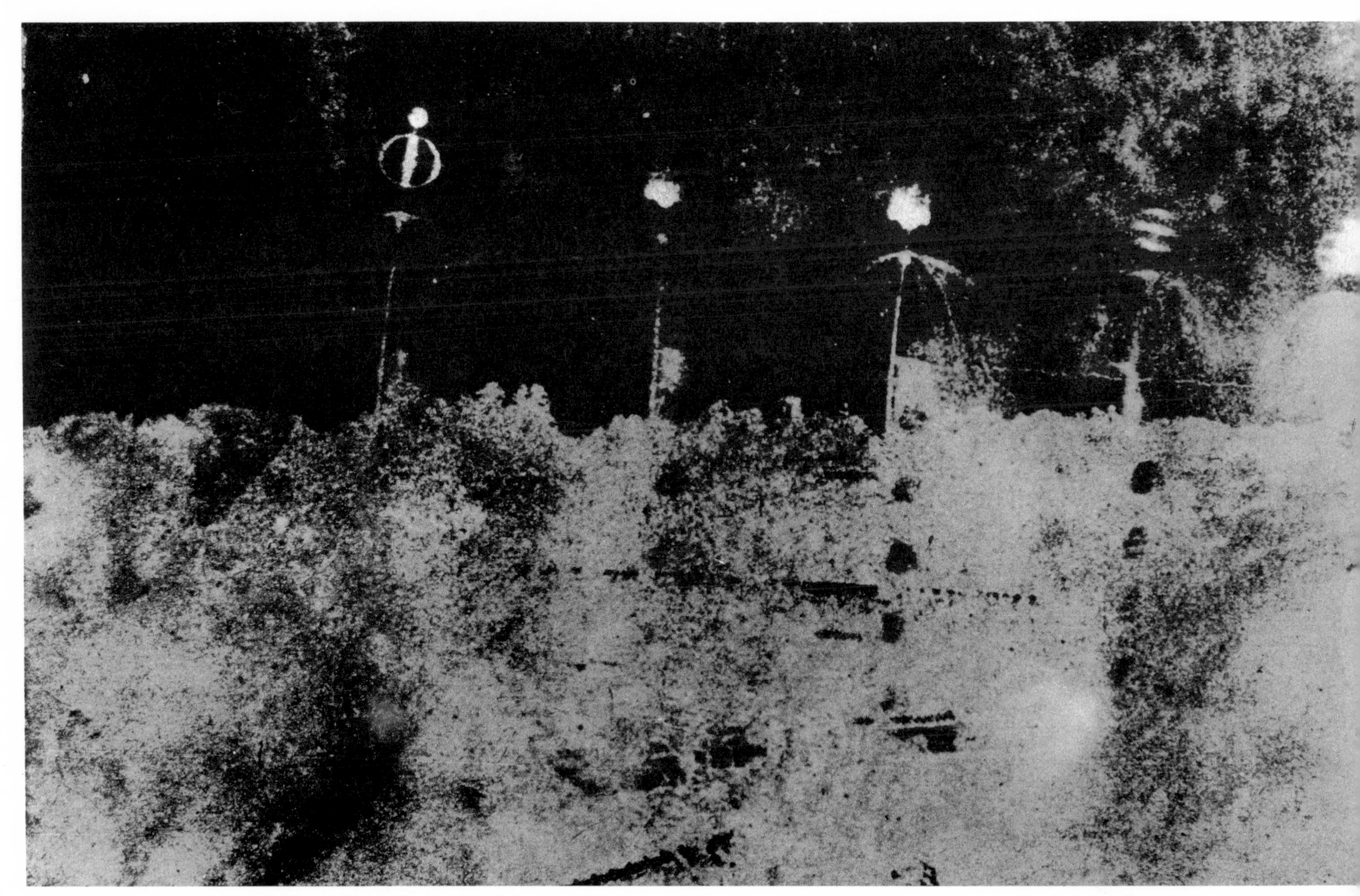

9. Negative of the May (Boys' Day) Festival celebration. Shimazu Nariakira. 1854–1860.

10. Government forces departing on the warship En-nen *for the Hakodate War. 1869.*

11. Samurai. 1853–1867.

12. Shintō functionary. 1868–1882.

oldiers about to depart for the Boshin War. Nakamura Masatomo. 1868.

14. *Samurai family. Hori Yohe-e. 1853–1867.*

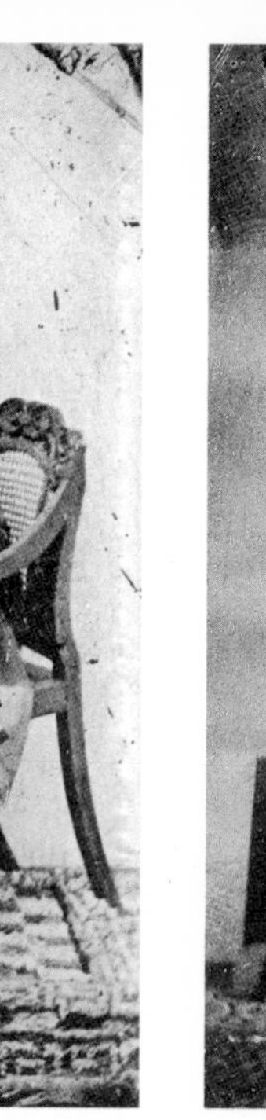

15. *Three men. Ryō Tenshinken. 1868–1882.*

16. *Samurai and woman. 1865–1867.*

17. *Three samurai. 1875.*

18. *Portrait of Katsuragi Yoshimasa. 1872.*

ung man. 1868–1882.

20. Soldiers from Satsuma. Miyauchi Studio. 1869.

23. Portrait of the photographer Matsuo Kanryō. 1868–1882.

rtrait of Ono Takahira. 1868–1882.

22. Man. 1868–1882.

24. Portrait of Ino Harufusa. Nakagawa Nobusuke. 1865.

TWO ▪ THE PERIOD OF ENLIGHTENMENT

'he harbor at Nagasaki. Ueno Hikoma. 1868–1882.

26. Foreigner in jinrikisha. Ueno Hikoma. 1868–1882.

27. Outdoor commemorative photograph. 1868–1882.

28. *Geisha. Ueno Hikoma. 1868–1882.*

29. *Old woman. Ueno Hikoma. 1868–1882.*

30. *Foreigners' mistresses. 1860s or early 1870s.*

Foreigner. Ueno Hikoma. 1868–1882.

32. Foreigner. Ueno Hikoma. 1868–1882.

33. Group photograph. Ueno Hikoma. 1860s or early 1870s.

Chinese woman. Ueno Hikoma. 1868–1882.

35. Chinese man. Ueno Hikoma. 1868–1882.

36. Samurai and foreigner. Ueno Hikoma. 1860s or early 1870s.

37. *Group photograph. Ueno Hikoma. 1860s or early 1870s.*

38. *Three samurai. Ueno Hikoma. 1860s or early 1870s.*

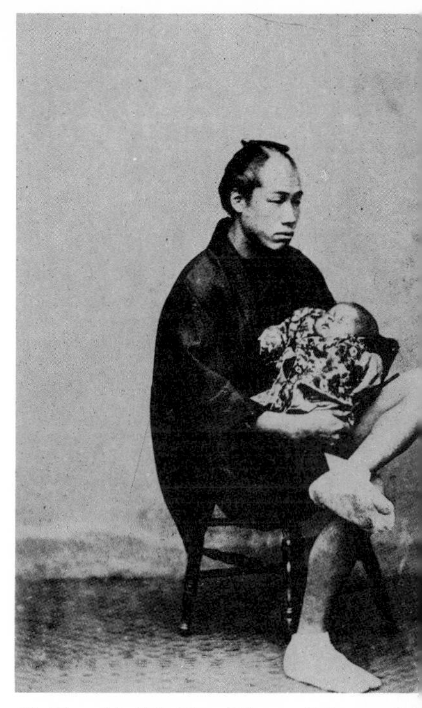

39. *Man with child. Ueno Hikoma. 1860s or early*

40. *Three men. Ueno Hikoma. 1860s or early 1870s.*

41. *Samurai. Ueno Hikoma. 1860s or early 1870s.*

Samurai. Ueno Hikoma. 1860s or early 1870s.

43. Samurai. Ueno Hikoma. 1860s or early 1870s.

46. Samurai. Ueno Hikoma. 1860s or early 1870s.

Samurai. Ueno Hikoma. 1868–1882.

45. Samurai. Ueno Hikoma. 1860s or early 1870s.

47. Battlement in the Shiroyama area of Kagoshima (Seinan War). Ueno Hikoma. 1877.

48. Solar eclipse. Shiina Sukemasa. 1894.

49. Ichinomura village (present-day Sapporo). c. 1871.

50. Construction of the Sapporo highway near Akagawa. 1872–1873.

51. Ōno village, on the outskirts of Hakodate. 1868–1882.

Road construction. 1868–1882.

53. The port of Hakodate. 1868–1882.

54. Hakodate street scene. 1868–1882.

55. Reclamation in Kuttyan. 1908–1909.

Agricultural experimental station on the outskirts of Hakodate. 1880.

57. Log bridge over the Toyohira River in Sapporo. c. 1871.

58. Construction of the Toyohira River bridge in Sapporo. 1875.

59. Test run on the Horonai Railroad. 1880.

60. The mouth of the Ishikari River. c. 1871.

. *Emigrants to Hokkaidō from Yamanashi prefecture. 1909.*

62. Housing of the farmer-militia in Muroran county. c. 1889.

63. Prisoner. Takebayashi Seiichi. 1868–1882.

Prisoner. Takebayashi Seiichi. 1868–1882.

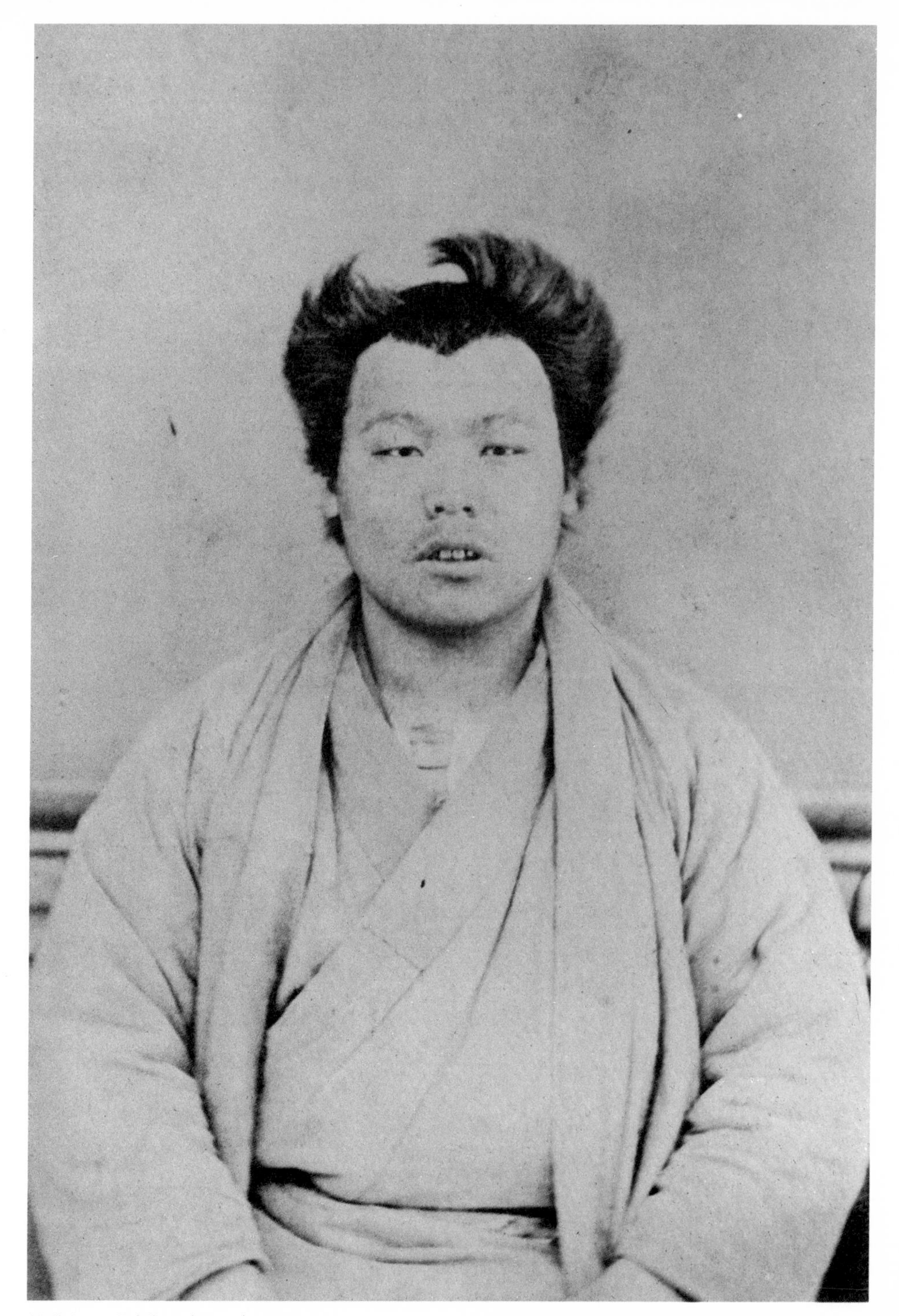

65. Prisoner. Takebayashi Seiichi. 1868–1882.

66. Ainu. 1868–1882.

River coolies. 1868–1882.

68. Family of the photographer Nagata Tomitarō. Nagata Tomitarō. 1926.

Cat of Sakhalin. 1898–1912.

70. *Woman and fishermen in Matsumae. Nagata Tomitarō. 1898–1912.*

71. *Shitakara coal mine in Kushiro. 1895.*

72. *Yūbari coal mine. 1898–1912.*

claimed land in Kuttyan. 1908–1909.

74. Drifting ice off the island of Etorofu. Endō Mutsuo. 1892.

od damage in Otaru. 1879.

76. *Ainu. Kajima Seizaburō. 1895.*

77. (left) *Lacquer-and-gold cover of a Meiji photo book.* (right) *Chiyoko, a geisha of the Nihonbashi district, Tokyo. From a photo book published around 1883–1897.*

78. A merchant. 1868–1882.

79. Buddhist priests. 1860s or early 1870s.

ıysician. 1868–1882.

81. Girls tending infants. 1860s or early 1870s.

82. "Kago, Travelling Chair." 1868–1882.

83. Street tumblers with lion masks. 1860s or early 1870s.

A post-town prostitute. 1860s or early 1870s.

85. "Prisoner." 1868–1882.

86. Woman in Western dress, child with doll. Kizu Kōkichi. 1868–1882.

Comic entertainer. 1883–1897.

88. Nihonbashi Bridge in Tokyo. 1883–1897.

89. The beacon at Kudanzaka in Tokyo. Uchida Kuichi. 1870–1882.

90. *"View of Main Street, Tokio." 1883–1897.*

91. *Rokumeikan pavilion. 1883–1897.*

92. *Kenshunmon gateway at the Kyoto Imperial Palace. Uchida Kuichi. 1868–1882.*

93. *Shintomiza Kabuki theater in Tokyo. 1868–1882.*

Suruga Tagonoura Bridge, to Fujiyama." 1883–1897.

95. *"Enoshima." 1868–1882.*

yomizu Temple in Kyoto. Uchida Kuichi. 1868–1882.

97. *"View of Imaichi, at Nikko Road." 1883–1897.*

98. Shinbashi train station. Mitsumura Risō. 1900.

99. Azuma Bridge in Tokyo. Mitsumura Risō. 1900.

100. "Mitsui-gumi House" in Tokyo. Uchida Kuichi. 1872–1882.

101. "Gion-machi, Kioto." 1868–1882.

Pagoda of the Yasaka Shrine in Kyoto. Uchida Kuichi. 1868–1882.

103. "English Club at Kobe." 1868–1882.

Sanjūsangendō Temple in Kyoto. Uchida Kuichi. 1868–1882.

105. Shureinomon gate in Okinawa. Mitsumura Risō. 1901.

106. *Test blasting of a torpedo on the Sumida River. Ezaki Reiji. 1883.*

107. *Egyptian mummy. c. 1874.*

"Carved Cat, Nikko." 1868–1882.

Construction site in Hokkaidō. Shimizu Tōkoku. 1868–1882.

110. Guardian deity at Kōfukuji Temple. Ogawa Kazumasa. 1883–1897.

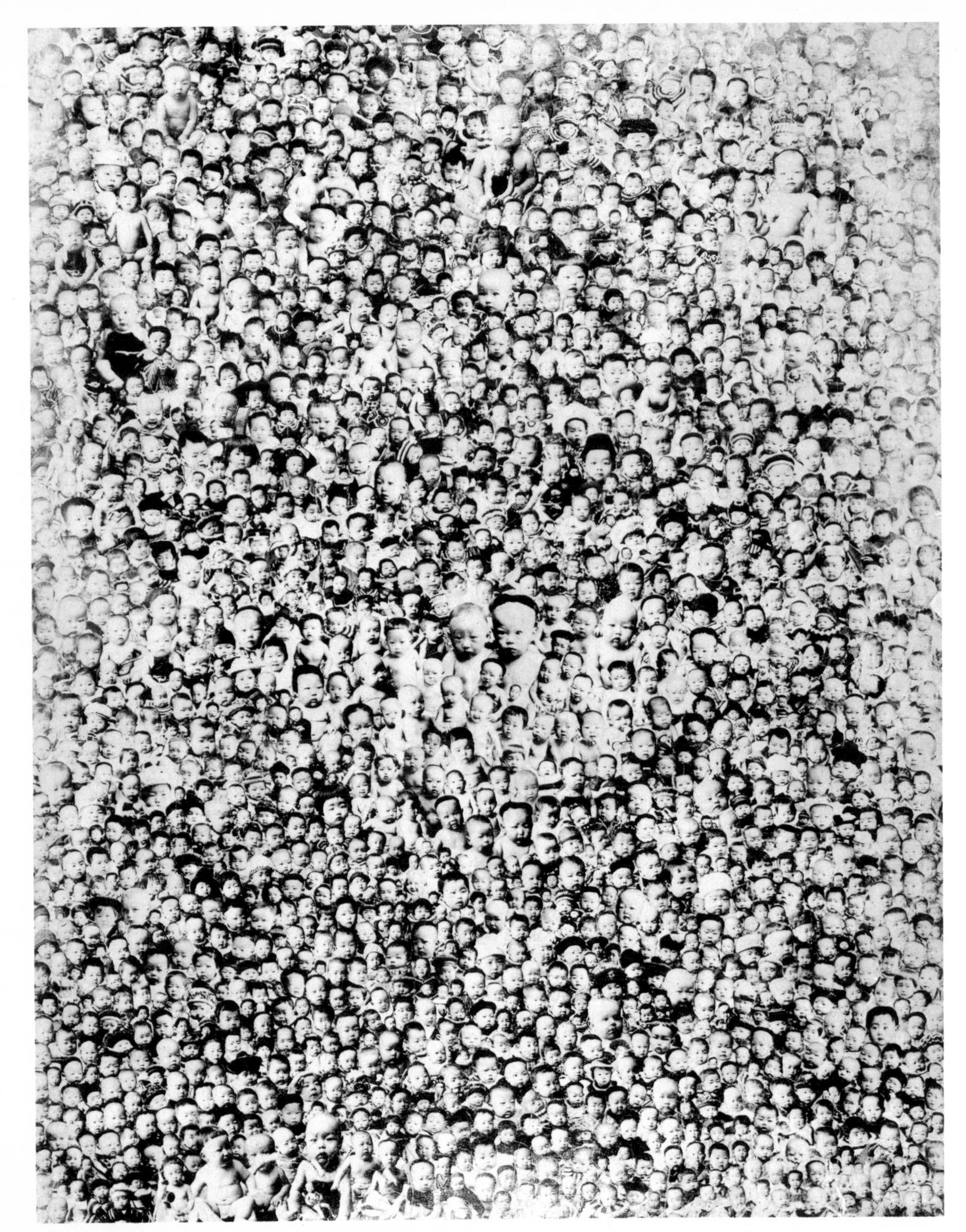

111. Collage of 1,700 babies. Ezaki Reiji. 1893.

112. Dilapidated interior of Edo Castle. Yokoyama Matsusaburō. Pre-1871.

113. *"Home Bathing." 1883–1897.*

114. *"Harakiri." 1883–1897.*

115. *"Jinrikisha." 1883–1897.*

116. *"Girls in Bed Room." 1883–1897.*

"Bronze Image (Daibutsu) at Uyeno, Tokio." 1883–1897.

118. "Shimoda." 1883–1897.

"Shiraito Waterfall, at Fujiyama." 1883–1897.

120. "Scene Sumida River, at Mukojima, Tokio." 1883–1897.

121. *A courtesan. 1868–1882.*

122. *Kokiyo, a geisha of the Shinbashi district. 1883–1897.*

THREE ■ COMMERCIAL PHOTOGRAPHY

123. A family in New York. Kikuchi Tōyō. 1909–1919.

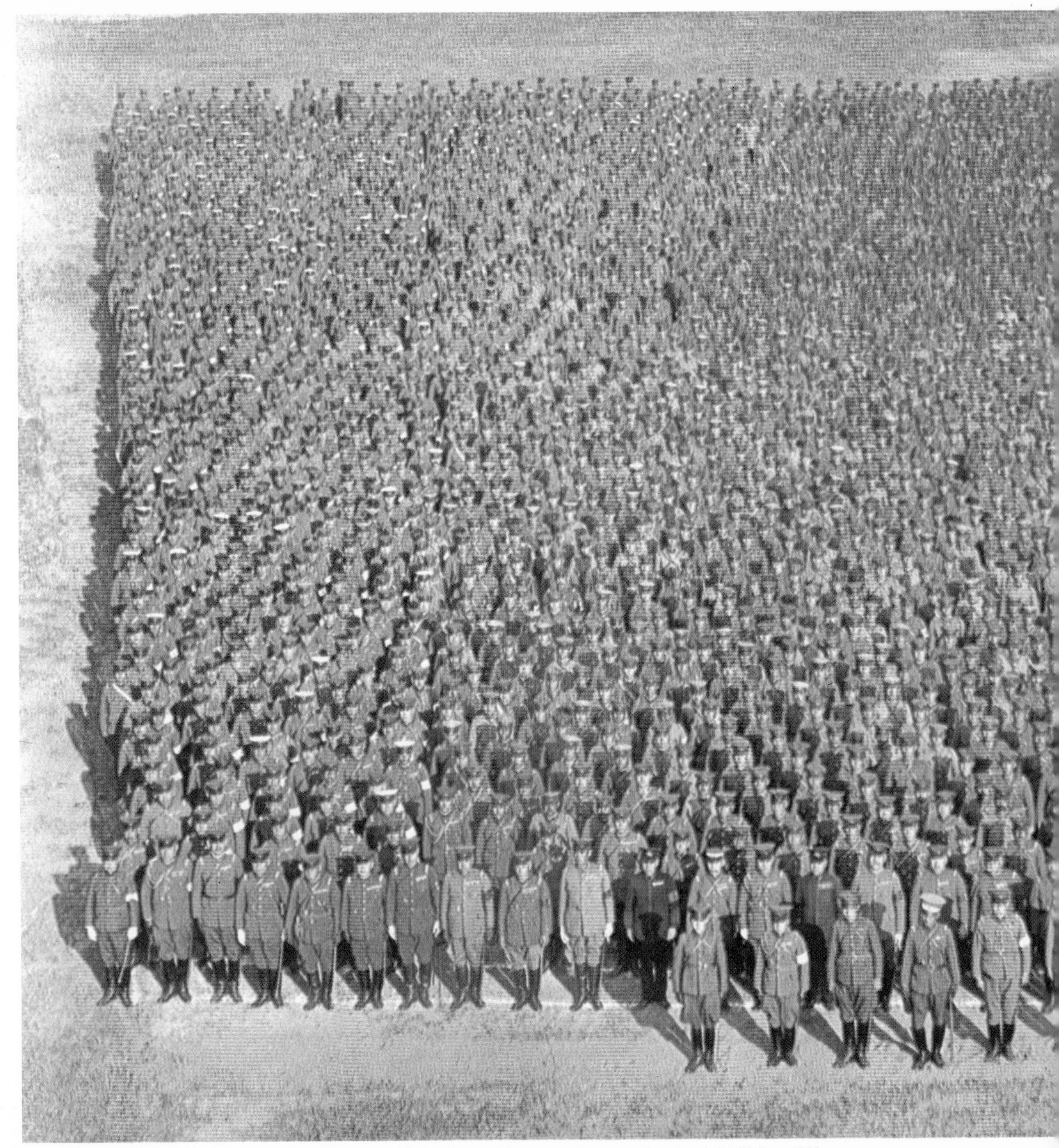

124. Officers and soldiers participating in grand maneuvers in Fukui prefecture. The emperor is in center foreground. G. T. Sun. 1933.

125. "Self-portrait." Harry K. Shigeta (Shigeta Kinji). Late 1920s or 1930s.

126. "The Venerable Tagore." Igarashi Yoshichi. 1929.

127. Shimazu Hisanori, seventh son of Shimazu Tadayoshi. Shunsho-kan Studio. 1880.

128. The Meiji emperor. 1883–1897.

The Taishō emperor wearing the Order of the Garter received from the King of England. 1912.

130. Emperor Hirohito. 1928.

131. Little girl. Tamoto Kenzō. 1887.

ittle boy. Nagata Tomitarō. 1912.

133. "Young Girl." Ezaki Kiyoshi. 1928.

134. Siblings. Fujimoto Otokichi. 1898–1912.

en wearing mantles. Kajima Seibe-e. 1898–1912.

136. "Portrait of Teru." Miyauchi Kōtarō. 1901.

137. *Bride and groom. Maruki Riyō. 1918.*

138. *Siblings. Hori Masumi. 1898–1912.*

139. *Family. Masuda Photograph Studio. 1900.*

140. *"Portrait Study." Shibata Tsunekichi. 1889.*

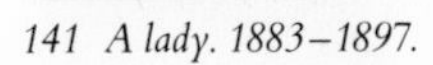

141 *A lady. 1883–1897.*

142. *Portrait of Tokugawa Tameko. Maruki Riyō. 1908.*

143. *A lady. Itani Photograph Studio. 1898–1912.*

144. *A lady. Itō Ryūkichi. 1927.*

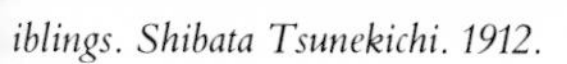
iblings. Shibata Tsunekichi. 1912.

146. Sisters. Maruki Riyō. 1912.

147. "Portrait of Fujita Yōko." Kikuchi Tōyō. 1928.

young lady. Ariga Toragorō. 1924.

149. A woman. Yasukōchi Jiichirō. 1935.

150. "Child." Ogawa Gesshū. 1928.

151. Vice Admiral Enomoto Takeaki (Buyō). 1880–1881.

152. The statesman Itō Hirobumi. Maruki Riyō. 1898–1910.

The parliamentarian Ozaki Yukio. Kobayashi Hiroshi. 1930.

154. Chaliapin. Nakayama Shōichi. 1936.

155. *"Portrait of Three Geisha."* 1898–1912.

lderly couple (a portrait of his parents). Ogawa Kazumasa. 1892.

157. Actresses in the Imperial Theater, Tokyo. Morikawa Aizō. 1929.

158. Leaders of the Constitutional Democratic Party. 1929.

159. *Faculty and students of the Naval Academy. Uchida Kuichi. 1873.*

160. Satsuma riflemen departing for the front during the Boshin War. 1867–1868.

. *Officers at the siege of Kumamoto Castle during the Seinan War. Tomishige Rihei. 1877.*

162. Japanese and Korean dignitaries in Seoul. Mitsumura Risō. 1909.

163. Women at the Shimazu residence in Kagoshima. Sugimoto Photograph Studio. 1902.

164. A gathering in honor of the head of a university. Iizuka Photograph Studio. 1886.

165. A gathering of elementary-school children. Suzuki Shinichi. 1898–1912.

166. The women's class of the Iwate Teachers School. Nara Photograph Studio. 1914.

167. Students in the orchestra and chorus of the Tokyo Music Academy. Miyauchi Kōtarō. 1898–1912.

168. The emperor (center front) and naval officers and men on the flagship Nagato. *1929.*

FOUR RECORDS OF WAR, I

9. *A battalion of farmer-militia prior to departure for the Chinese front. Suzuki Shinichi. 1895.*

170. *The battle of the Yellow Sea. 1894.*

. Artillery shelling near Port Arthur. 1894.

172. A military bridge near Mukden. Hosaka Kōtarō. 1905.

Practice firing from a warship. Ichioka Tajirō. 1905.

174. Japanese infantry in battle near Likiatun. Ogura Kenji. 1904.

175. Russian war dead on 203-Meter Hill. Ōtsuka Tokusaburō. 1904.

176. Japanese infantry by an uncompleted Russian military railroad bridge. Saitō Jirō. 1905.

177. Japanese infantry in Sakhalin. 1905.

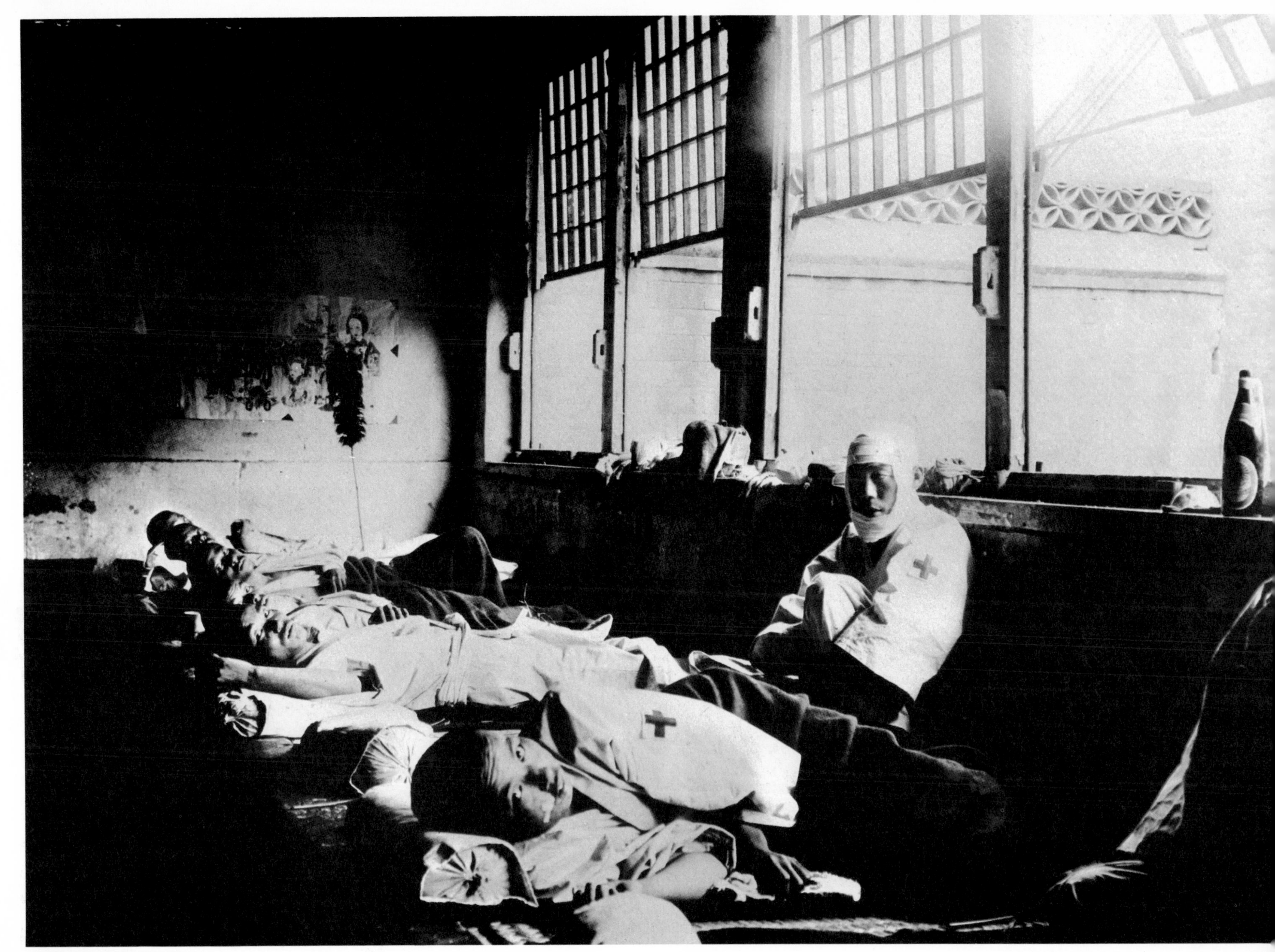

178. Wounded soldiers in Kai-pingting. Hosaka Kōtarō. 1904.

9. Street in Changtu. Morikane Shūgaku. 1905.

180. Explosion on the outskirts of Port Arthur. Ōtsuka Tokusaburō. 1904.

. *Japanese soldiers killed in the battle of Tashihkiao. Ogura Kenji. 1904.*

182. Beheading of a spy on the outskirts of Kaiyuan. 1905.

183. Russian and Japanese truce delegations in Changtu. Ogura Kenji. 1905.

184. A storm-tossed landing place in Shantung. 1914.

185. Vendors catering to German prisoners of war at the Ōita depot in Japan. 1917.

186. The corpse of Private Yamamoto. 1919.

187. Japanese infantry near Nerchinsk. 1919.

188. Corpses of partisans massacred by the Japanese army near Chita. 1920.

Weapons confiscated by the Japanese in a Siberian village. 1919.

190. Japanese workers in an engine shed near Chita. 1919.

191. Trains containing Russian refugees in the Chita railroad yard. 1920.

192. A reception in northern Manchuria for a delegation from the Japanese House of Representatives. 1919.

FIVE ART PHOTOGRAPHY

193. "Bullfight." Nakayama Iwata. Spain, 1926.

194. "Peony." Umesaka Ōri. 1931.

"Woman under a Tree." Nojima Kōzō. 1915.

196. "White Flower." Tamura Sakae. 1931.

197. "Flowing Quietly in the Ravine." Ogawa Gesshū. 1927.

"The Clatter of People and Horses." Yonetani Kōrō. 1926.

199. "After the Rain." Umesaka Ōri. 1933.

"Loquat." Nojima Kōzō. 1930.

201. "Snow on Bamboo." Takahashi Kinka. 1907.

202. "Moonlit Night by the Lake Shore." Fujii Shimei. 1907.

"Quiet Temple in the Autumn Woods." Urahara Seiho. 1926.

204. "Estuary." Ogawa Gesshū. 1925.

205. *"The Shade of Trees." Hidaka Chōtarō. 1921.*

206. *"Moonlight on Snow." Itō Fumikazu. 1922.*

207. *"Scene of Fura." Hirao Keiji. 1926.*

8. *"Scene with Myself." Itō Ryōzō. 1932.*

209. "Snow." Yonetani Kōrō. 1922.

0. *"Winter." Izumi Toshirō. 1928.*

211. "Faint Sunlight." Yamanaka Hekisui. 1922.

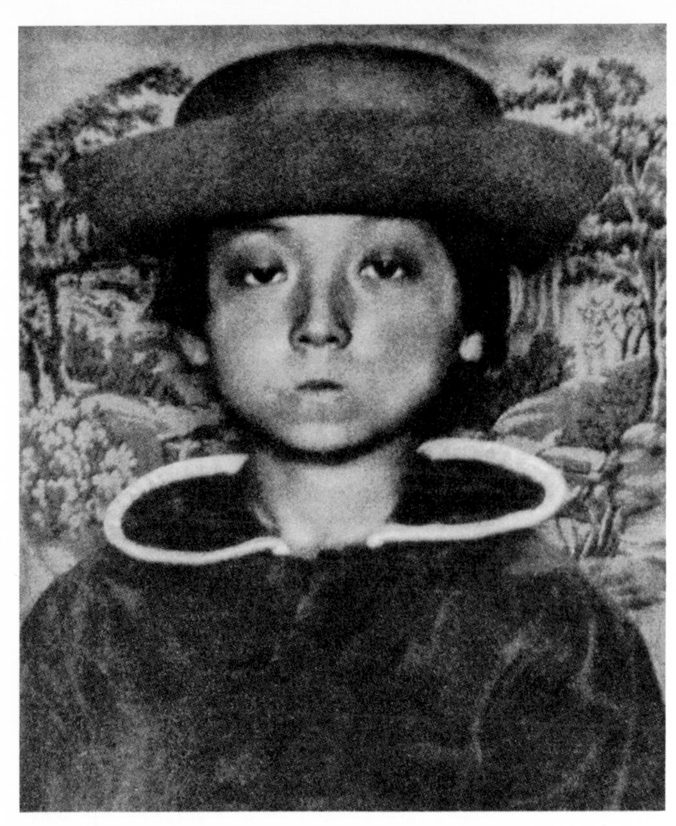

212. "Portrait of a Little Girl." Yamamotó Makihiko. 1929.

213. "Portrait of Sisters Standing Outdoors." Takao Yoshirō. 1929.

4. *"Person in a Room." Matsugi Fujio. 1930.*

215. *"Scene with Factory." Takayama Toshio. 1930.*

216. "Mr. Takada Minayoshi." Tsusaka Jun. 1929.

217. "Young Boy Toying with a Snake." Hagiwara Roshū. 1928.

8. *"Backyard." Matsugi Fujio. 1930.*

219. *"Scene." Tōyo Kichisaburō. 1930.*

220. "Woman in Paris." Fukuhara Shinzō. 1926.

1. “Pond at Shuzenji Temple.” Fukuhara Shinzō. 1926.

222. “Autumn in Okutama.” Fukuhara Shinzō. 1925.

223. "Nara Scene." Fukuhara Rosō. 1925.

224. "Fifty Subjects in Tokyo (No. 1)." Nishiyama Kiyoshi. 1926.

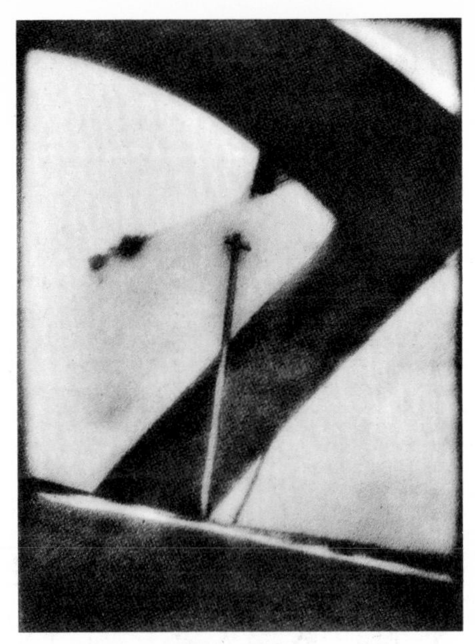

225. "Bridge." Tsusaka Jun. 1926.

226. "Still Life." Fukuda Katsuji. 1926.

227. "Still Life." Takayama Masataka. 1926.

. "Lines." Sugimoto Saburō. 1928.

229. "Composition of Lines." Yamazaki Masuzō. 1926.

230. "Study (1)." Matsuo Saigorō. 1926.

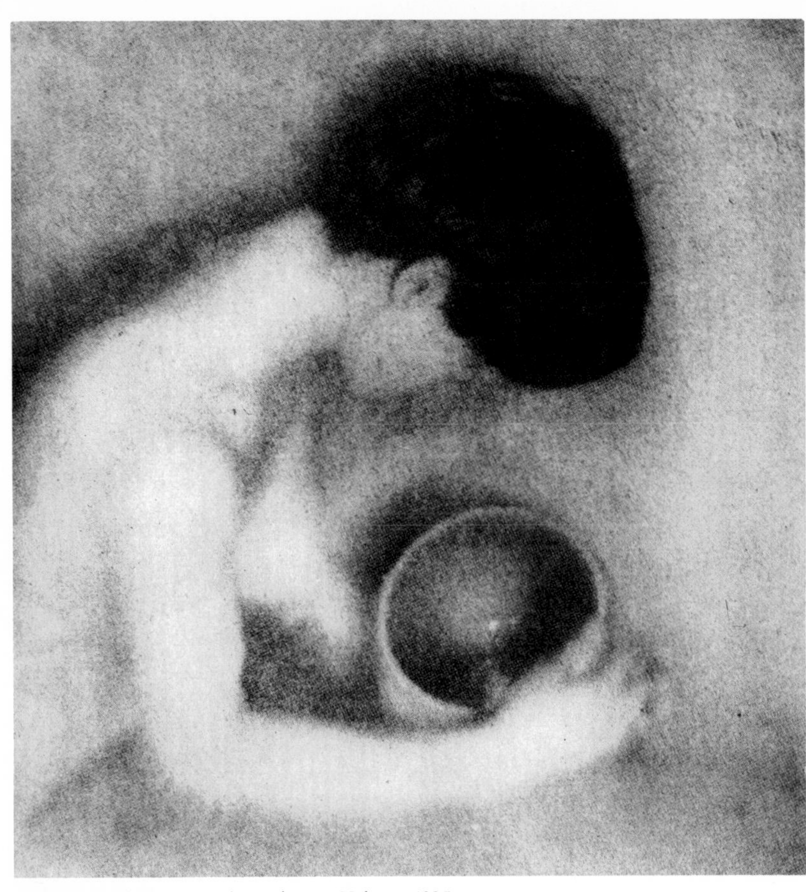

231. "Man Holding a Bowl." Fuchigami Hakuyō. 1925.

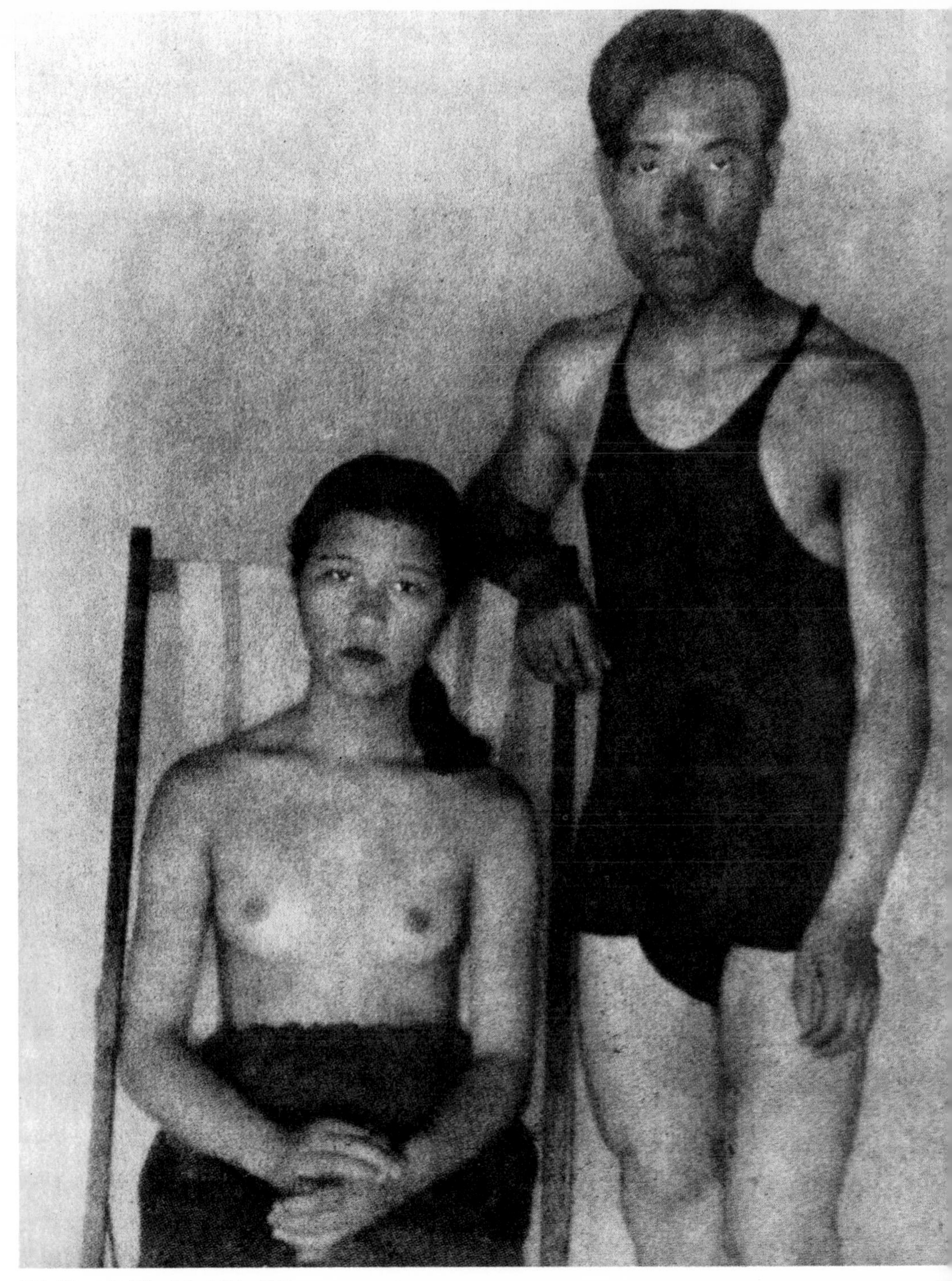

232. "Portrait of Two." Satō Shin. 1932.

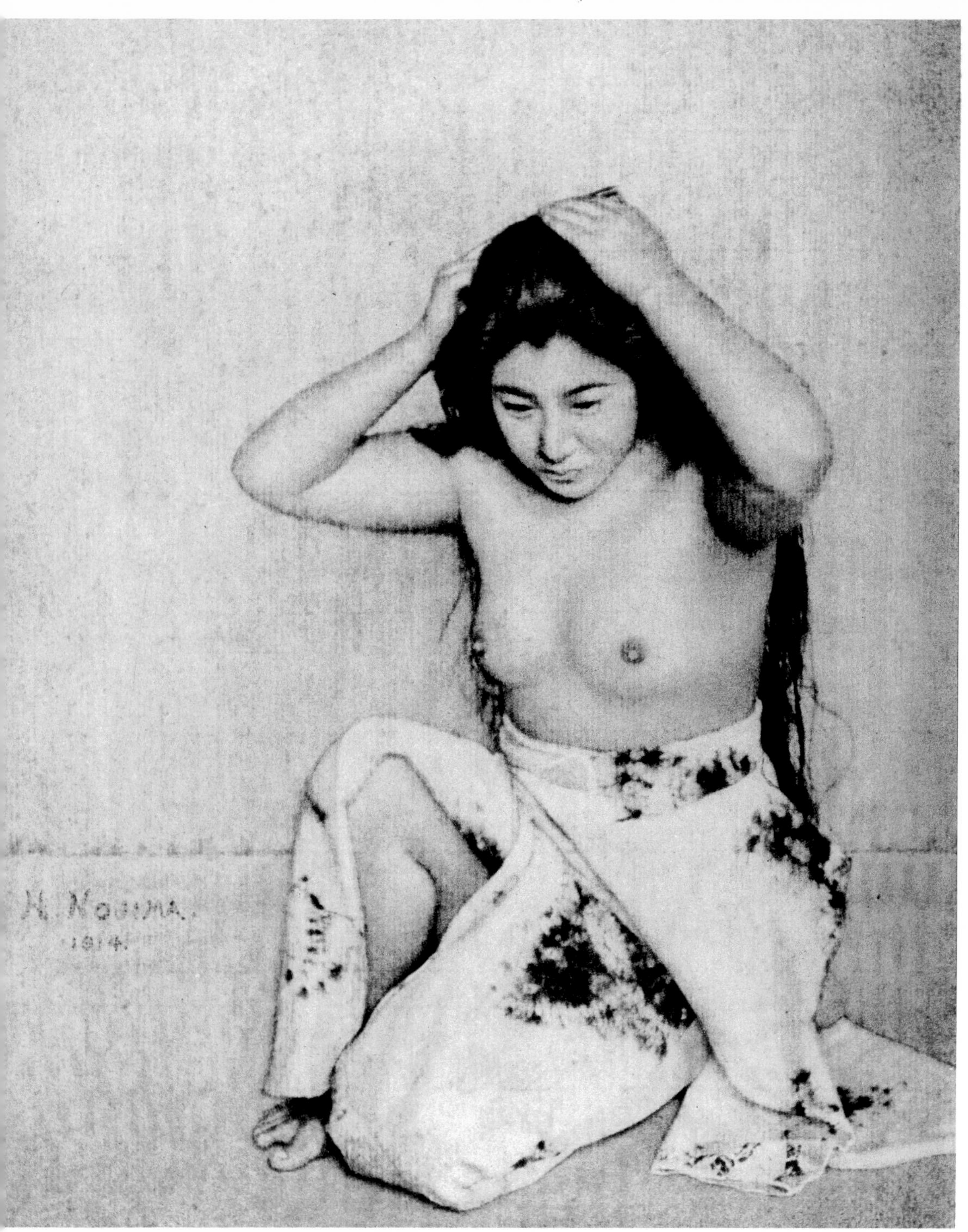

"Woman Combing Hair." Nojima Kōzō. 1914.

234. "Strength." Tamamura Kihei. 1922.

235. *"A Lonely Person." Eguchi Nanyō. 1920.*

236. *"Portait of a Lady." Yasumoto Kōyō. 1938.*

237. "People Serving God." Ono Ryūtarō. 1915.

238. "Portrait." Yoshikawa Tomizō. 1924.

239. *"Street Scene." Nakayama Iwata. New York, 1922.*

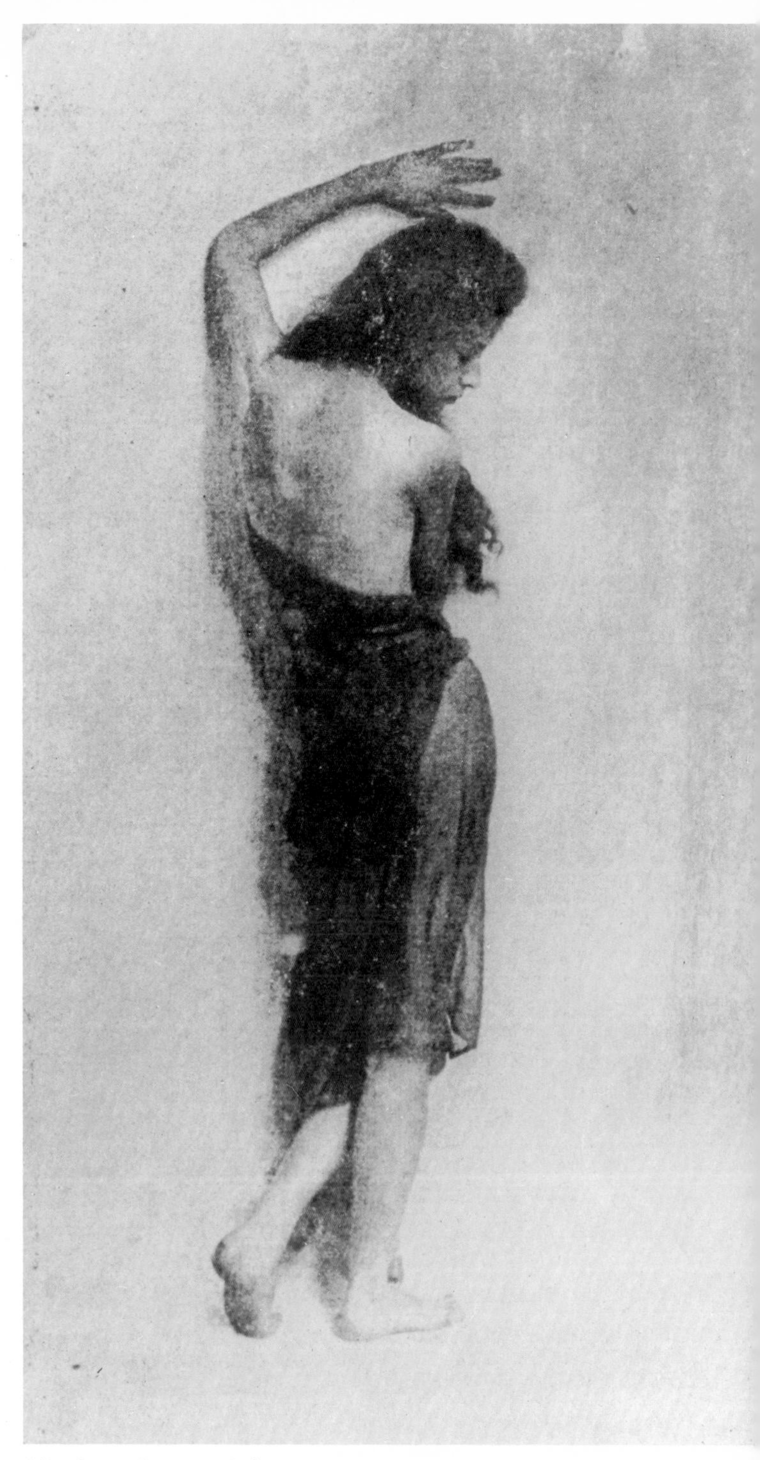

240. *"Portrait." Kajiwara Takuma. St. Louis, 1926.*

. *"Tamiris in 1927." Suminami Sōichi. New York, 1928.*

242. "Portrait of a Dancer." Nakayama Iwata. New York, 1922.

243. "Priest Taking a Stroll." Yamamoto Makihiko. 1927.

SIX THE EPOCH OF DEVELOPMENT

244. "Woman." Nojima Kōzō. 1933.

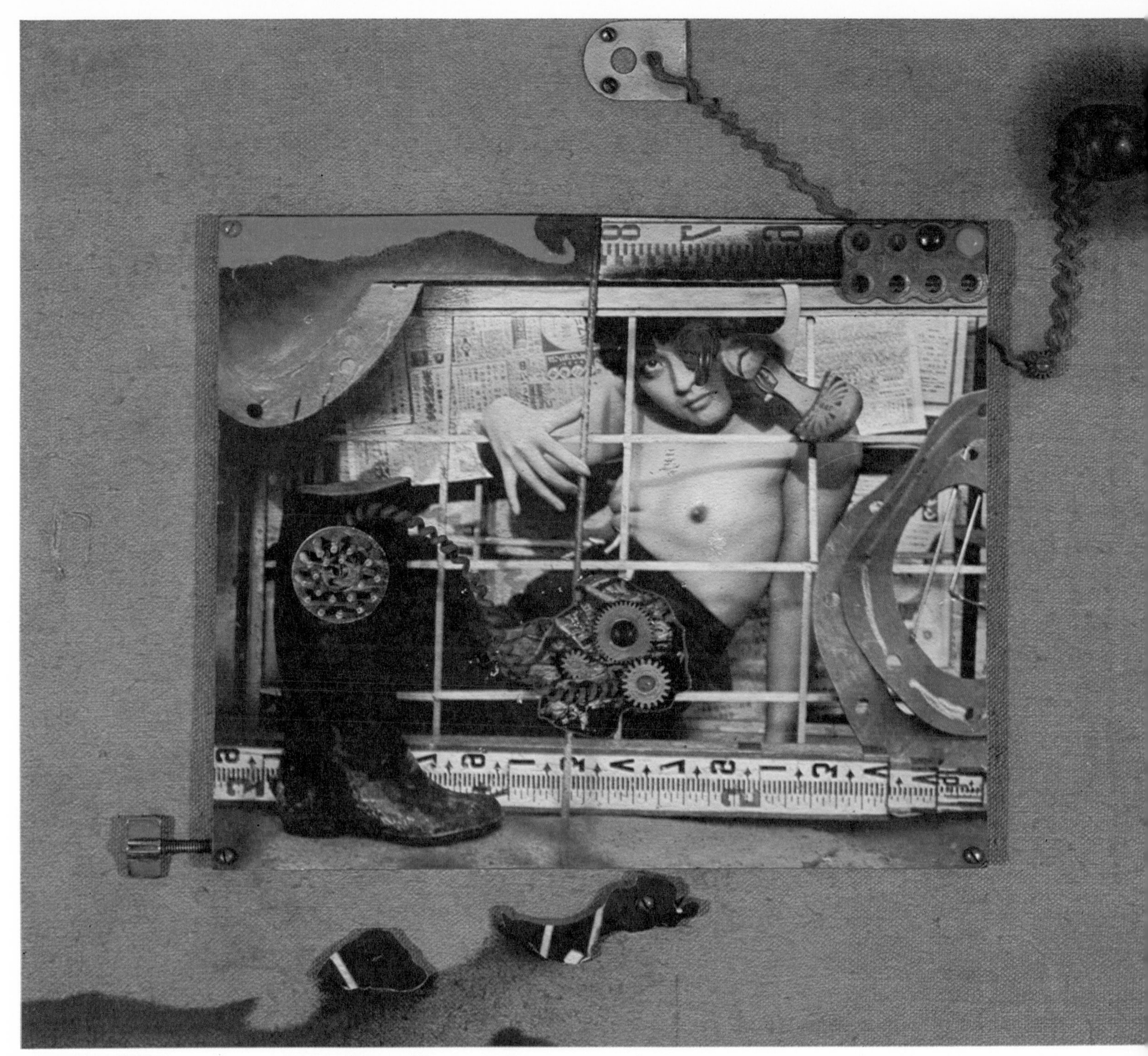

245. "Concept of the Machinery of the Creator." Hanawa Gingo. c. 1930.

"Fashion." Hirai Terushichi. 1938.

247. "A Dream of the Moon." Hirai Terushichi. 1938.

248. "Balinese Dancers." Kitazumi Genzō. 1942.

249. "A House." Kondō Tatsuo. 1937.

250. "Paper." Kōmura Kiyohiko. 1936.

251. "Ochanomizu Station." Watanabe Yoshio. 1933.

252. "Water Flowers." Aida Tamon. 1941.

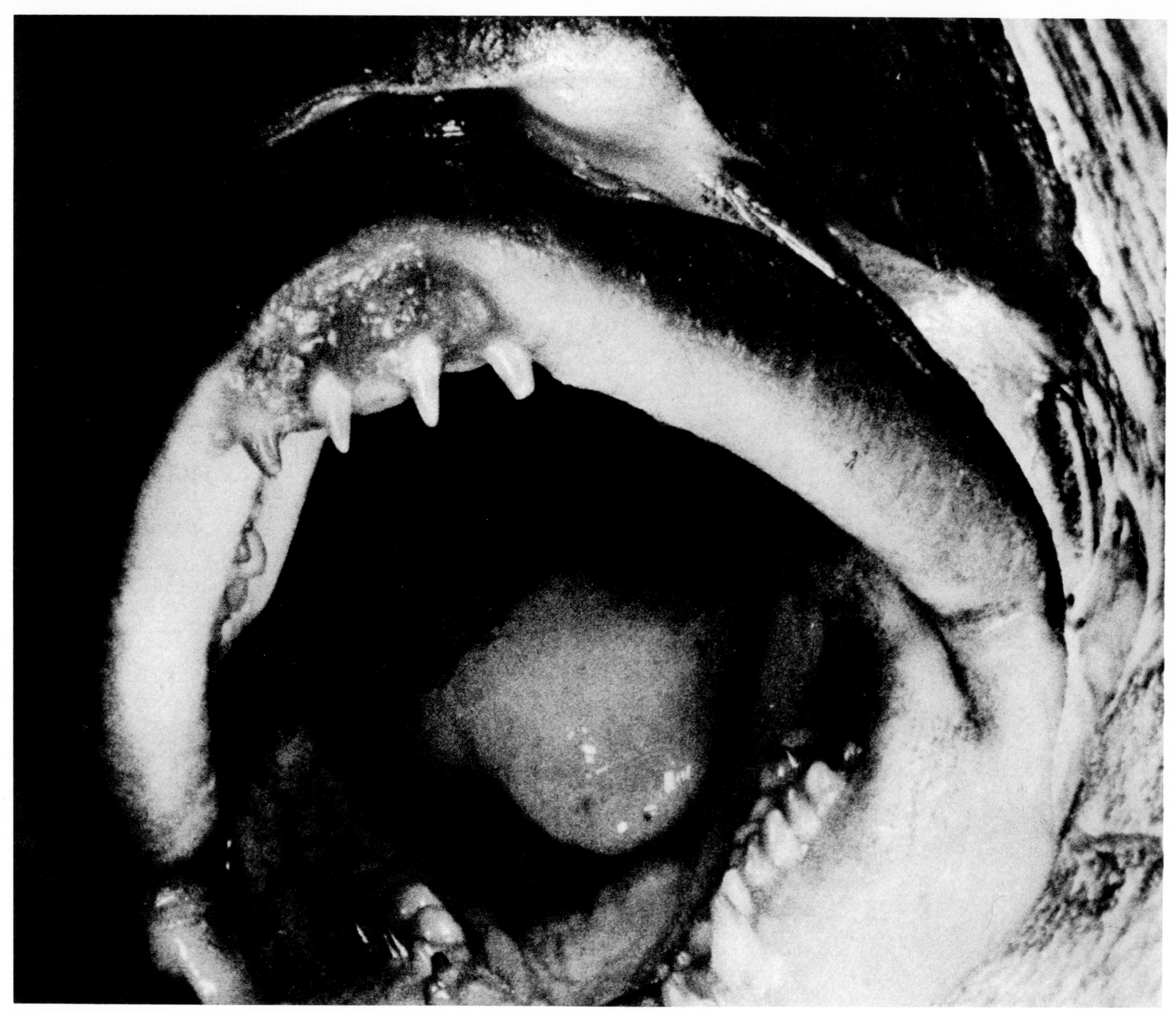

253. "Sea Bream." Benitani Kichinosuke. 1932.

254. "Crushed Expression." Majima Shōichi. 1940.

255. "Sweat." Narita Shunyō. 1937.

. "Temptation: the Passion of Steel." Koishi Kiyoshi. 1933.

257. "Hands of Amida, the National Treasure at Kōryūji Temple." Domon Ken. 1941.

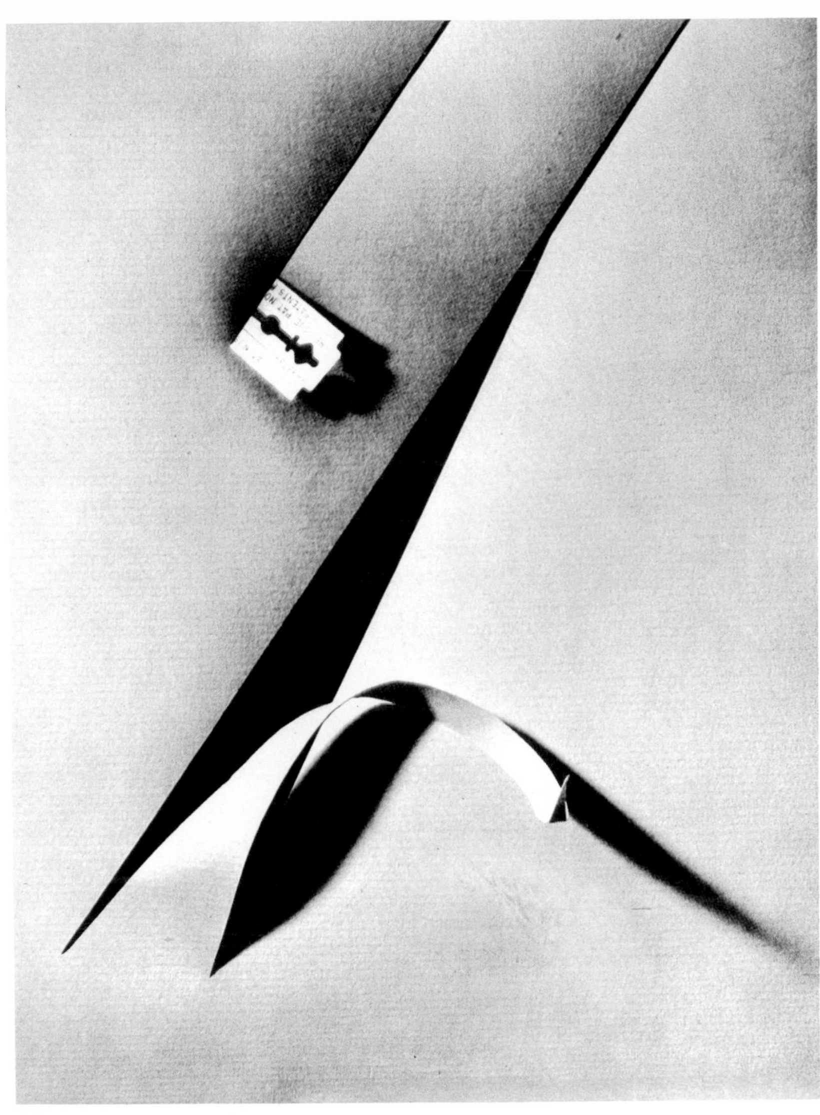

258. "Composition." Wakayanagi Yoshitarō. 1933.

259. "Chimney." Kōno Tōru. 1940.

260. "Camera: Eye × Steel • Composition." Horino Masao. 1932.

261. "......" *Yamakawa Ken-ichirō. 1933.*

262. *"Merchandise at a Store." Iida Kōjirō. 1931.*

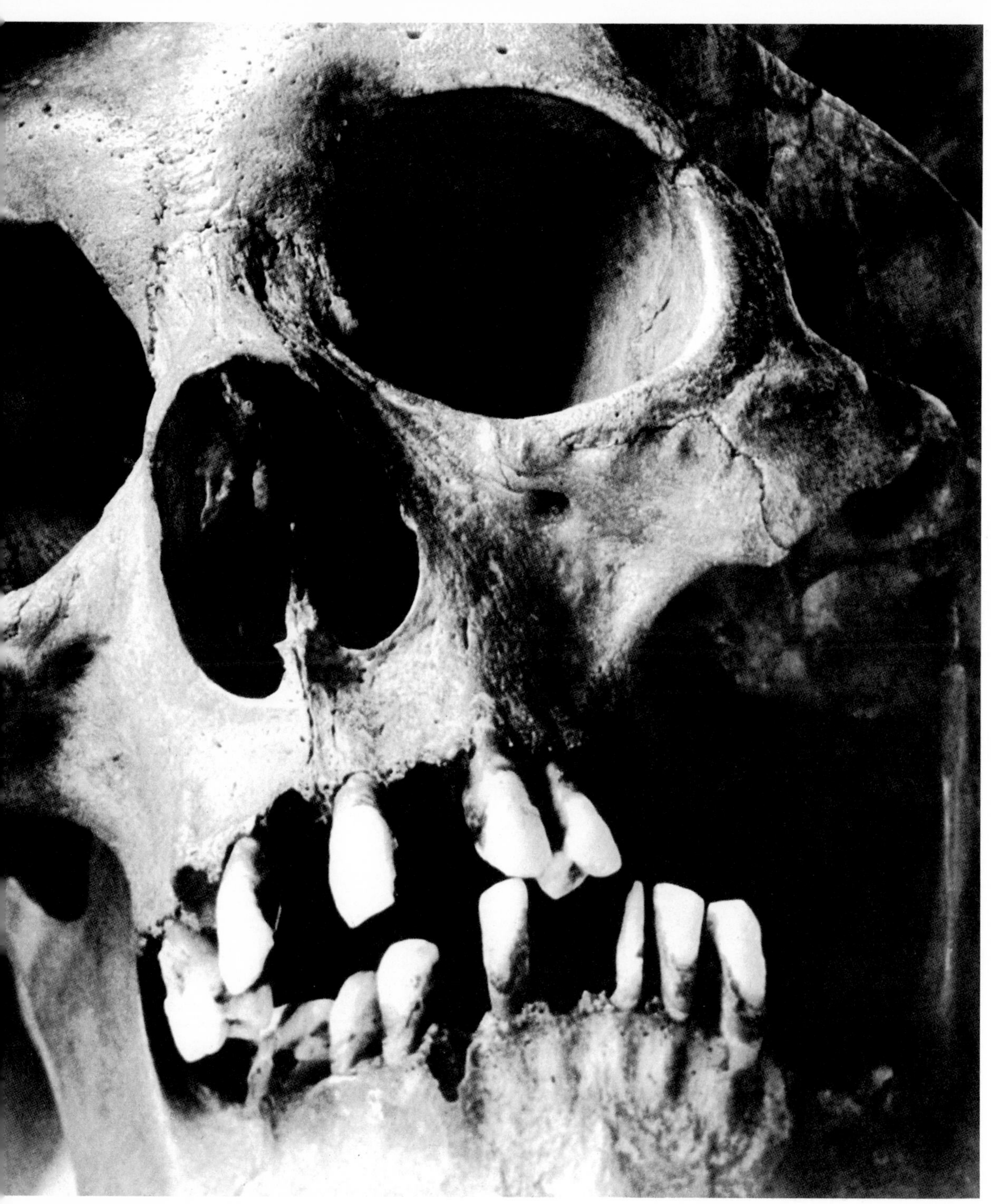

"Skeleton." Nakamura Kenji. 1934.

264. "Chrysanthemum Wedging." Domon Ken. 1941.

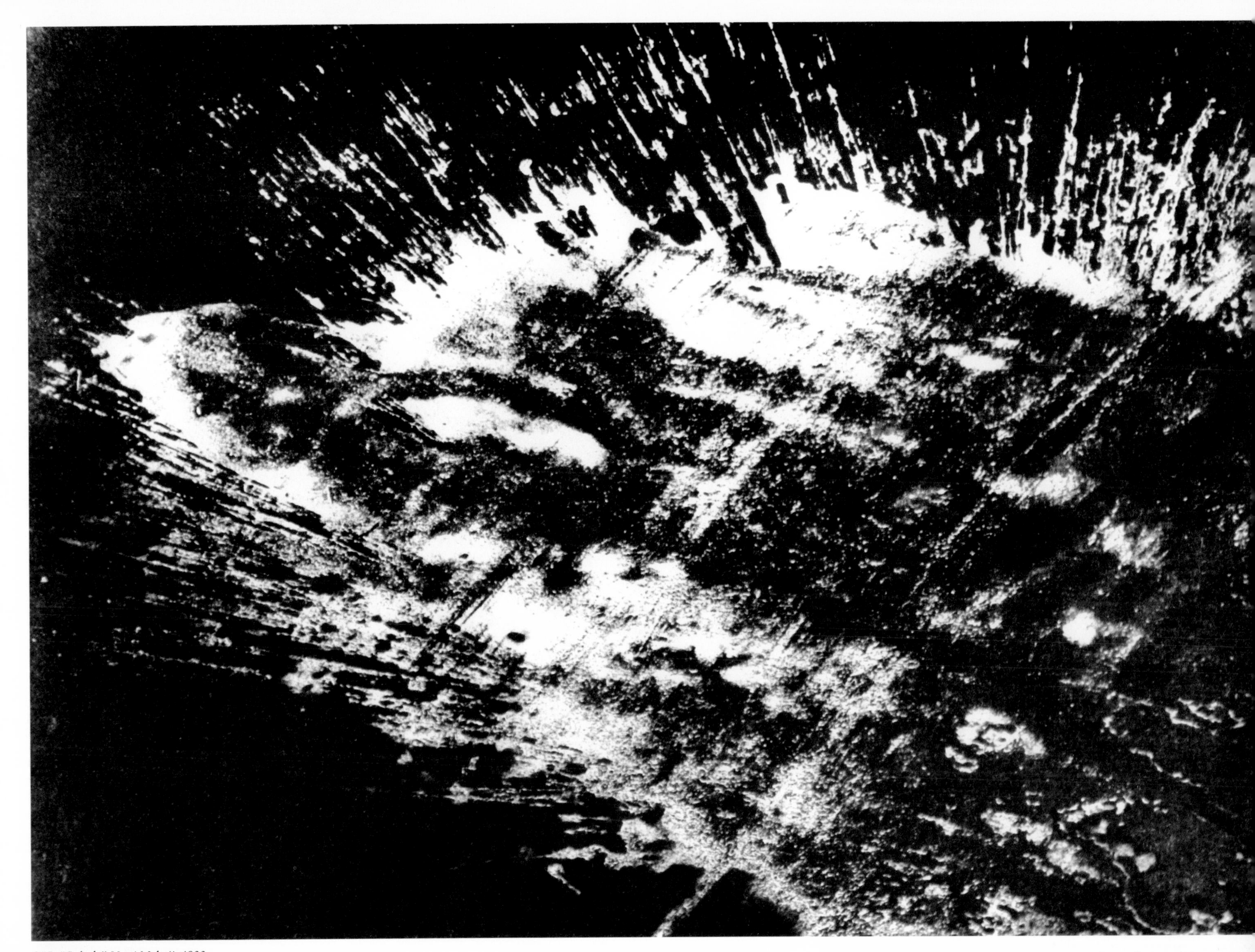

265. "Splash." Yasui Nakaji. 1933.

66. "Swimming." Shibata Ryūji. 1937.

267. "Silhouette." Ueda Shōji. 1936.

268. "So What!" Hanaya Kanbe-e. 1937.

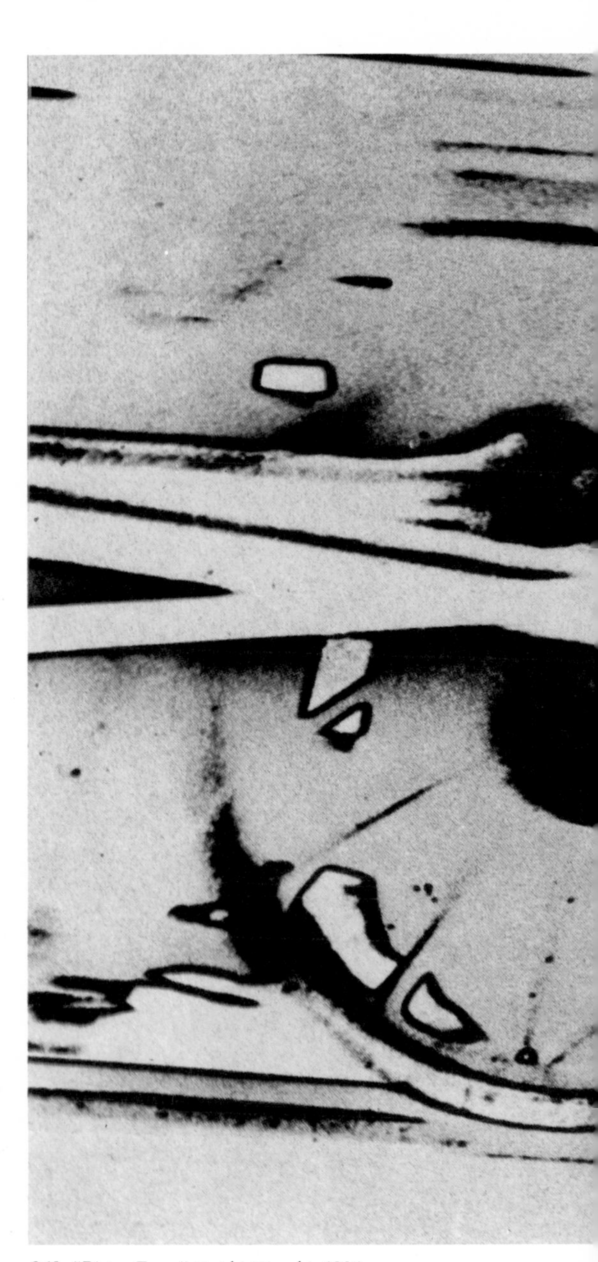

269. "Piston Fury." Koishi Kiyoshi. 1934.

270. "Delight." Ueda Bizan. 1940.

1. *"Feeling of Fatigue." Koishi Kiyoshi. 1936.*

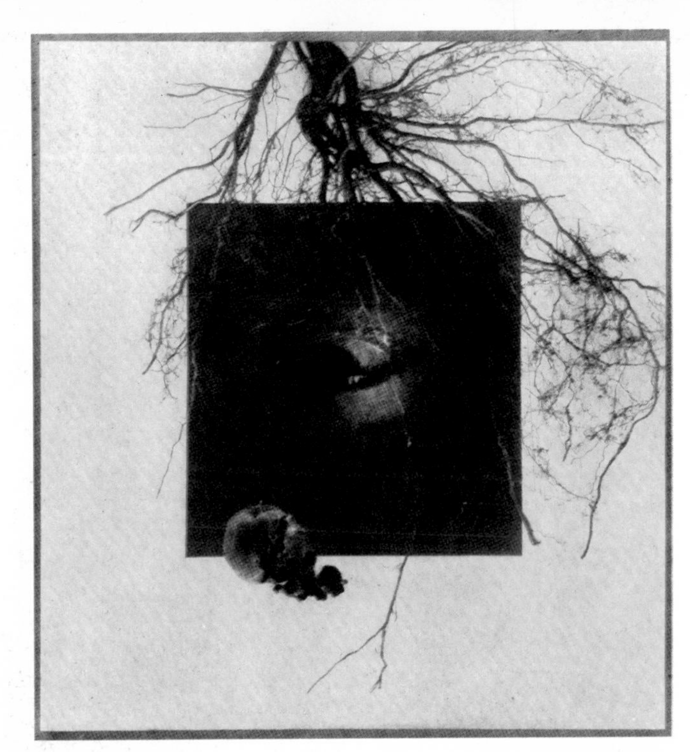

272. "Taste of Autumn." Tanaka Shinpei. 1932.

273. "No Title." Matsubara Jūzō. 1935.

274. "Legend of Night." Hattori Yoshifumi. 1938.

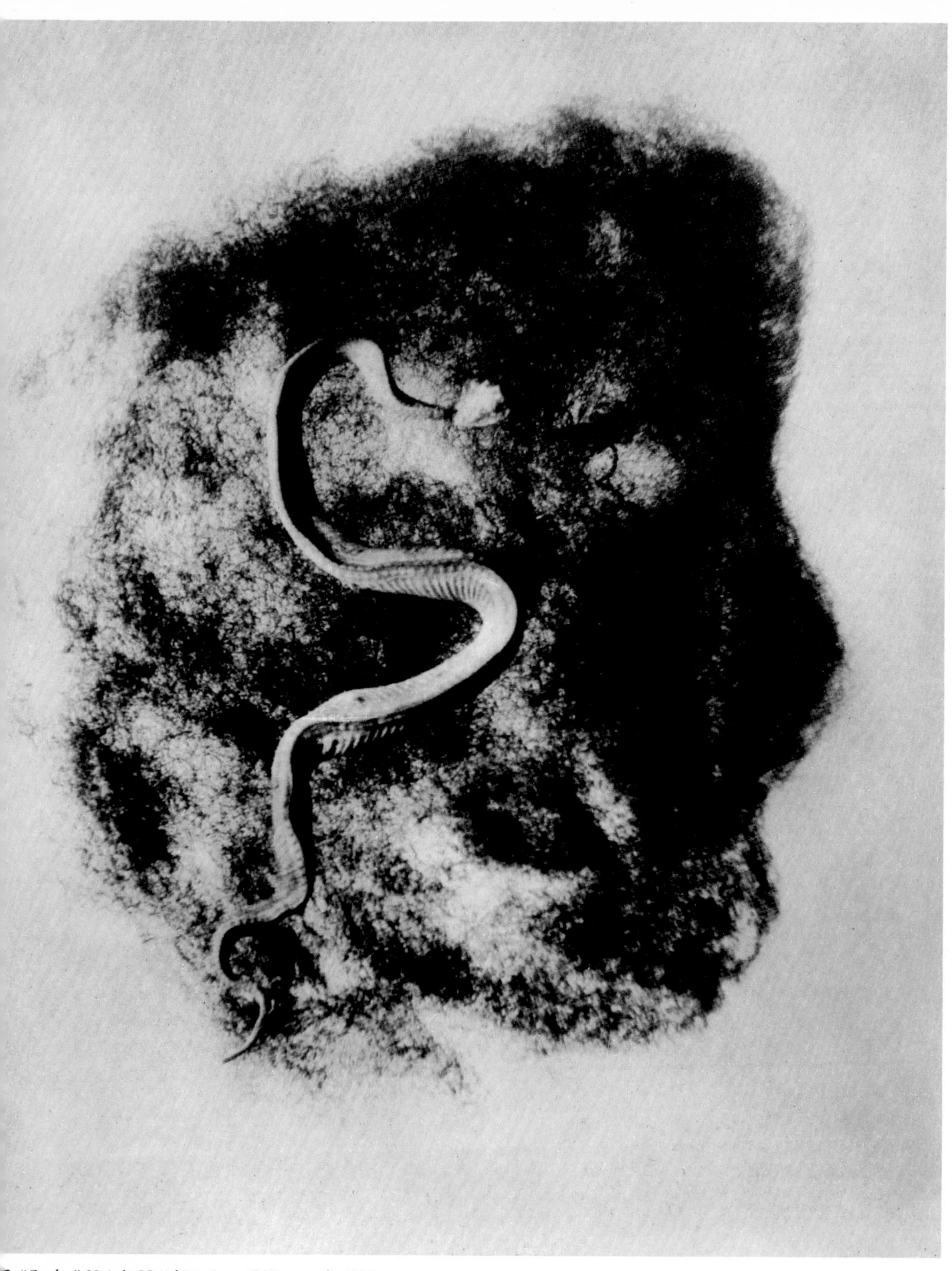

5. *"Snake." Kaieda Heiichirō. Late 1920s or early 1930s.*

276. *"From Nature." Tajima Tsuguo. 1940.*

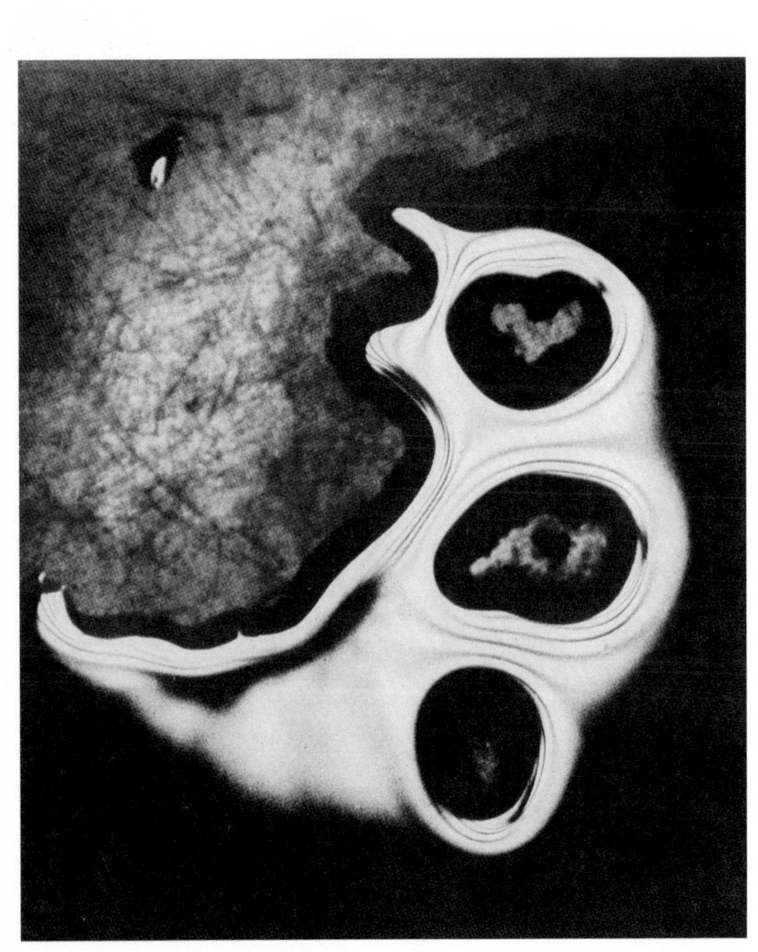

277. *"Plastic in a Ghost Image." Shimogō Yōyū. 1939.*

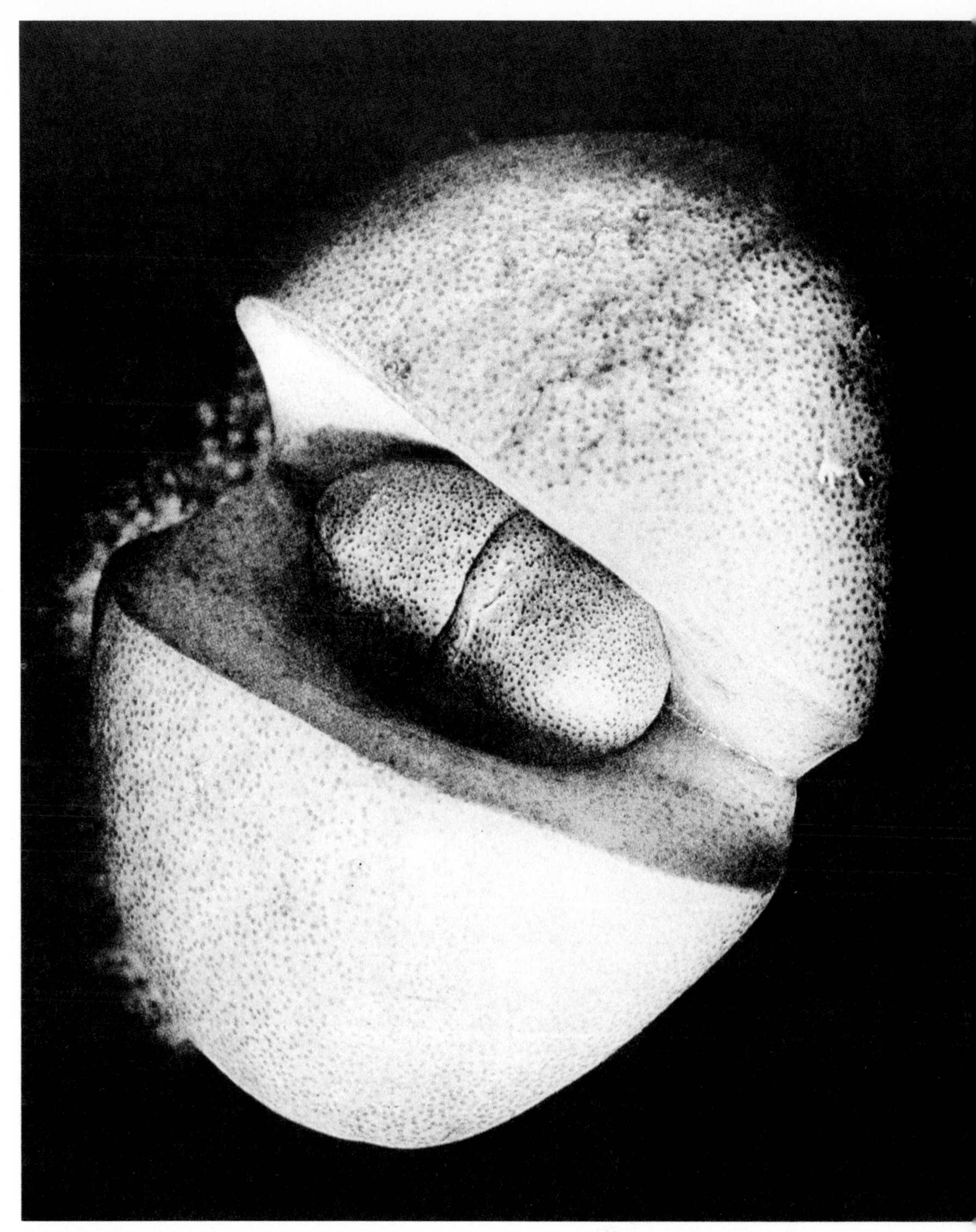

278. *"Mesembryanthema." Shimogō Yōyū. 1939.*

79. "......" Nakayama Iwata. 1932.

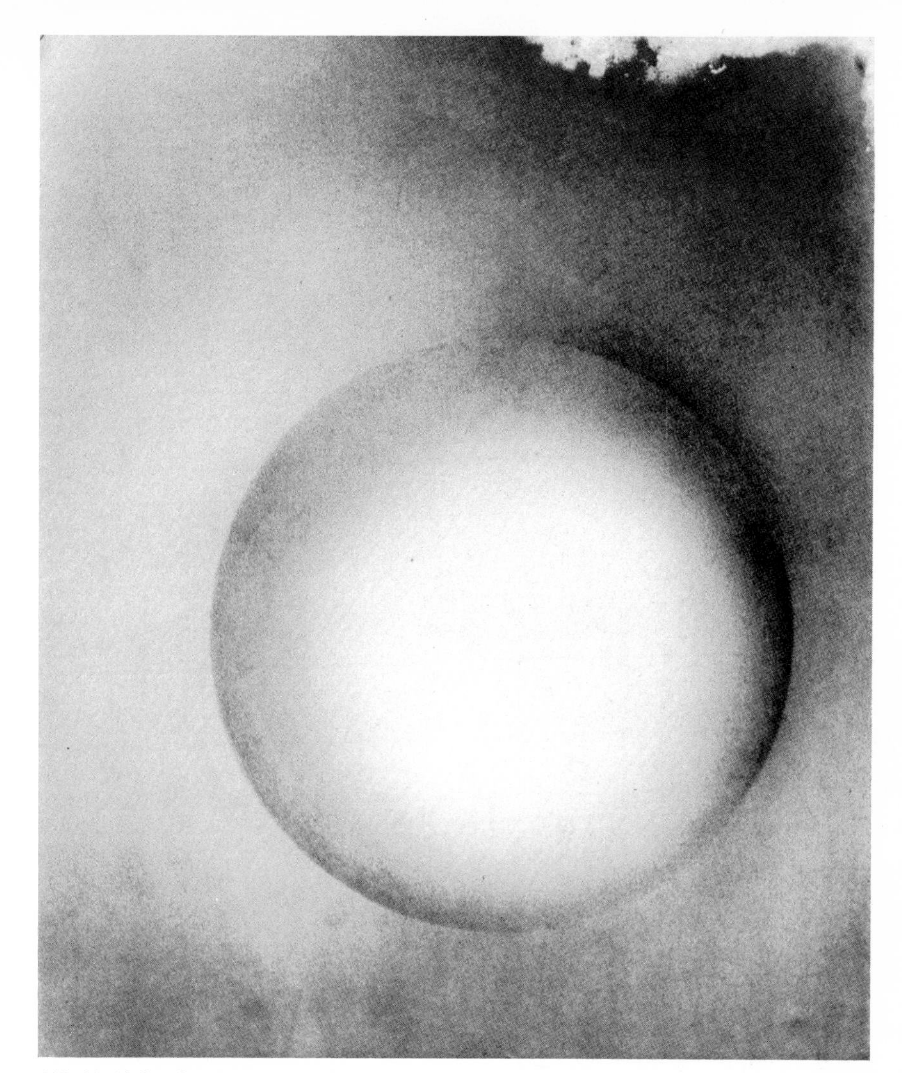

280. Untitled. Sakata Minoru. 1940.

281. "Elephant." Koishi Kiyoshi. 1939.

282. *"Shell Mound." Koishi Kiyoshi. 1939.*

283. *"Butterflies." Nakayama Iwata. 1941.*

284. "Uemura Shōen." Hamaya Hiroshi. 1936.

285. "Takada Tamotsu." Kimura Ihe-e. 1933.

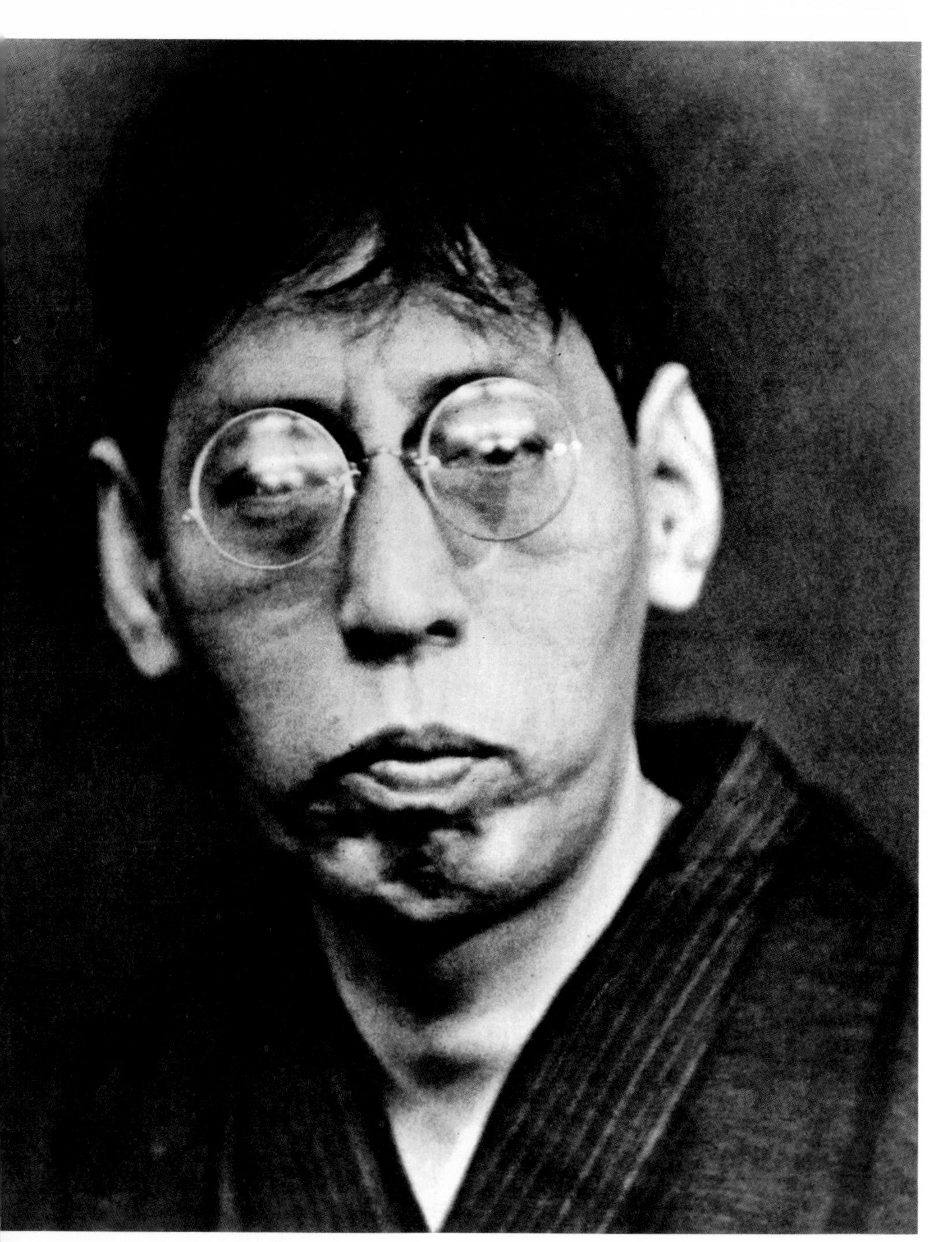

6. "Satō Haruo." Kimura Ihe-e. 1933.

287. "Go Seigen." Katō Kyōhei. 1941.

288. "Fujita Tsuguji." Nakayama Iwata. 1926.

289. "A Master: Yoshida Bungorō." Domon Ken. 1942.

0. "The Late Naoki Sanjūgo." Yamamura Takao. 1936.

291. "Senda Koreya." Nojima Kōzō. 1932.

292. "No Title." Nojima Kōzō. 1933.

293. "Model F." Nojima Kōzō. 1931

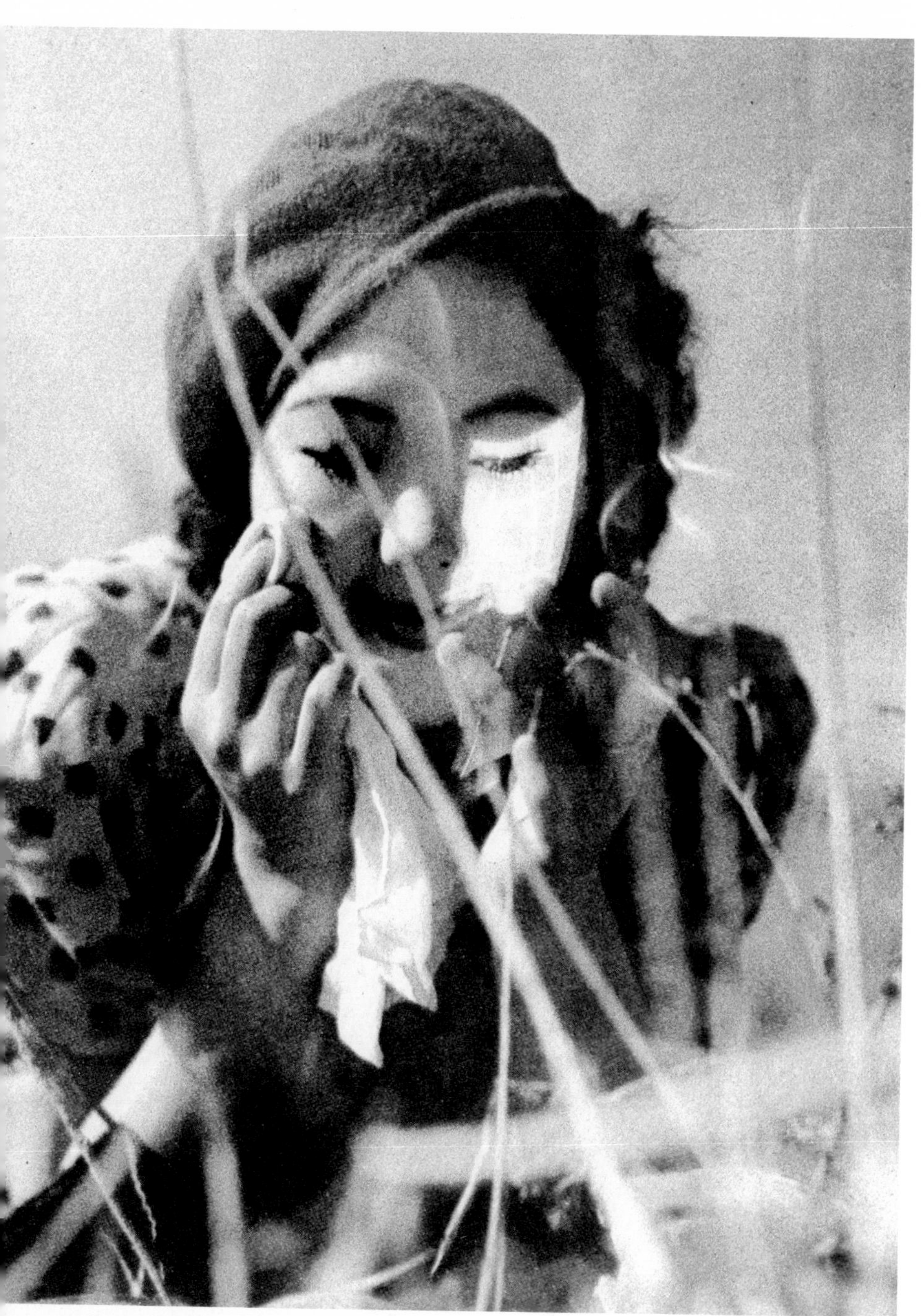
"Woman." Fukuda Katsuji. 1937.

303. Fashion photograph for a hat. Tamura Shigeru. 1940.

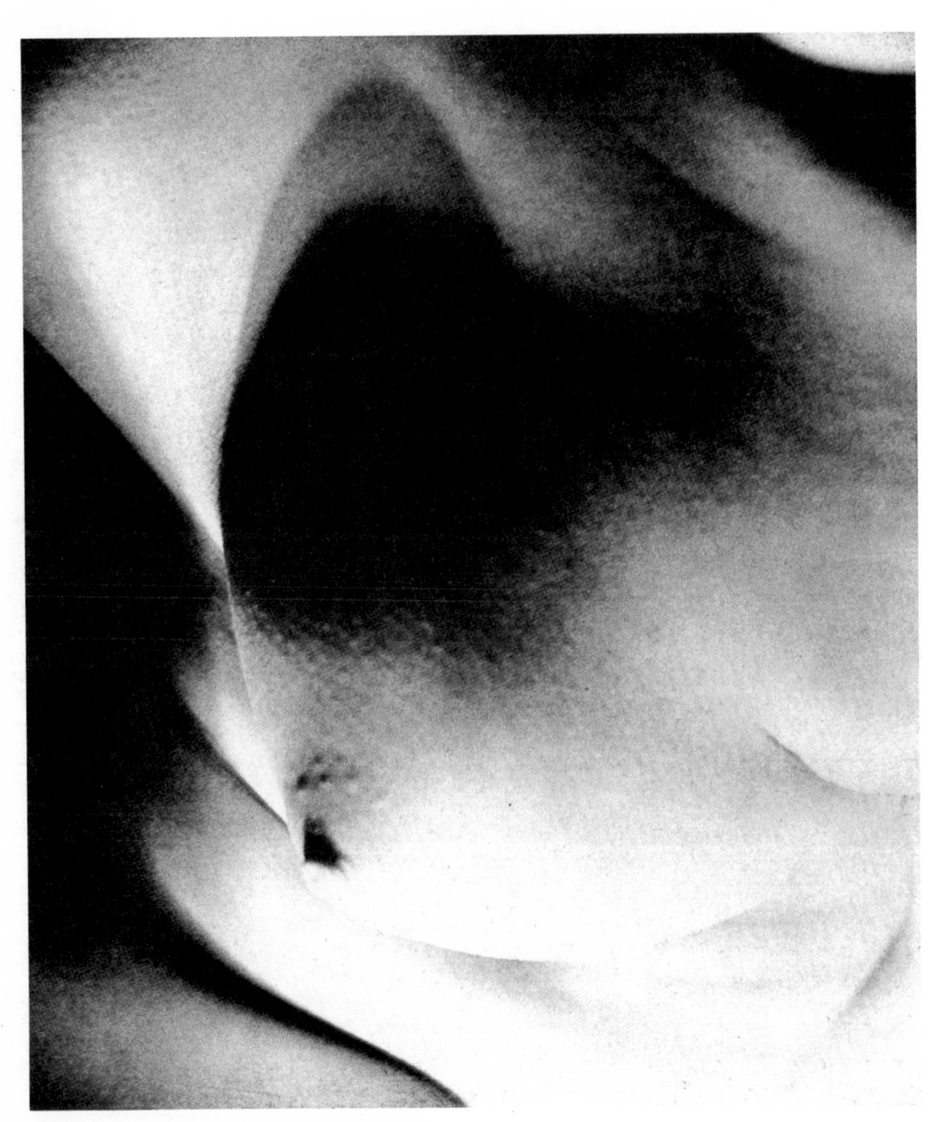

304. "……" Saeki Ryō. 1933.

305. "Nude Woman." Benitani Kichinosuke. 1931.

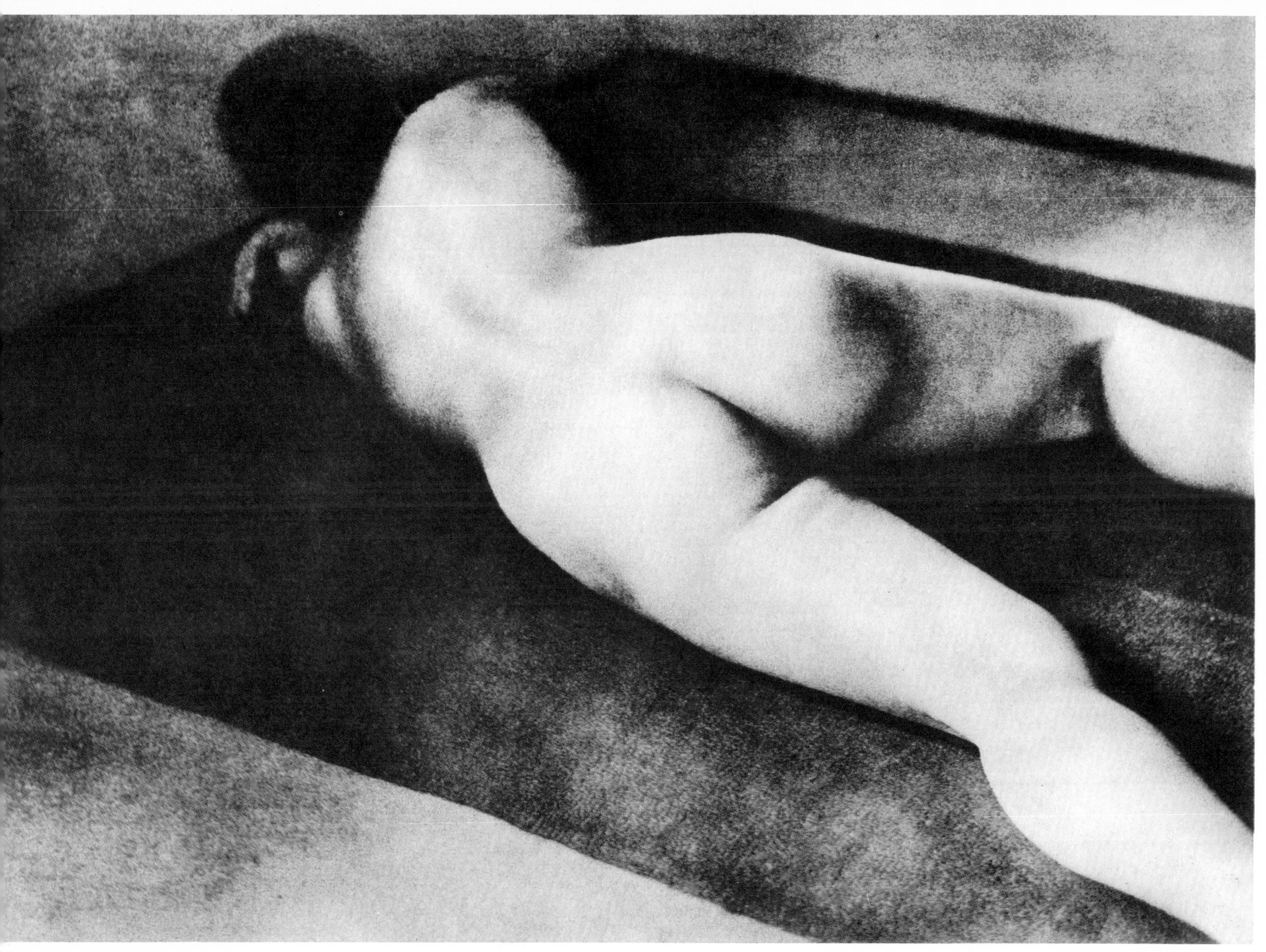

5. "Woman." Nojima Kōzō. 1931.

307. "Woman from Shanghai." Nakayama Iwata. 1932.

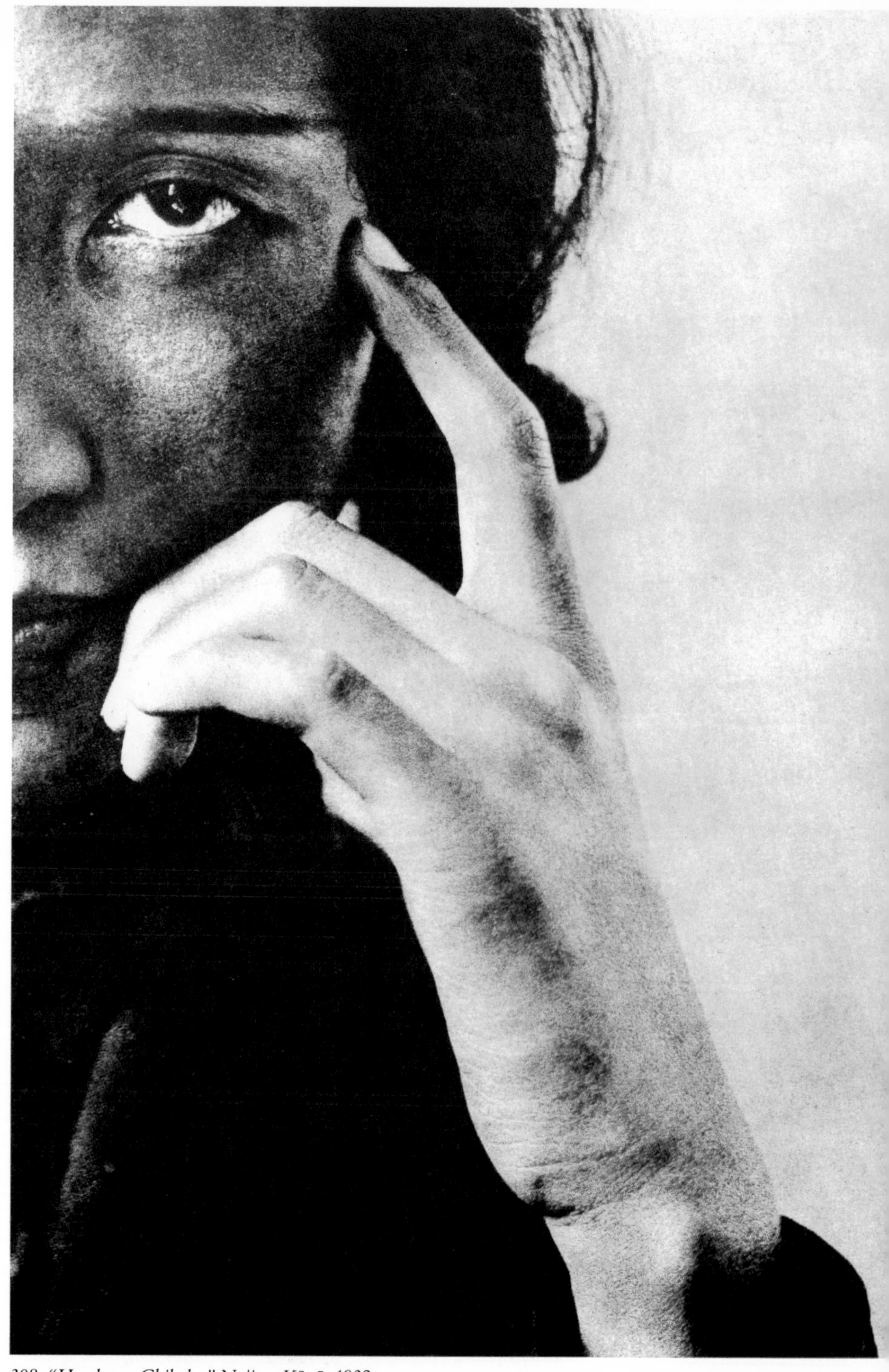

308. "Hosokawa Chikako." Nojima Kōzō. 1932.

. "Hair." Kimura Ihe-e. 1935.

310. "Expression of a Woman." Kimura Ihe-e. 1934.

311. "Scene with Clouds." Narita Shunyō. 1938.

312. *"The Torii Pass from Kakuma." Suzuki Hachirō. 1936.*

313. *"Train Rushing." Fuchigami Hakuyō. Manchuria, 1930.*

. "In Front of an Eatery." Fuchigami Hakuyō. Manchuria, 1930.

315. "Shoeshine Man." Yoneshiro Zen-emon. Manchuria, late 1920s or early 1930s.

316. "A Shepherd Boy." Sakakibara Shōichi. Manchuria, 1935.

317. "Proceeding on a Wild Plain." Baba Hatchō. Manchuria, 1935.

318. *"Man." Okada Nakaharu. Manchuria, 1937.*

319. *"Beggar." Kitano Kunio. Manchuria, 1939.*

20. "Milk." Isshiki Tatsuo. Manchuria, 1938.

321. "Laundering." Okada Nakaharu. Manchuria, 1939.

322. "A Hamlet." Emi Mitsuo. Manchuria, 1938.

323. "Pigs." Shibuya Shōyō. Manchuria, 1939.

324. "Still Life of a Lamp." Baba Hatchō. Manchuria, 1938.

325. "Coal." Nakada Shiyō. Manchuria, 1937.

326. "Setting Sun." Baba Hatchō. Manchuria, 1938.

327. "Locomotive." Tanaka Seibō. Manchuria, 1937.

328. "Three People." Yasui Nakaji. 1941.

329. "Sick Dog." Yasui Nakaji. 1934.

330. *"Singing Men." Yasui Nakaji. 1936.*

331. "Children Shooing Away Sparrows." Chiba Teisuke, 1942.

332. *"Warming at the Fire." Iwase Sadayuki. 1934.*

333. "Kadonyū Village." Sakata Minoru. 1941.

4. *"Fisherman at Hitachi Seashore." Hamaya Hiroshi. 1940.*

335. *"Old Man." Miki Shigeru. 1944.*

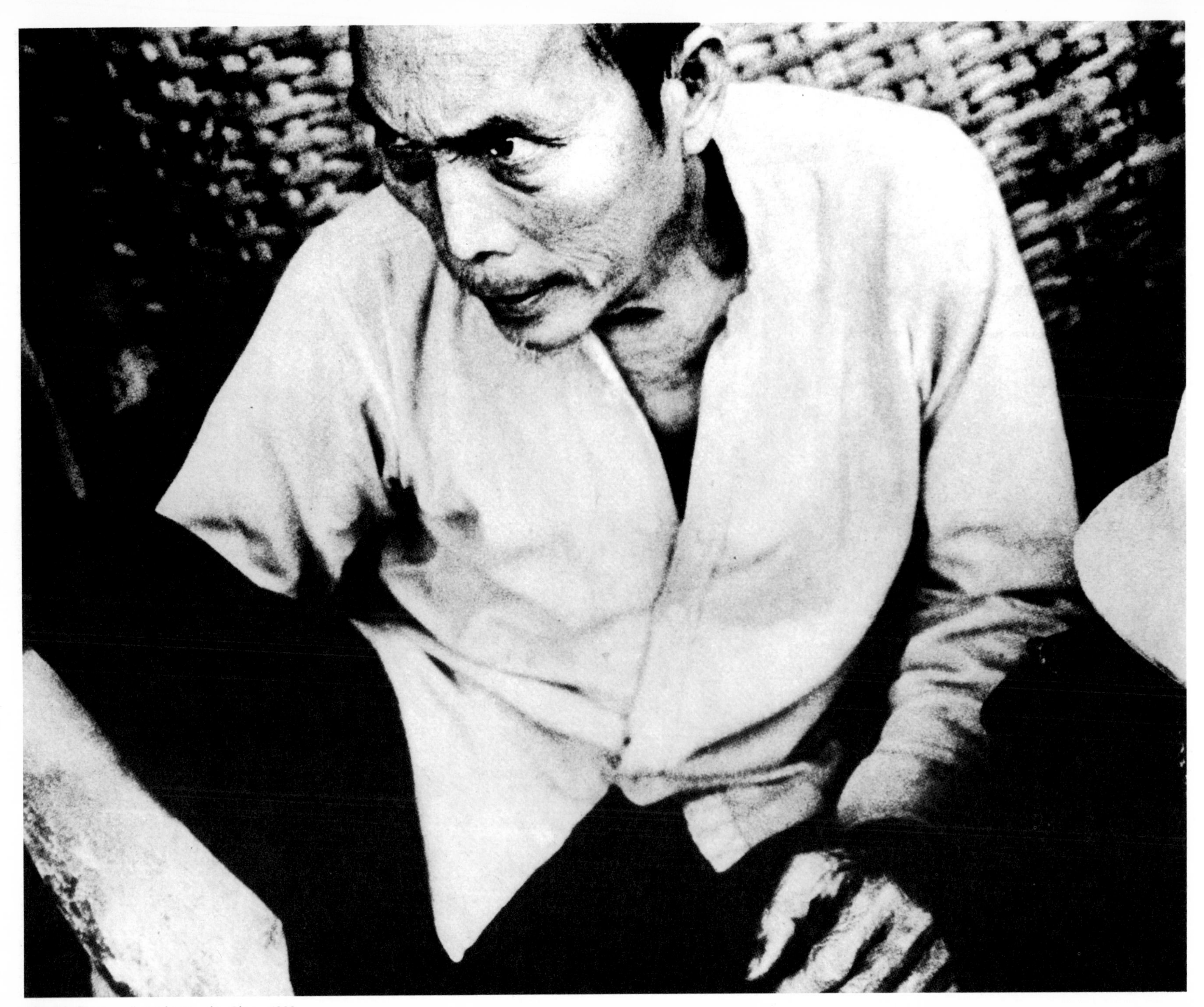

336. "A Cantonese." Koishi Kiyoshi. China, 1939.

337. *"An Orphanage in Harbin." Hamaya Hiroshi. Manchuria, 1940.*

338. *"Transient Coolie." Hamaya Hiroshi. Manchuria, 1940.*

339. "People." Tanahashi Shisui. China, 1940.

340. "Slow-going." Kuwabara Kineo. Manchuria, 1940.

341. *"A Monk of Senzan." Kimura Ihe-e. Manchuria, 1939.*

342. *"At the Shōwa Steel Works." Nishino Kazuo. Anshan, Manchuria, 1939.*

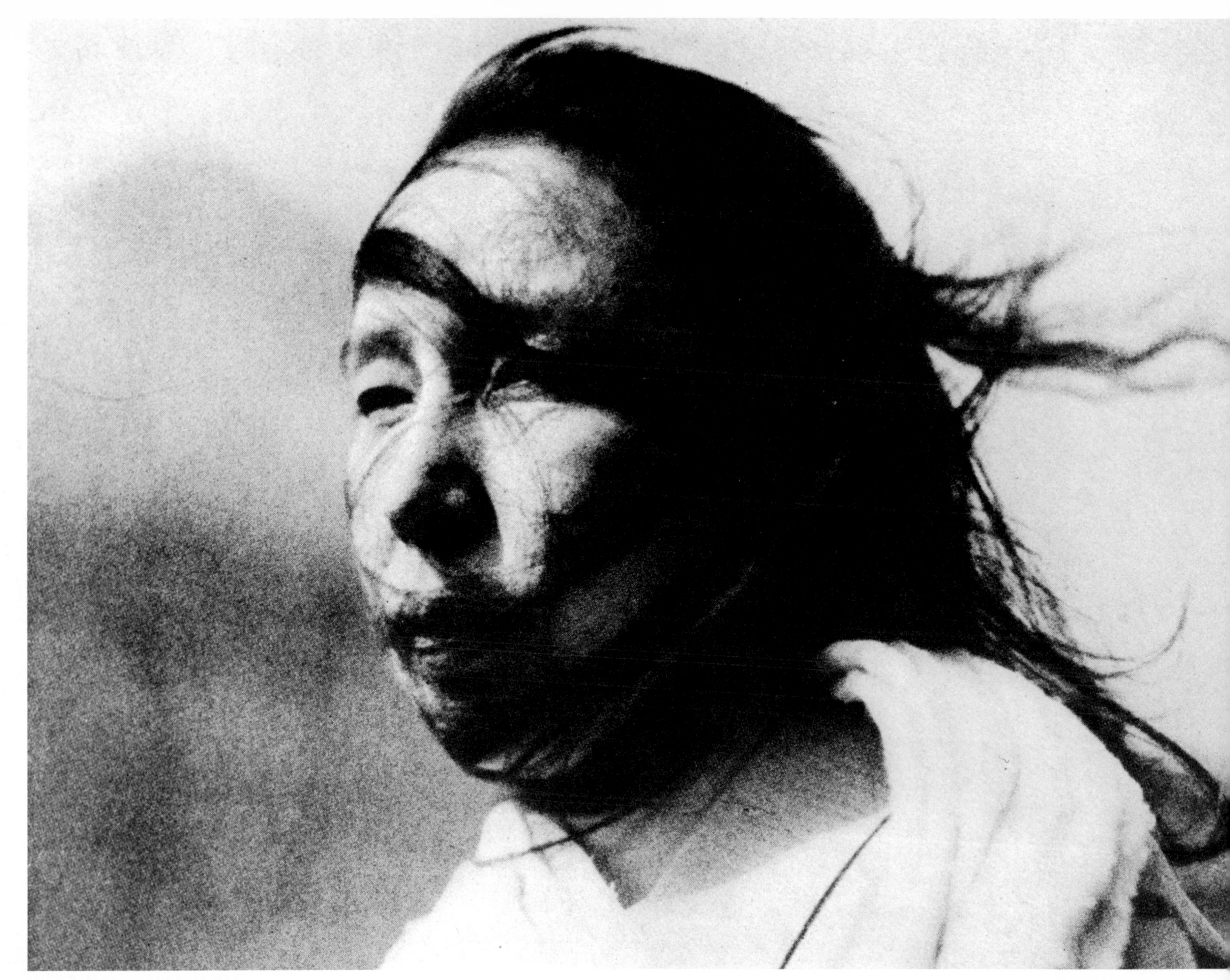

343. "Wind." Mizutani Chikushi. 1935.

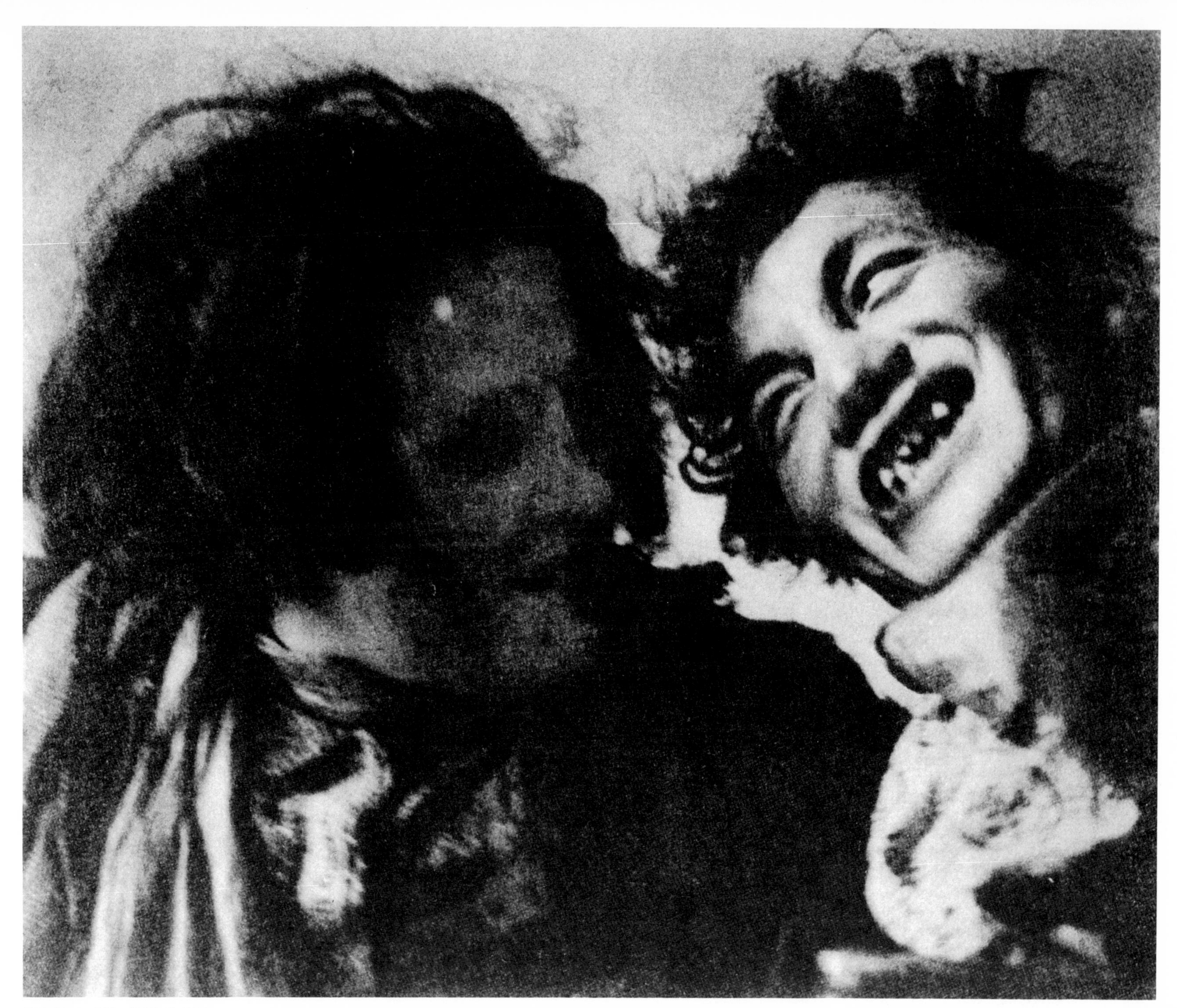

344. "Actors." Yasui Nakaji. 1937.

345. *"Strolling Musicians." Horino Masao. 1934.*

346. *"Man Sleeping in a Trash Cart." Iida Kōjirō. 1933.*

. "Poster." Iida Kōjirō. 1931.

348. "Child." Yasui Nakaji. 1935.

349. *"Beggar." Horino Masao. 1932.*

350. *"Laborer at a Calcium Factory in Kuwana." Ōhashi Isao. 1938.*

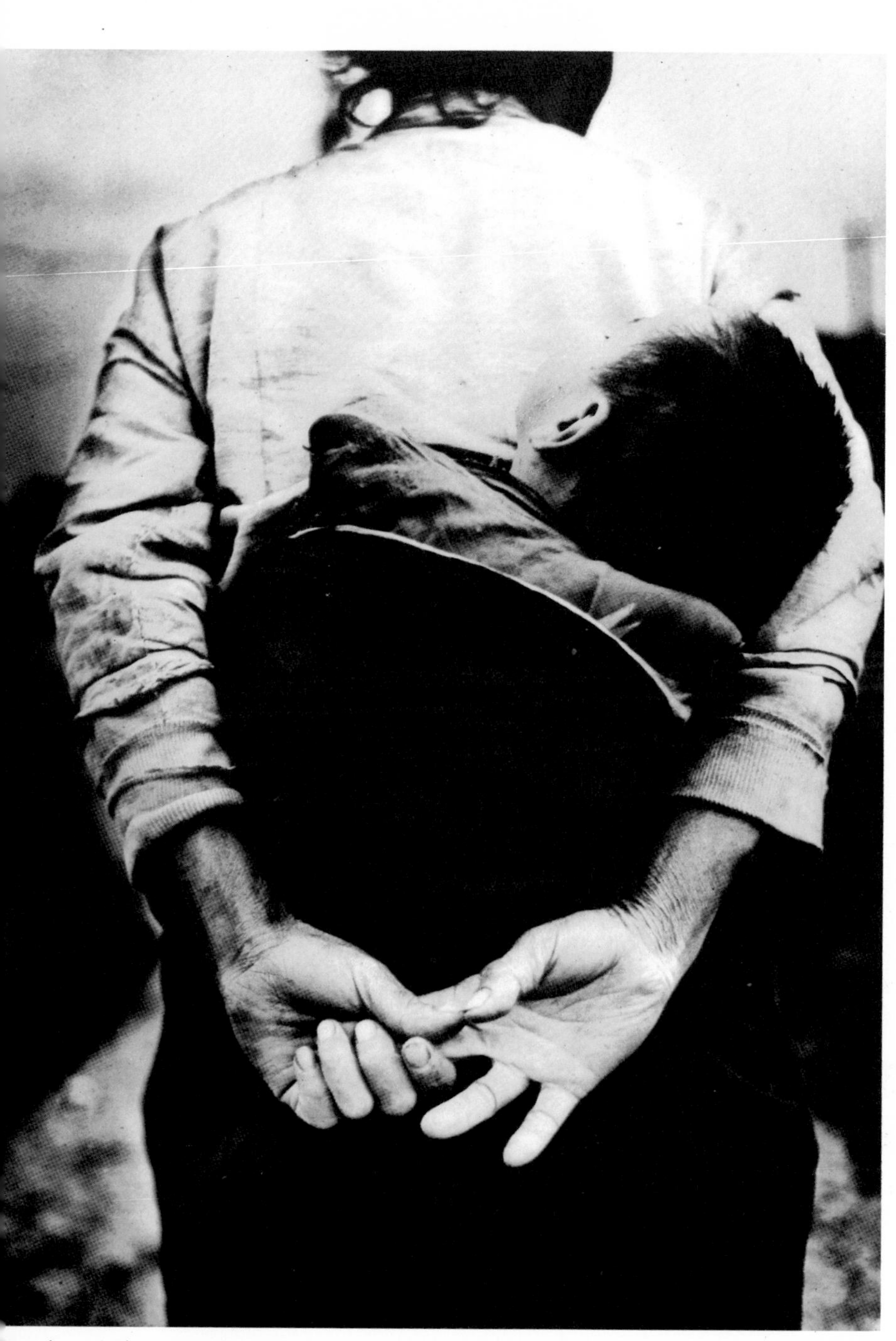

"Mother and Child." Kōno Tōru. 1935.

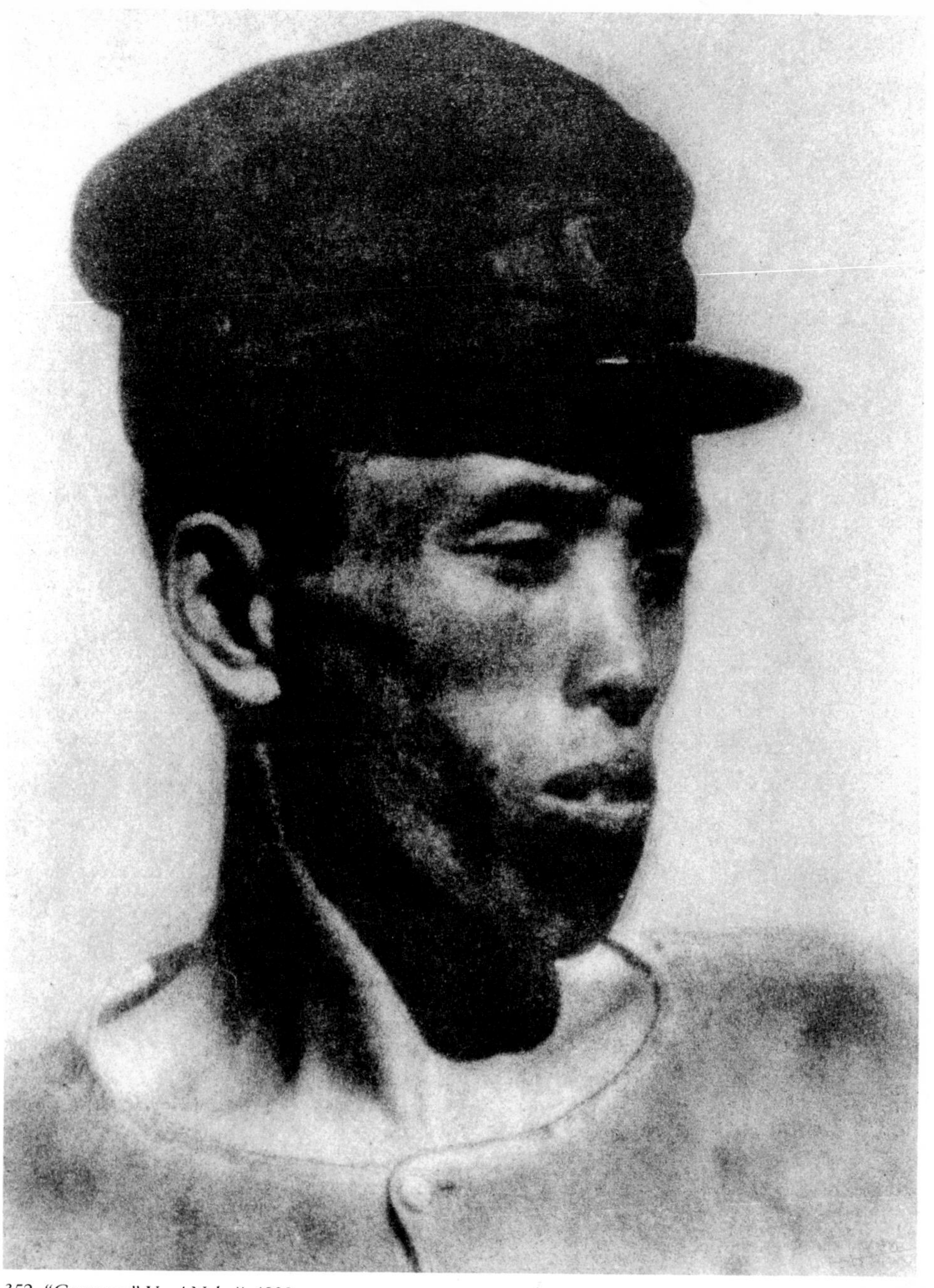

352. "Crewman." Yasui Nakaji. 1930.

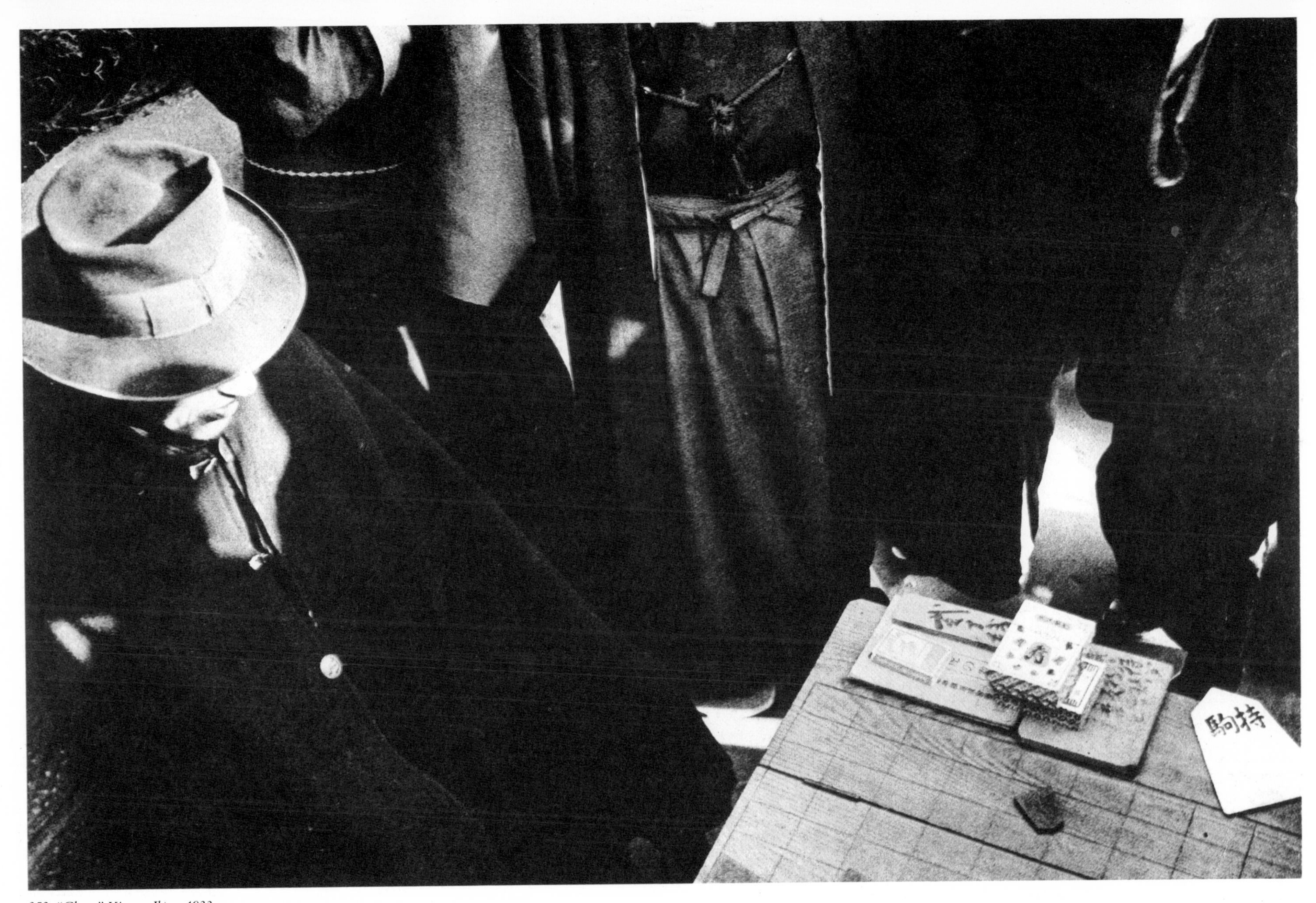

353. "Chess." Kimura Ihe-e. 1933.

354. "Western Clothing Store." Kimura Ihe-e. 1933.

355. "……" Kimura Ihe-e. 1932.

356. "Downtown Children." Kimura Ihe-e. 1933.

357. *"Street Merchant." Kuwabara Kineo. 1942.*

358. *"Flea Market in Setagaya." Kuwabara Kineo. 1936.*

ne at a Fair." *Kuwabara Kineo. 1936.*

360. "Tākī." Hamaya Hiroshi. 1939.

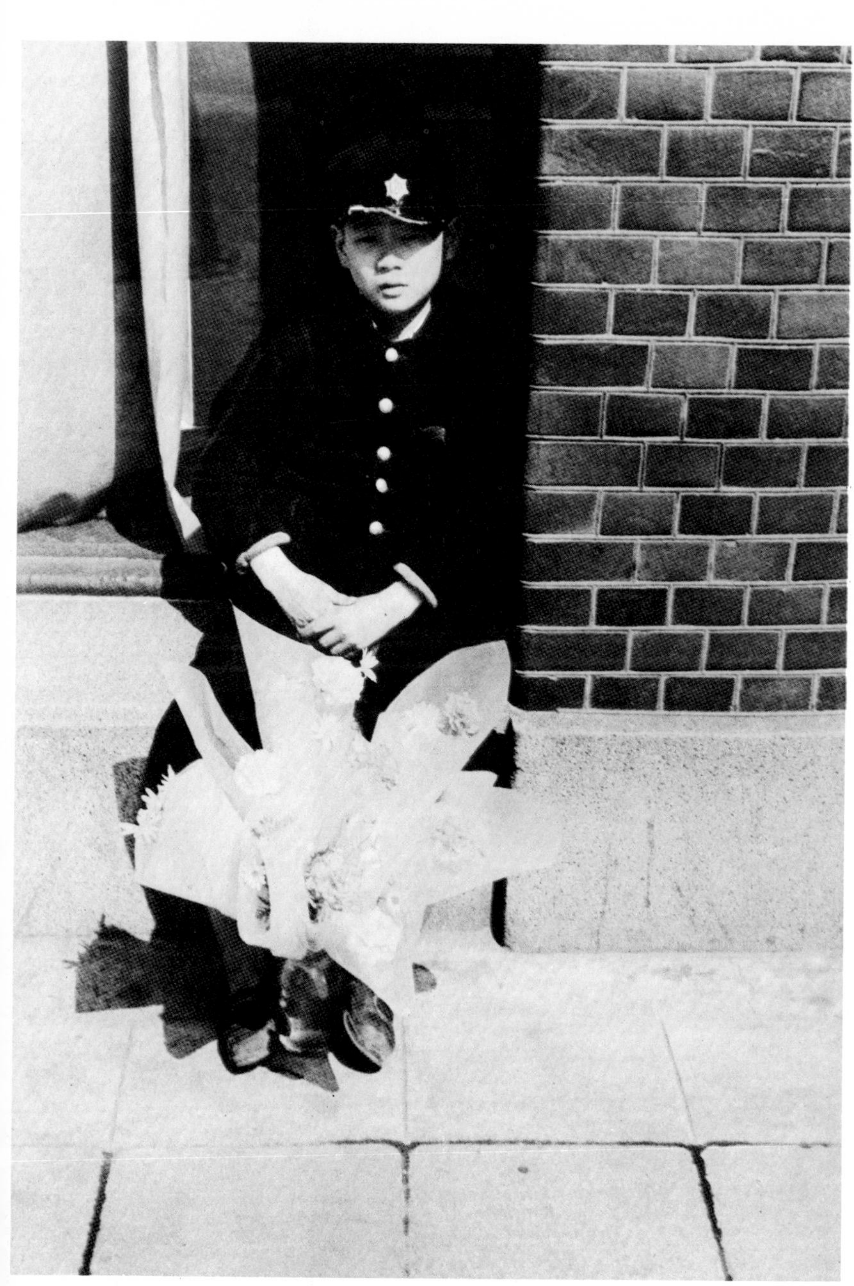

361. *"Boy Selling Flowers at Ginza."* Hamaya Hiroshi. 1936.

362. *"Backstage at a Cabaret."* Horino Masao. 1931.

363. *"Looking at a Review: the Tokyo Shōchiku Musical Theater." Watanabe Yoshio. 1932.*

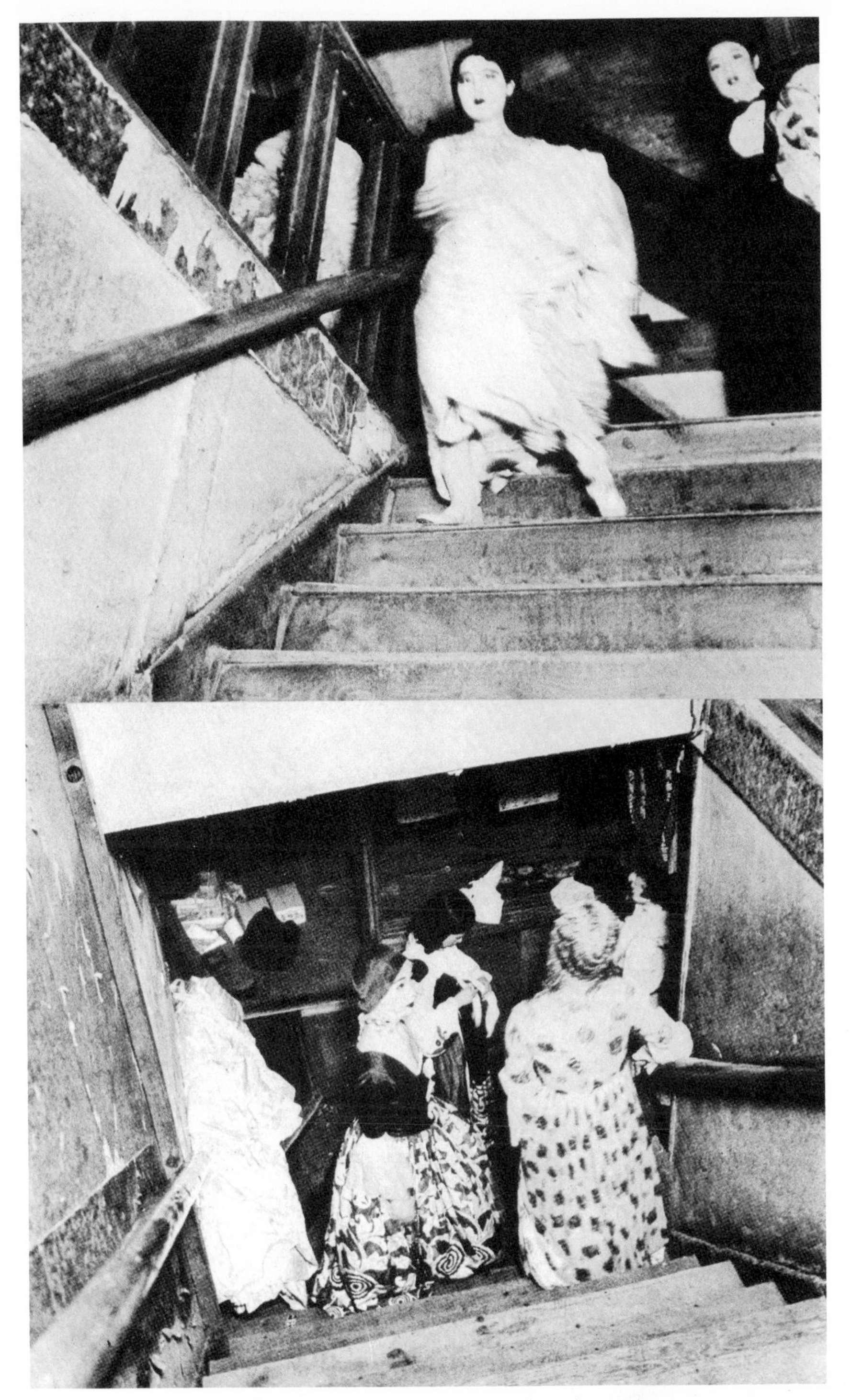

364. *"Looking at a Review: the Tokyo Shōchiku Musical Theater." Watanabe Yoshio. 1932.*

365. *"Looking at a Review: the Tokyo Shōchiku Musical Theater." Watanabe Yoshio. 1932.*

366. *"Looking at a Review: the Tokyo Shōchiku Musical Theater." Watanabe Yoshio. 1932.*

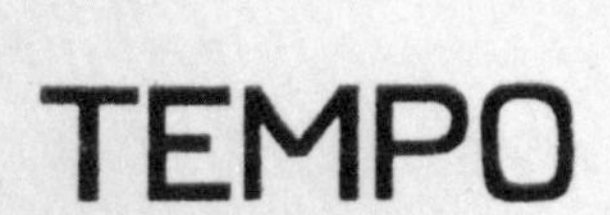

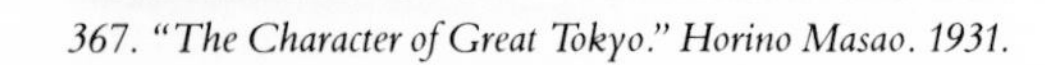

367. "The Character of Great Tokyo." Horino Masao. 1931.

368. *"The Character of Great Tokyo." Horino Masao. 1931.*

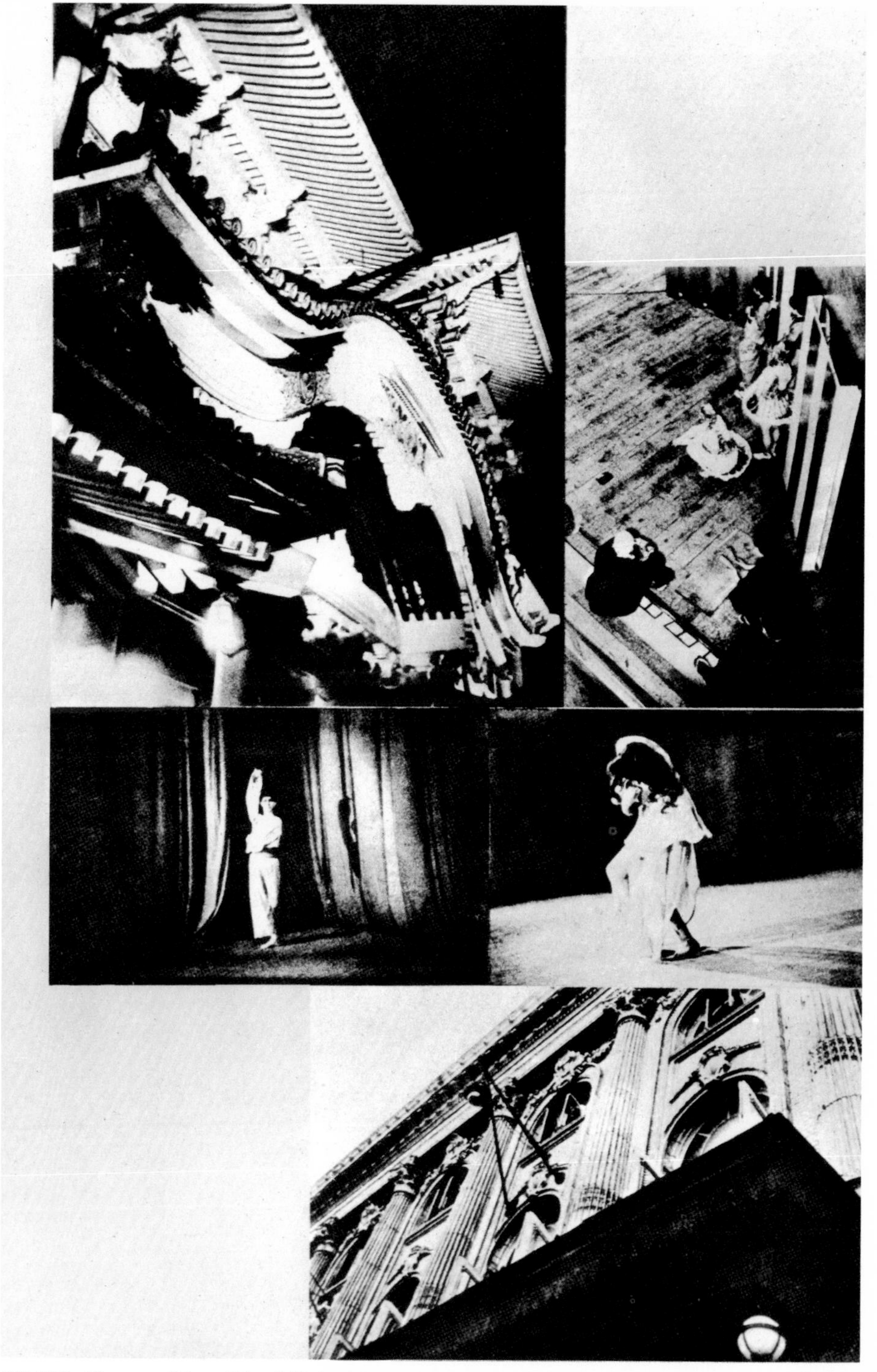

369. *"The Character of Great Tokyo." Horino Masao. 1931.*

370–4. From Snow Country, *a record of folk customs during the lunar New Year celebrations in Niigata prefecture. Hamaya Hiroshi. 1940–1944.*

370. "Strolling Boys Reciting Chants to Drive Away Pests."

. "Praying to a Young Tree."

372. "Congratulating a Groom."

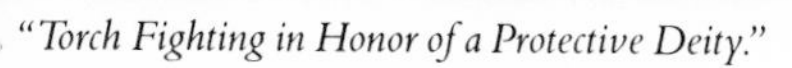

"Torch Fighting in Honor of a Protective Deity."

374. "Retreat in a Community Hall."

375. "Marketplace in Naha." Kimura Ihe-e. 1937.

SEVEN ▪ THE CAMERA'S EYE

376. A send-off rally for student conscripts departing for the front. 1943.

377. Sailors and retainers of the Shōgun on the deck of Mount Fuji, *a warship built in the United States. 1868.*

78. Ryōgōku Bridge. 1868–1882.

379. Exposed head of a criminal executed for matricide. 1872.

380. Exposed head of Etō Shimpei. 1874.

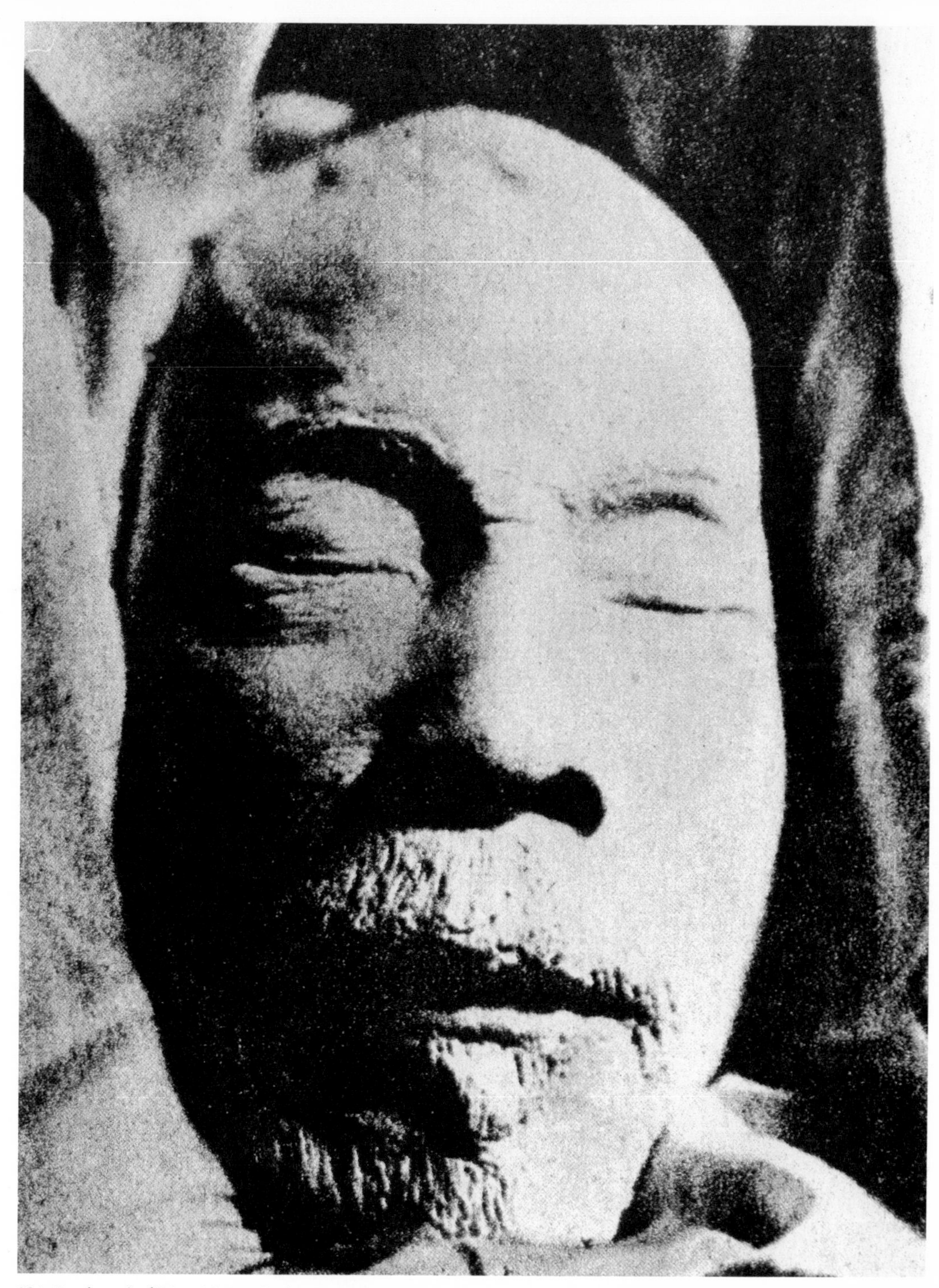

381. Death mask of Prime Minister Inukai Tsuyoshi. 1931.

382. Farmhouse buried under volcanic ash. 1914.

383. *Earthquake damage in Aichi prefecture. Miyashita Kin. 1891.*

384. The great Kantō earthquake of September 1, 1923: fire in the Hibiya area.

85. The great Kantō earthquake: charred bodies in the Honjo district, where 38,000 persons burned to death.

386. The great Kantō earthquake: women bathing in the puddles amidst the debris at Ginza.

387. The great Kantō earthquake: charred bodies in front of the Yokohama Shōkin Bank at Nihonbashi.

388. Man killed by the eruption of Mount Bandai in Aizu. 1888.

9. *Victims of an earthquake in the northern part of Hyōgo prefecture. 1925.*

390. Women and children of Tochigi prefecture, in the copper-poisoned area surrounding the Ashio copper mine. 1887.

Construction workers who were physically abused at the Watanabe labor quarters in Hokkaidō. 1926.

392. Female miners at the mouth of a coal pit. 1898–1912.

3. Pit workers in Mitsui Company's Miike coal mine. c. 1925.

394. Farmers in Iwate prefecture. 1896.

5. Victims of a severe rainstorm flocking to buy cheap white rice offered as a relief measure in Tsukishima, Tokyo. 1917.

396. Children eating white radishes (daikon) *during a famine caused by crop failure in Iwate prefecture. 1934.*

397. Farmers suffering from cold-weather damage to their crops in Iwate prefecture. 1935.

398. Female workers making nets at a factory in Sapporo, Hokkaidō. 1868–1882.

9. Courtesans in the Yoshiwara pleasure quarters. c. 1905.

400. Crowd at Tokyo station greeting the Duke of Connaught, representative of the British monarch. Sawa Kurō. 1918.

1. Police guarding Tokyo city hall in preparation for a citizens' demonstration against the merging of gas companies. 1911.

402. Rally protesting a fare hike for Tokyo streetcars, sponsored by the Japan Socialist Party at Hibiya Park. 1906.

403. Handcuffed prisoners disguised with straw hats being led to a secure place following the great Kantō earthquake. 1923.

404. Police and protesters struggling in front of the residence of Prime Minister Hara Takashi after a gathering in support of universal male suffrage. 1920.

Demonstration led by the Yūaikai labor organization, opposing the government's chosen delegate to the First International Labor Conference. 1919.

406. Protest against the Public Peace Preservation Law at Arimagahara, Shiba district, Tokyo. 1925.

Rural response to the first general election under universal male suffrage. The wall writing reads:
solutely do not talk about anything related to the election. Let sleeping dogs lie." 1928.

408. A longshoreman being arrested. 1932.

409. *A demonstration by Osaka steel-factory workers. 1921.*

410. *The first May Day demonstration in Otaru city. 1926.*

411. Struggle between students and police in front of the former University of Commerce in Tokyo. 1931.

412. Arrest of participants in a protest meeting against the Public Peace Preservation Law. 1925.

. Devotees of the Tenri religious sect praying after 385 of their members were arrested for lese majesty. 1928.

414. Armed Koreans arrested in Manchuria after the March 1 Movement for Korean independence. 1919.

415. Itō Hirobumi, the first Japanese resident-general in Korea, and the Korean crown prince. c. 1907.

416. Persons executed in Korea for participating in the March 1 Movement for Korean independence. 1919.

417–21. The February 26 Incident of 1936, in Tokyo.

417. Troops dispatched to suppress the rebels.

418. Navy land-combat unit heading for Nagatachō, where the rebels were assembled.

419. Tokyo under martial law.

420. Evacuees from the Shiba district returning home after calm had been restored.

21. Scene in front of the restaurant "Kōraku," which served as headquarters for the rebel army.

422. The uniform of commander-in-chief which was given by the Meiji emperor to Viscount Hinonishi. 1927.

EIGHT ■ ADVERTISEMENTS AND PROPAGANDA

423. *"Akadama Port Wine." Kawaguchi Photograph Studio (Inoue Mokuta and Kataoka Toshirō). Poster, 1922.*

424. *"Lait Cream." Sawa Reika. Poster, 1935.*

425. *"Shiseidō Soap." Ibuka Akira. Poster aimed at the Asian continent, 1941.*

. *Cover of Shiseidō company magazine* Hanatsubaki. *Ibuka Akira. August 1938.*

427. Oriental Can Company advertisement in a propaganda magazine distributed abroad. Kamekura Yūsaku. 1941.

428. *Cover of* Front, *a magazine distributed abroad. 1942.*

429. *Cover of* Front, *a magazine distributed abroad. 1942.*

430. *"Dai Nippon Beer." Taishō period (1912–1926) poster.*

431. "Kunji Perfumed Oil." 1909.

432. "Daigaku Face Powder." 1909.

433. "Hasegawa Cabinet Store." 1909.

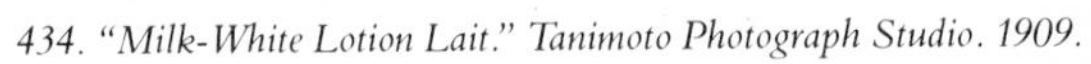

434. "Milk-White Lotion Lait." Tanimoto Photograph Studio. 1909.

435. "Club Washing Powder." 1909.

36. “Misono Face Powder.” 1909.

437. “Beauty Lotion.” 1909.

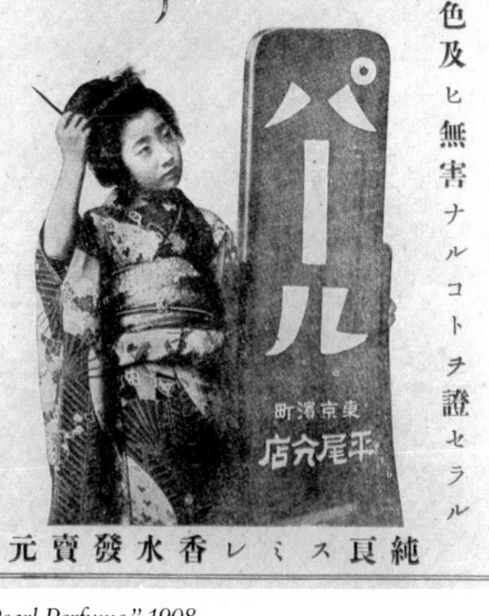

38. “Pearl Perfume.” 1908.

439. “Pastamusk Soap.” 1909.

440. “Kaneda Watch Store.” 1909.

441. "Fuji Bicycle." Koishi Kiyoshi. 1936.

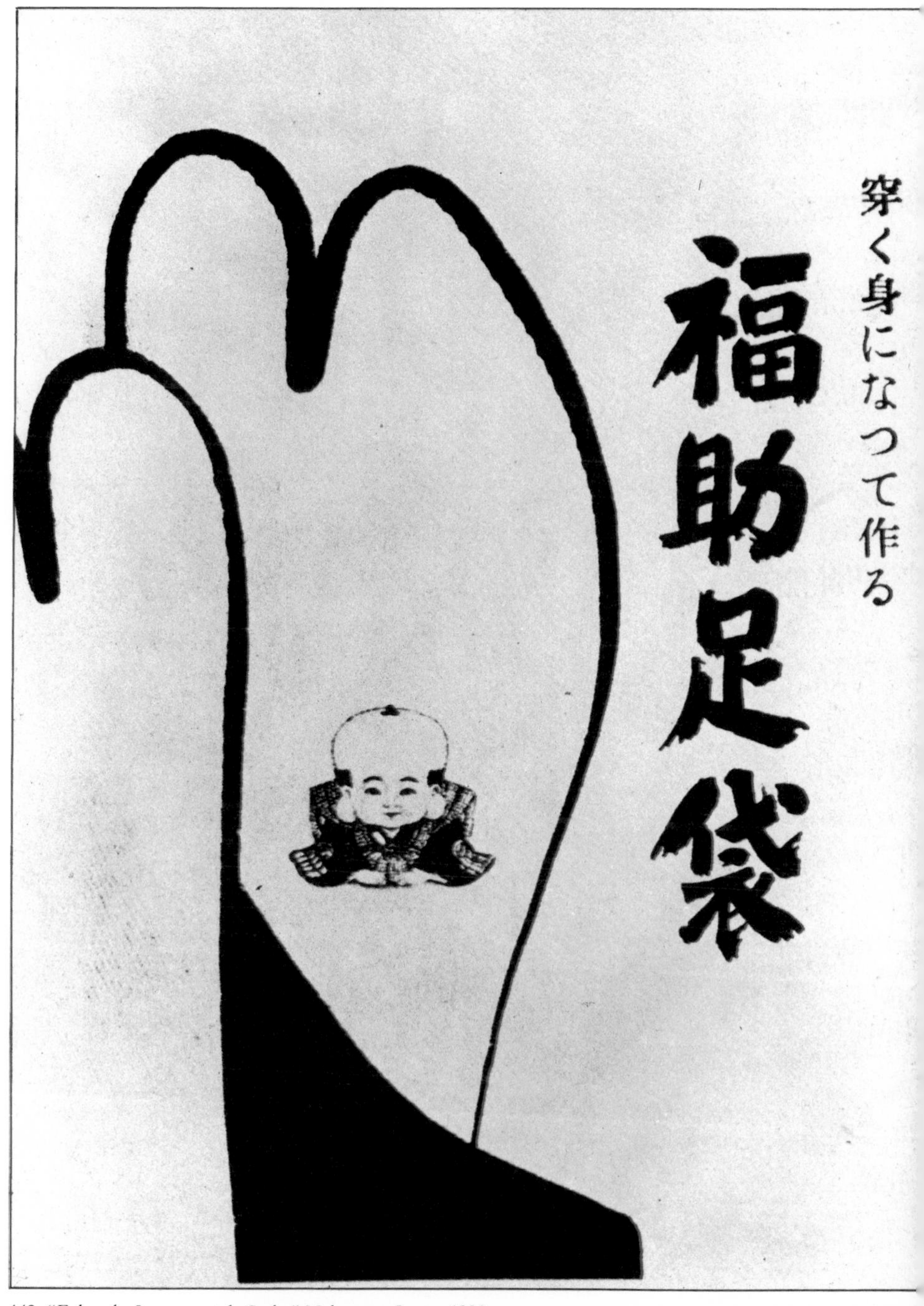

442. "Fukusuke Japanese-style Socks." Nakayama Iwata. 1930.

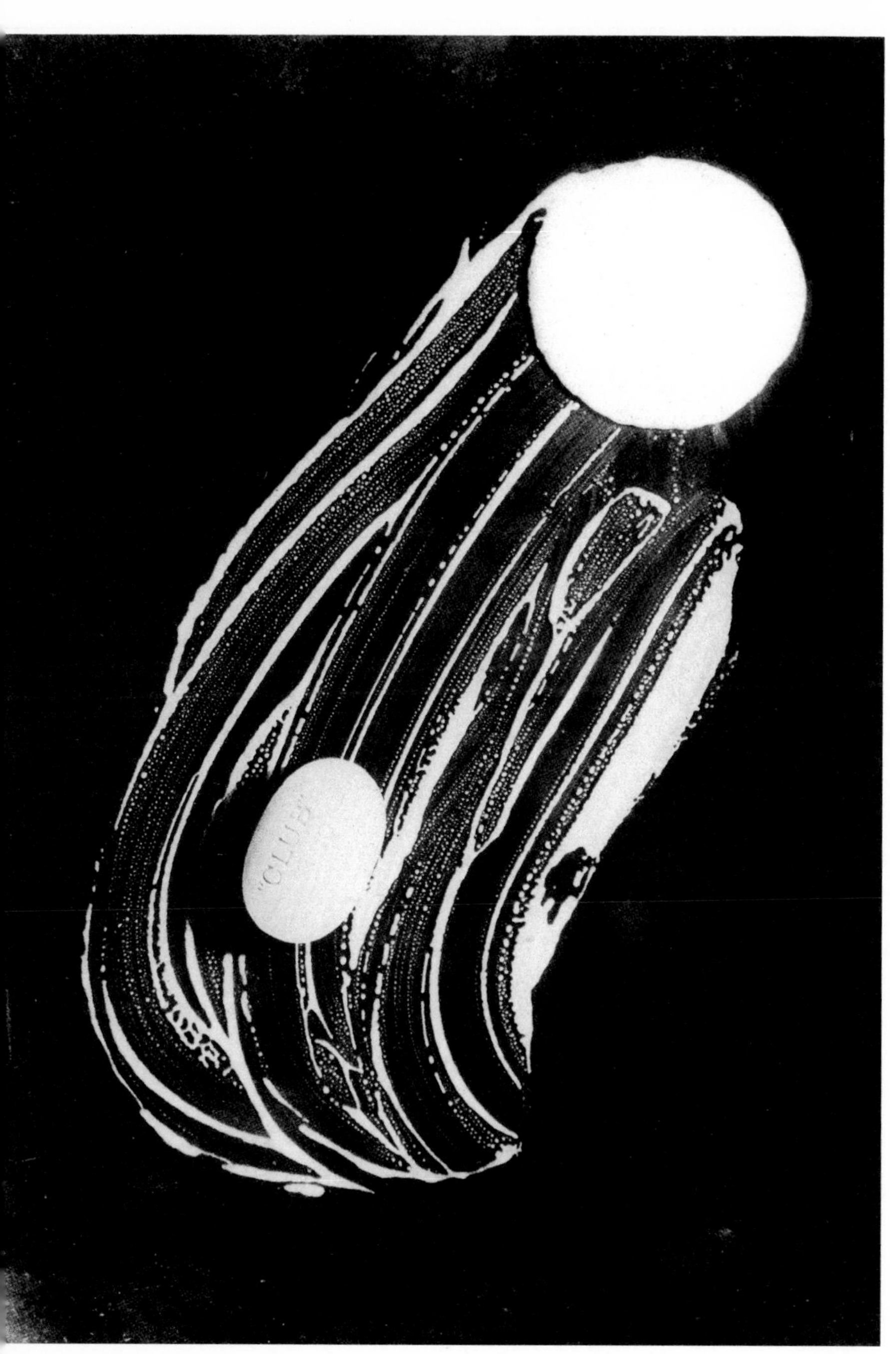

. *"Club Soap." Koishi Kiyoshi. 1931.*

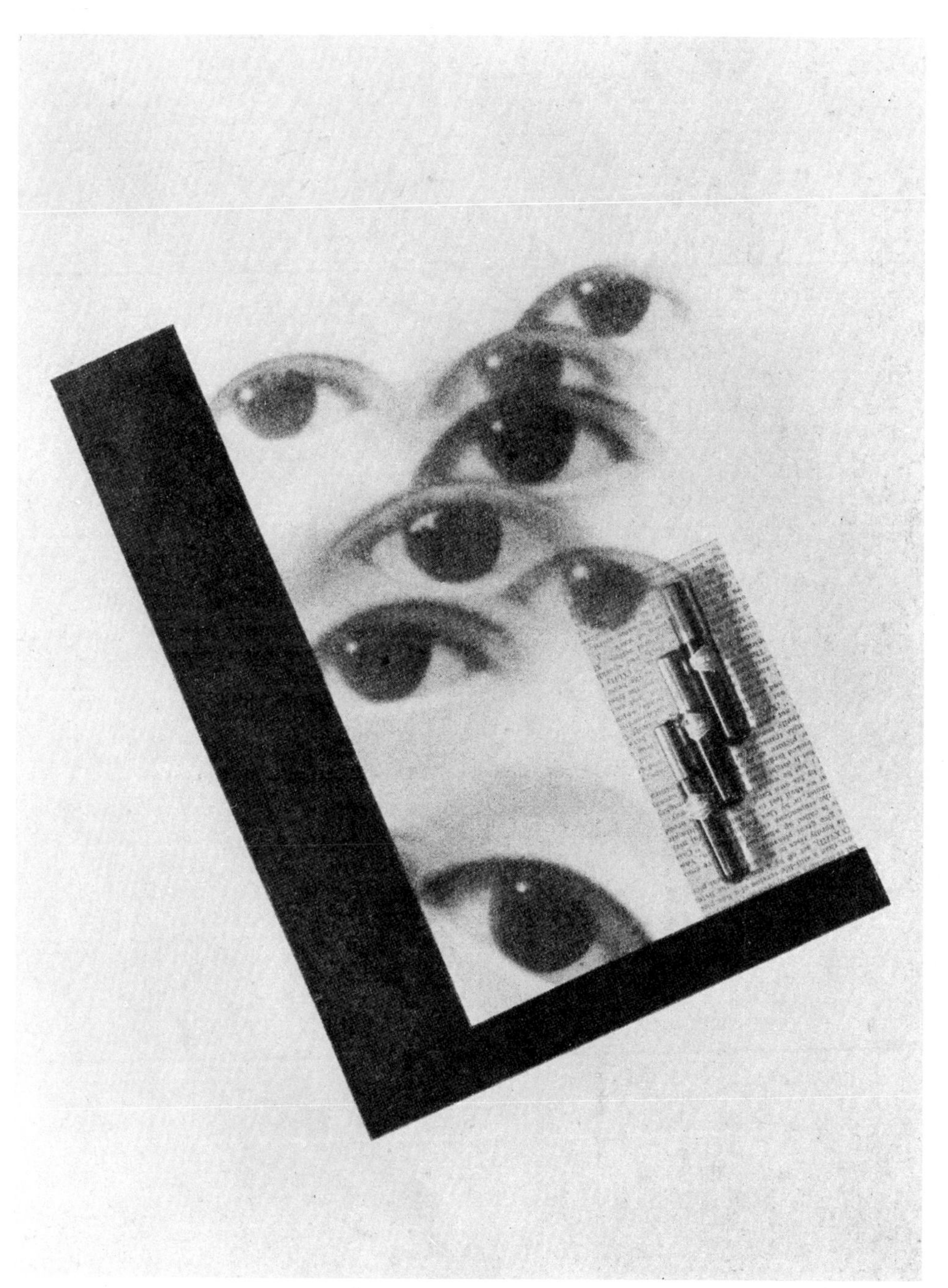

444. "Smile Eye-Drops." Koishi Kiyoshi. 1930.

445. "Kikkōman Soy Sauce." Ueda Bizan. 1932.

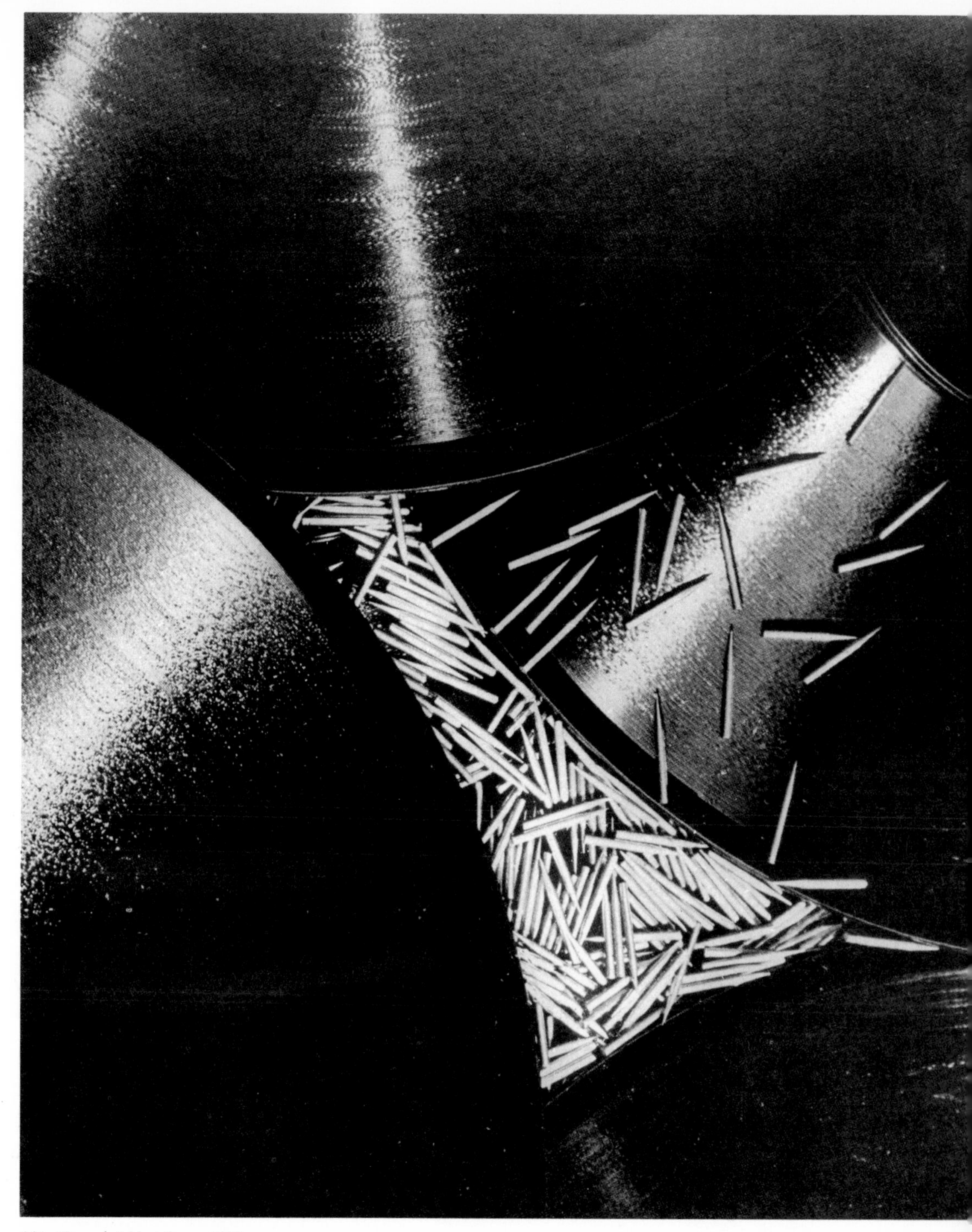

446. "Records." Hori Fusao. 1932.

47. *“Salomethyl.” Ogawa Taigi. 1933.*

8. *“Morinaga Chocolate.” Fukuzawa Tomizō. 1933.*

449. *“Lion Tooth Paste.” Takahashi Yoshio. 1932.*

450. *"Shibaura Motors." Domon Ken. Poster, 1938.*

451. *"Great Tokyo Architecture Fair." Poster, 1935.*

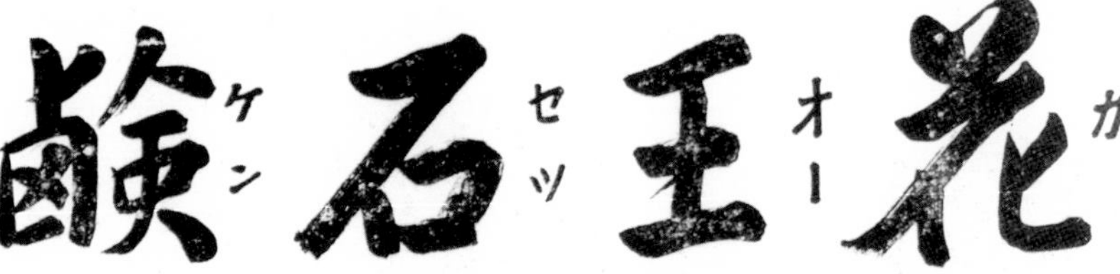

452. *"Kaō Soap." Kimura Ihe-e. Newspaper advertisement, 1931.*

453. "Datsun." *Advertisement in* Nippon, *a magazine distributed abroad, 1935.*

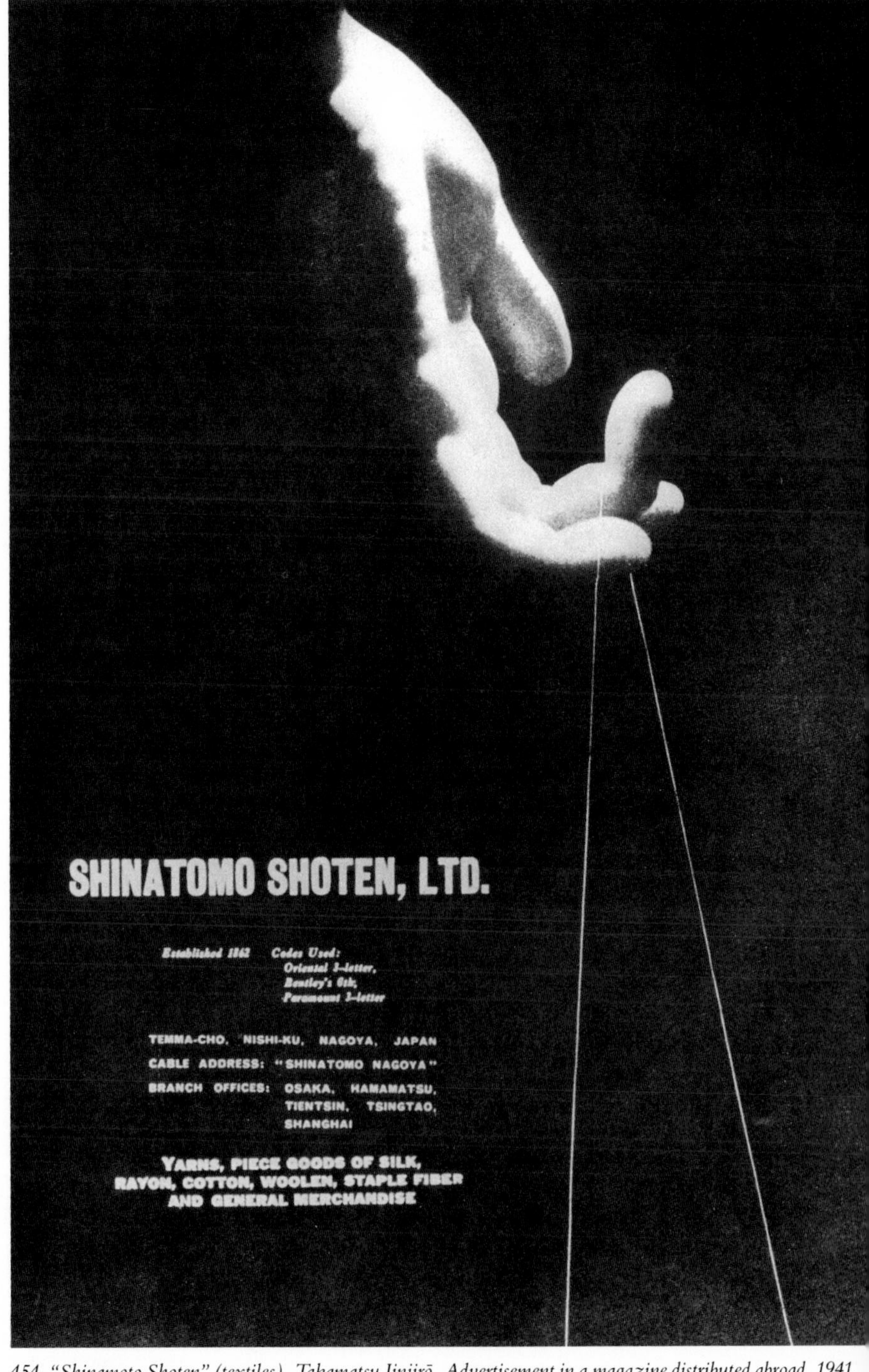

454. "Shinamoto Shoten" (textiles). Takamatsu Jinjirō. Advertisement in a magazine distributed abroad, 1941.

, "Tōyō Bōsuifu" (waterproof cloth). Fujimoto Shihachi. Advertisement in a magazine distributed abroad, 1941.

456. Light-bulb advertisement. Natori Yōnosuke. Advertisement in Commerce Japan, a magazine distributed abroad, 1941.

457. Composite photograph (14 x 6 feet) displayed at the Chicago Trade Fair. Photographs by Kimura Ihe-e and Koishi Kiyoshi; composition by Hara Hiroshi. 1938.

458. Composite photographs in a collection designed to introduce Japan abroad. Nihon Kōbō (Japan Atelier). 1934.

Premier Prince Fumimaro Konoye
Le Président du Conseil, le Prince Fumimaro Konoyé
Ministerprasident Prinz Fumimaro Konoye

459. *Cover of* Manshū Gurafu *(Pictorial Manchuria). December 1940.*

460. *Spread in* Manshū Gurafu *(Pictorial Manchuria). June 193*

461. *Cover of* Gurafikku *(Graphic). July 1938.*

462. *Spread in* Shashin Shūhō *(Photo Weekly). Koishi Kiyoshi. August 1942.*

463. *Spread in* Front. *1942.*

464. *Spread in* Asahi Gurafu *(Asahi Pictorial). October 1940.*

465. *Prime Minister Tōjō Hideki. Kikuchi Sōzaburō. Cover of* Asahi Kamera *(Asahi Camera). February 1942.*

466. *An officer. Published in* Nippon-5, *edited by Natori Yōnosuke. 1932.*

467. *The emperor at a military review at the Yoyogi Parade Grounds, Tokyo. G. T. Sun. 1936.*

468. *The army flying school at Akeno. Kikuchi Shunkichi. 1944.*

469. *Wartime day-care service in Tokyo. Hayashi Tadahiko. 1942.*

470. *Care packages made by students of the Tokyo Second Public Girls High School to be sent to the front. The packages are arranged to read "To the Imperial Forces." 1937.*

471. *Labor service in farming by a student. Yamada Eiji. c. 1942.*

472. *A female defense corps training with bamboo spears in preparation for the landing of United States forces. Kikuchi Shunkichi. April 1945.*

473. *Labor service by female students: raking leaves to be used as fertilizer. Katō Kyōhei. 1941.*

. *Young factory workers praying before a meal.*
·ashi Tadahiko. 1943.

475. Elementary-school children in Tokyo jogging during physical-education class. Kikuchi Shunkichi. c. 1940.

476. Tank force exercising at the foot of Mount Fuji (a composite photograph to give the appearance of many tanks). Published in Front, *1942.*

477. Left: *a battle exercise above the Tokorozawa Airfield, photographed by Hamaya Hiroshi in 1942.* Right: *the same photograph with a falling P-38 fighter painted in, published in 1944 to boost morale.* Mainichi *newspaper. January 26, 1944.*

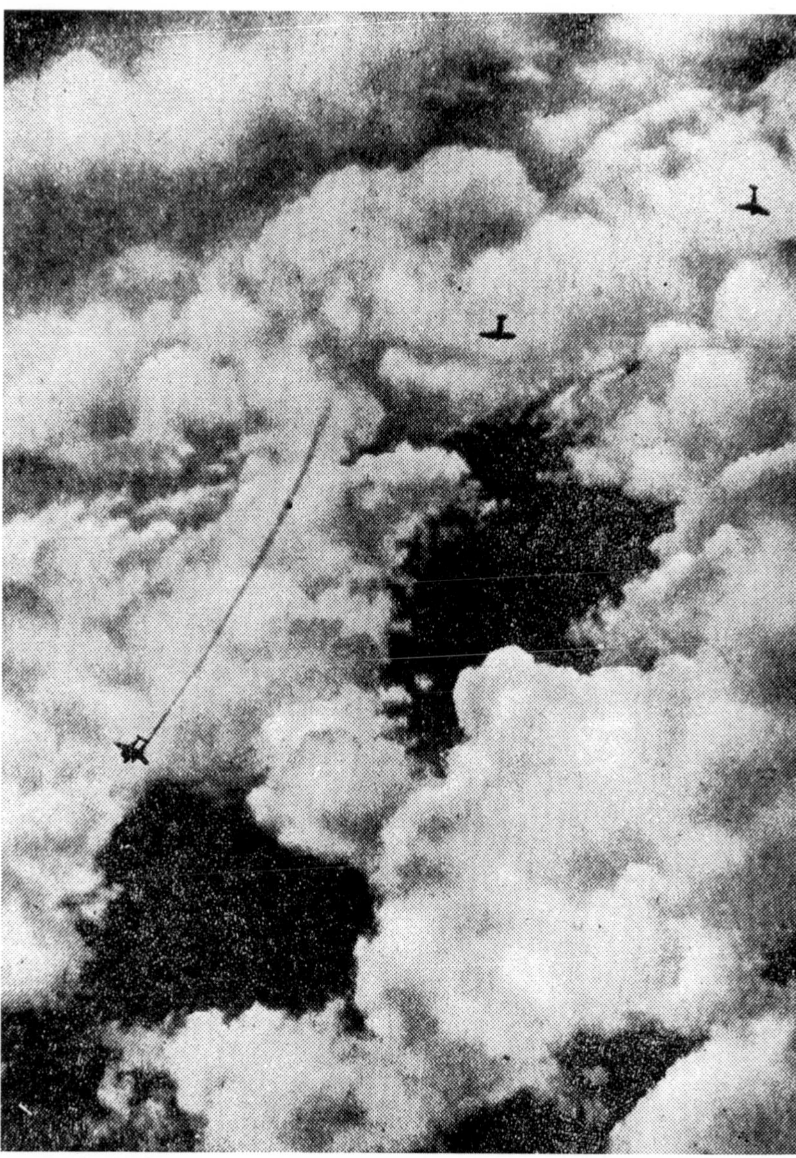

478. "Fight to the Bitter End"—a composite photograph made from originals by Kanamaru Shigene. First displayed as a billboard in 1943.

NINE ■ RECORDS OF WAR, II

479. A skull among the weeds on a battlefield in central China. Takada Masao. February 1938.

480. Special naval combat troops landing against the enemy on the shore of the Yangtze River. Hada Manzō. July 1938.

481. The attack on Canton. 1938.

482. The Rape of Nanking. Fudō Kenji. December 1937.

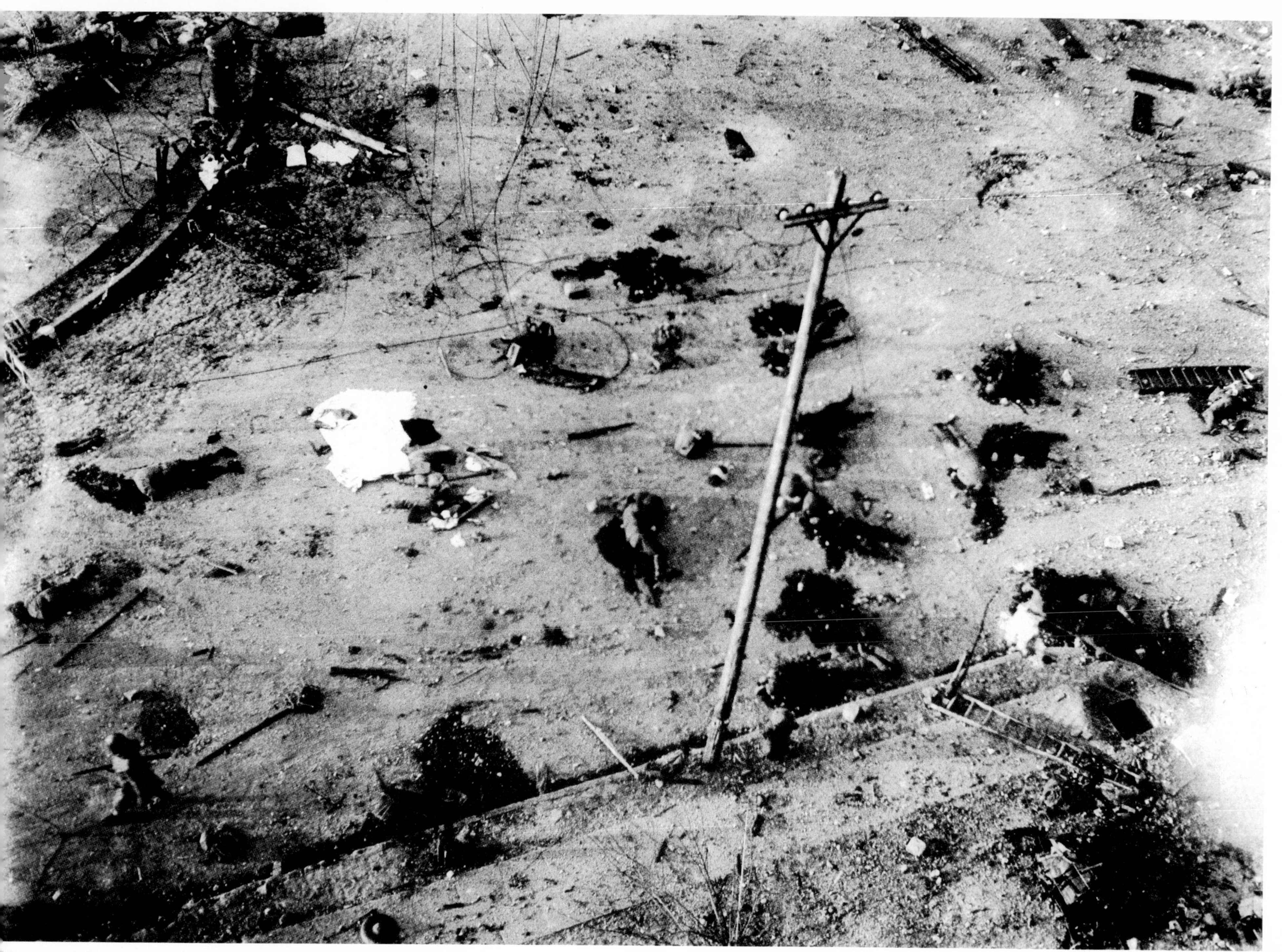

83. *Corpses of Chinese soldiers in Nanking immediately following the capture of the city. December 1937.*

484. The Japanese army entering Ku-shin in the battle for Wuhan. September 1938.

485. Soldiers taking a brief rest during the Japanese advance through the Tai-hsing range in northern China. Iwamoto Shigeo. May 1941.

86. Soldiers marching in the mud during the China War. Photographer, place, and date unknown.

487. *Interior of the Tientsin station immediately after the Japanese capture. July 1937.*

488. *Chinese in the south being investigated by Japanese soldiers. January 1940.*

489. *Cheng Pen-hua, a twenty-four-year-old woman soldier captured in central China. April 1938.*

. Chinese citizens apprehended by the Japanese military police after the capture of Canton. Matsuo Kunizō. October 1938.

491. Regular Chinese soldiers captured by the Takeshita unit of the navy land-combat forces in central China. August 1937.

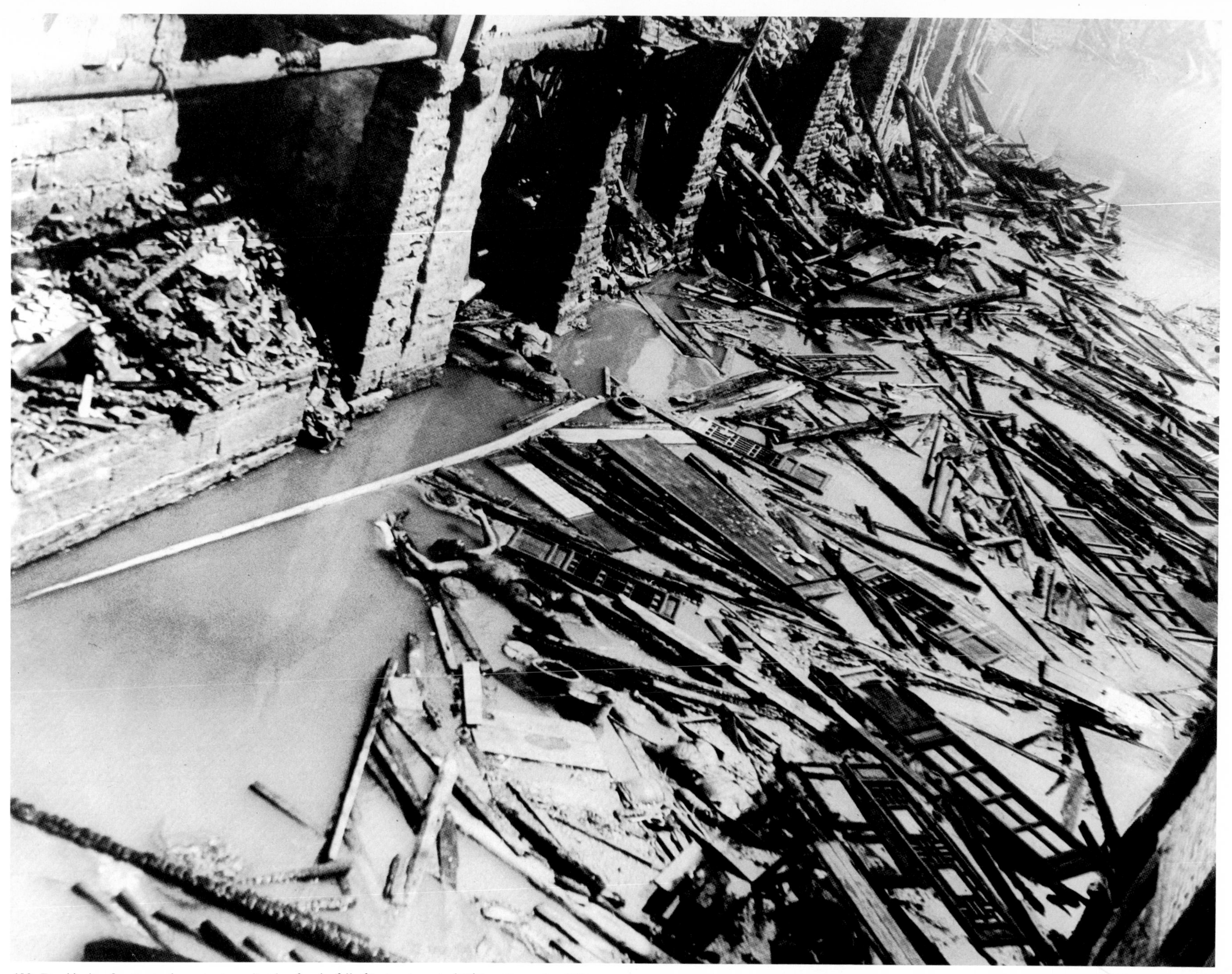

492. Dead bodies floating in the water immediately after the fall of Lotien in central China. September 1937.

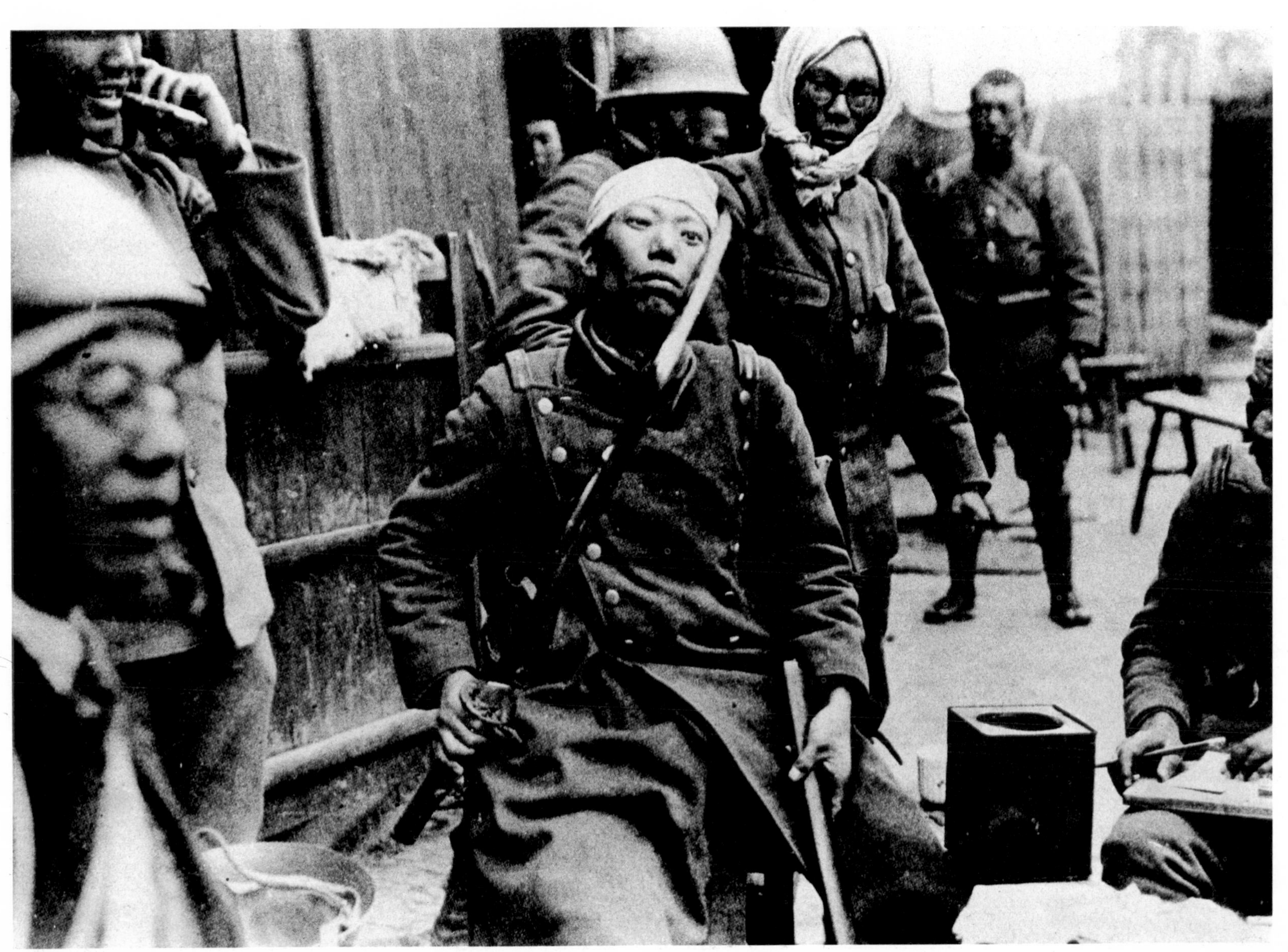

493. The Manchurian Incident: Sublieutenant Kurihara inspecting his sword after a battle with the Chinese forces in Manchuria. March 1932.

494. Chinese residents of Nanchang in central China made homeless by the Japanese attack. Koyanagi Jiichi. March 1939.

495. The attack on Pearl Harbor. December 7, 1941.

496. The battle of the Coral Sea. May 1942.

497. The surrender of General Percival at Singapore. Kageyama Kōyō. February 1942.

498. United States prisoners of war at the battle of Bataan in the Philippines. Miyauchi Jūzō. April 1942.

499. An intellectual soldier from the Shizuoka Regiment who committed suicide with a bayonet during training. Yanagida Fumio. 1938.

500. Student enlistees. December 1943.

501. Manchurian youths at a physical examination for prospective conscripts. 1941.

502. A female volunteer corps in Kokura preparing for the decisive battle in the homeland. 1944.

503. Bombardment of Osaka by B-29s. Yamagami Entarō. March 1945.

504. Burned corpses collected in the streets of Yokohama after a carpet bombing with incendiary bombs. Bessho Yahachirō. May 1945.

505. Charred bodies of a mother and child near Kikukawa Bridge in Honjo, following the air raid that turned Tokyo into a city of ashes and death. Ishikawa Kōyō. March 1945.

506.

506. (left) "Heroic Air Commandoes," a suicide unit departing from Kumamoto prefecture to attack air bases in Okinawa. Unit members are facing in the direction of their native places and bidding farewell to their distant families. Koyanagi Jiichi. May 1945.

507. (below) Girl students seeing off kamikaze pilots at Chiran Airfield with flags and branches of cherry blossoms. Hayakawa Hiroshi. May 1945.

507.

508. Atomic bomb, Hiroshima: applying oil to bomb victims' burns in the streets approximately three hours after the first atomic bomb was dropped. Matsushige Yoshito. August 6, 1945.

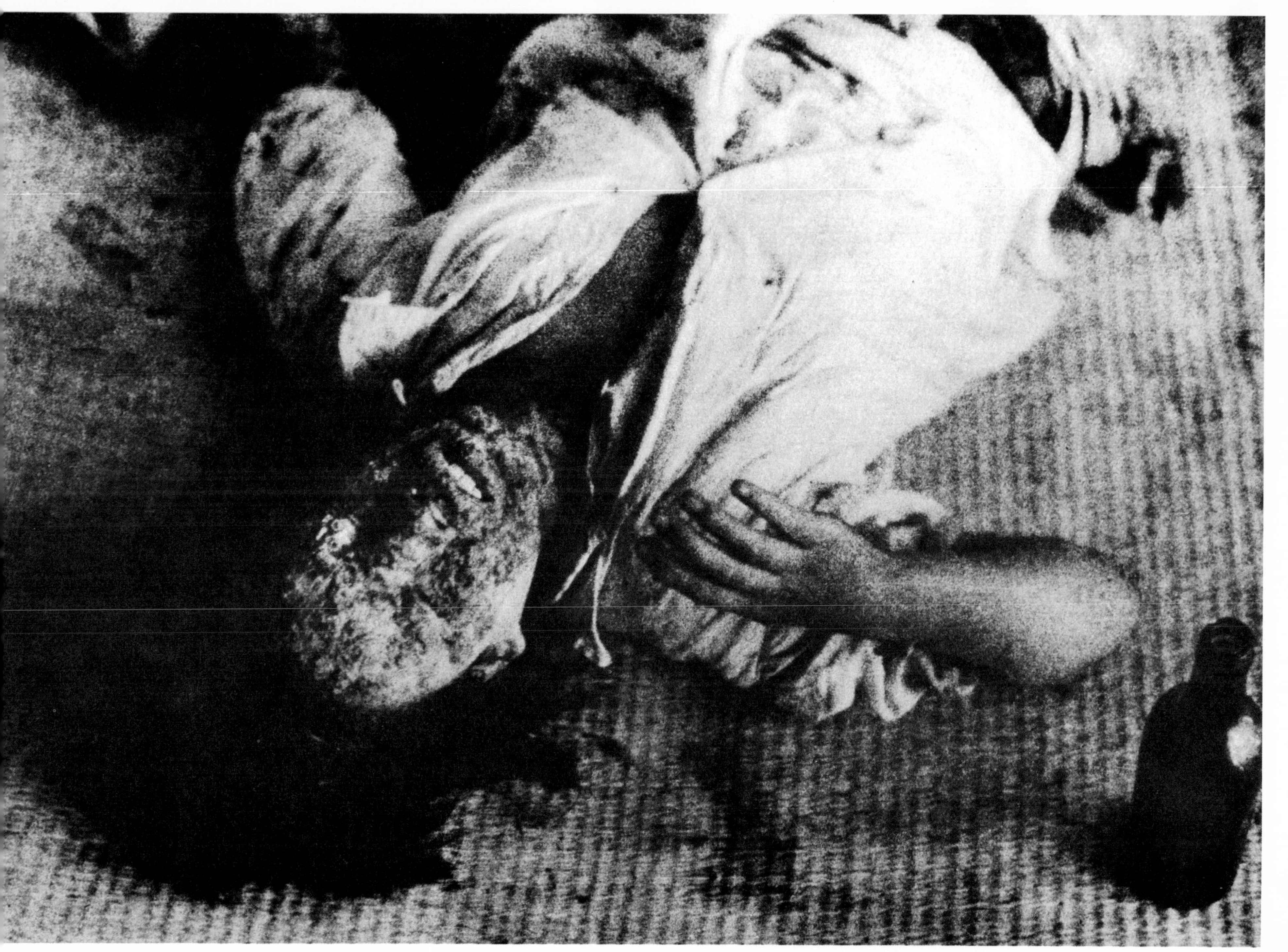

509. Atomic bomb, Hiroshima: a bomb victim at the Red Cross hospital four days after the bombing. August 10, 1945.

510. Atomic bomb, Nagasaki: scene near Uragami in Nagasaki on the day after the second atomic bomb was dropped. Yamahata Yōsuke. August 10, 1945.

511. Atomic bomb, Nagasaki: bomb victims sharing water from a bottle. Yamahata Yōsuke. August 10, 1945.

512. Atomic bomb, Nagasaki: charred corpse of a young boy, near the epicenter area. Yamahata Yōsuke. 'August 10, 1945.

typed but still evocative, particularly for the early decades of the twentieth century. Félicien Challaye's *Le Japon illustré,* published by Librairie Larousse in Paris in 1915, for example, contains over seven hundred sharp illustrations, most of which are photographs. A comparably ambitious and technically laudable undertaking in English is a mammoth volume edited by W. Feldwick, compiled by W. H. Morton-Cameron, and published by the Globe Encyclopaedia Company of London in 1919: *Present Day Impressions of Japan: The History, People, Commerce, Industries and Resources of Japan and Japan's Colonial Empire, Kwantung, Chosen, Taiwan, Karafutó.*

The major photographic record of the Shōwa period is the previously mentioned *Ichiokunin no Shōwa Shi* series by Mainichi Shimbunsha. In 1972, Asahi Shimbunsha published two volumes of photographs on the Shōwa period titled *Me de Miru Shōwa* [Shōwa Observed], and the *Shūkan Yomiuri* [Weekly Yomiuri] of March 10, 1976, was devoted to "Fifty Years of Shōwa."

In addition to the war photography in *Ichiokunin no Shōwa Shi,* Mainichi Shimbunsha has published numerous other grim photographic collections on the war in China and the Pacific, such as the 1971 volume *Nihon Kūshū* [The Japan Air Raids] and, in 1970, *Hishō: Shōnen no Senreki—Heiwa no Ishizue to Natta 15-sai* [Misery: The War Experience of Young Soldiers—Fifteen-Year-Olds Who Became the Foundation for Peace]. In English, S. L. Mayer has edited a well-illustrated record titled *The Japanese War Machine* (Chartwell Books, 1976).

Hiroshima-Nagasaki, a volume of numbing photographs of the consequences of the atomic bombs, was published in Japanese and English editions in 1978 by a progressive citizens' group called the Hiroshima-Nagasaki Publishing Committee (Heiwa Kaikan, 1-4-9 Shiba, Minato-ku, Tokyo 105). This volume also includes drawings and paintings by victims of the atomic bombs who were requested to depict their personal experiences and recollections in a major project sponsored by NHK television in the mid-1970s. Many of the drawings were exhibited nationally, with selections reproduced in a catalogue titled *Gōka o Mita: Shimin no Te de Genbaku no E o* [The Holocaust Visualized: Pictures of the Atomic Bombings by the Hands of the People]. An English edition of these graphic recollections was published by NHK in 1977 as *Unforgettable Fire: Pictures Drawn by Atomic-Bomb Survivors.*

The stunning impact of seeing the atomic holocaust through both the eye of the camera and the hand and mind's eye of the victim is an unusually vivid reminder that photography is but one of many ways in which modern Japan prior to 1945 survives iconographically for the historian. Here it is possible to list only a few examples of the other graphic ways of seeing through which these years were experienced, and can be visualized now by those who are inclined to look back.

The richness of modern Japanese art in both the traditional and Western styles is conveyed in a handsome, compact volume published by Asahi Shimbunsha in 1967 under the title *Genshoku Meiji Hyakunen Bijutsukan* [Japanese Art Since the Restoration: A Collection in Full Color]. This contains two hundred color plates, with care taken to include the works of many different artists. For an overview in English translation, see Michiaki Kawakita, *Modern Currents in Japanese Art,* volume 24 in "The Heibonsha Survey of Japanese Art" (Weatherhill/Heibonsha, 1974).

Four hundred sixty-five samples of poster art from the Bakumatsu period to 1956 are reproduced, many in color, in an attractive collection edited by the Tokyo Art Directors Club and published by Bijutsu Shuppansha in 1967. This appeared as volume 1 of *Nihon no Kōkoku Bijutsu: Meiji, Taishō, Shōwa* [The Advertising Art of Japan: Meiji, Taishō, Shōwa], and carries the English subtitle "Posters in Japan, 1860–1956"; the second volume is devoted to newspaper and magazine advertisements.

Konishi Shirō has edited the most spectacular collections of *nishiki-e* ("brocade pictures," that is, woodblock prints) from the Bakumatsu and Meiji periods. *Nishiki-e: Bakumatsu Meiji no Rekishi* [Brocade Pictures: The History of the Bakumatsu and Meiji Periods] covers the years from 1853 to 1912 in twelve volumes of full-color reproductions; this was published in 1977 by Kodansha. *Shimbun Nishiki-e* [Newspaper Brocade Pictures], a single volume published in 1972 by Mainichi Shimbunsha, consists of full-color reproductions of the garish and often grisly covers of sensational newspapers in the early Meiji period. Both of these fascinating collections depict the flowering of the woodblock print as a vehicle of "reportage" prior to the technological breakthroughs that permitted mass reproduction of photographs after the turn of the century.

One of the most successful Japanese publishing ventures of the 1970s was a twenty-five volume series published in lavish color by Chikuma Shobō under the title *Edo Jidai Zushi* [Illustrated Chronicle of the Edo Period]. This pictorial vision of the Edo or Tokugawa period (1600–1867) was organized geographically, and is to be followed by a seventeen-volume sequel titled *Meiji Taishō Zushi* [Illustrated Chronicle of Meiji and Taishō], focusing on the key cities and regions of Japan from the Restoration to the 1920s.

Taiyō [The Sun], one of Japan's more elaborate monthly glossies, frequently devotes issues or special editions to historical subjects. Of particular interest to students of modern Japan are the May 1974 issue devoted to "The Taishō Period," and the July 1975 issue devoted to "The Shōwa Period"; the material possessions of the time are lovingly portrayed here. In the winter of 1973, *Taiyō* published a special edition titled *Meiji Ishin Hyakunin* [One Hundred Individuals from the Meiji Restoration], useful for portraits of the key figures of the Restoration, although the printing is excessively arty.

Fujin Gahō (subtitled in English "The Lady's Graphic" in its early years), a monthly magazine for comfortably situated women that was founded in 1905, celebrated its seventieth anniversary with a 1975 softback glossy titled *Fashion to Fūzoku no 70-nen* [70 Years of Fashion and Customs]. A slightly eccentric evocation of popular tastes, pastimes, and possessions is *Yomigaeru Shōwa Roman* [Shōwa Romance Revived], published in 1976 by Shogakkan; this bears the English subtitle "Roman Mook," a "mook" being explained as contemporary journalistic English for a cross between a magazine and a book.

Graphic impressions of nineteenth-century Japan by Westerners have been collected in several publications. The most brilliant engravings of Bakumatsu Japan appeared in Aimé Humbert's *Le Japon illustré,* published in two huge volumes in 1870 by Librairie de La Hachette, Paris. Humbert was a member of the first Swiss mission to Japan in 1863–1864, and records that he took copious photographs during his frequent trips outside the foreign settlement in Yokohama. Largely on the basis of these photographs, some eight or more illustrators produced the 476 engravings and line drawings that accompany Humbert's lengthy text. A fine abridged Russian edition of this work was published in one volume as *Zhivopisnaia Iaponīia,* also in 1870. In 1874, R. Bentley & Sons brought out an English translation titled *Japan and the Japanese: Illustrated;* although again a handsome work, the English version omits more illustrations than does the Russian abridgment. The Japanese were introduced to Humbert's opus in 1966, when Tōto Shobō published *Bakumatsu Nihon: Ihōjin no E to Kiroku ni Miru* [Bakumatsu Japan Seen Through the Pictures and Account of a Foreigner].

Foreign impressions of Bakumatsu and early Meiji Japan were collected in two volumes edited by Ikeda Masatoshi and published by Shunjūsha in 1955; this project includes a bibliography of illustrated Western sources on early modern Japan, and is titled *Gaijin no Mita Bakumatsu Meiji Shoki Nihon Zue* [Drawings and Pictures of Bakumatsu and Early Meiji Japan As Seen by Foreigners]. Visual impressions of Japan as printed in the *London Illustrated News* between 1853 and 1902 are collected in *Egakareta Bakumatsu Meiji* [Sketches of Bakumatsu and Meiji], published by Yūshōdō Shoten in 1968.

The uneven but occasionally effective cartoons of Georges Bigot, who worked in Japan during the Meiji period, are collected in Shimizu Isao, ed., *Georges Bigot Gashū: Meiji o Kassha Shita Futsujin Fūshi Gakka Den* [The Drawings of Georges Bigot: Biography of a French Satirist Who Cast Light Upon Meiji], published by Bijutsu Dōjinsha in 1970. *Japan Punch,* the Yokohama-based journal to which Bigot contributed, was published from 1862 to 1887; the full run was reprinted by Yūshōdō Shoten in ten volumes in 1975.

The selected works of Kitagawa Rakuten, the preeminent social and political cartoonist of prewar Japan, were published by Graphic-sha beginning in 1974; the three volumes of *Rakuten Mangashū Taisei* [Rakuten's Cartoons] cover Meiji, Taishō, and Shōwa. The work of other famous prewar cartoonists can be sampled in the March 1971 issue of *Taiyō* and the September 1975 issue of *Bungei Shunjū Delux*. The Mainichi Shimbunsha project on Shōwa history and culture includes a supplementary volume published in 1977 as *Shōwa Manga Shi* [History of Shōwa Cartoons].

Stills from prewar Japanese cinema have been assembled in several publications. These include the first of two volumes published by Asahi Shimbunsha in 1976 as *Aa, Katsudō Daishashin* [Ah, the Great Motion Pictures], and *Shōwa Nihon Eiga Shi* [History of Japanese Movies in the Shōwa Period], another volume published in 1977 as a supplement to Mainichi Shimbunsha's *Ichiokunin no Shōwa Shi*.

Given the vigor of left-wing perspectives in the Japanese social sciences, the relative paucity of quality illustrated works on explicitly radical subjects is somewhat surprising. A graphic evocation of repression in the 1930s, however, can be found in two books published in the United States by Yashima Tarō. Yashima is better known in the West today for his children's books, but he was imprisoned in Japan for involvement in the proletarian art movement before he succeeded in making his way to America in the early 1940s. Both his brutalization and his idealism are depicted in two moving pen-and-ink sketchbooks published by Henry Holt & Co.: *The New Sun* (1943) and *Horizon Is Calling* (1947). For a survey of prewar proletarian art with a few illustrations, see *Nihon Puroretaria Bijutsu Shi* [History of Proletarian Art in Japan], edited by Okamoto Tōki and Matsuyama Fumio and published in 1967 by Zōkeisha.

Excellent color reproductions of serious Japanese paintings portraying the Pacific War effort are included in parts 1 and 2 of volume 2 of *Reports of General MacArthur,* published by the United States Department of the Army in 1966. On the Japanese side, see *Taiheiyō Sensō Meigashū* [The Pacific War Art Collection], published by Nobel Shobō in 1967; this contains one hundred plates, many in color and all with English as well as Japanese captions. The war paintings were done in both Western and Japanese styles. Samples of the cruder levels of graphic Japanese war propaganda are included in Anthony Rhodes, *Propaganda, The Art of Persuasion: World War Two* (Chelsea House, 1976).

Finally, it should be noted that popular or mass-oriented books and periodicals in pre-1945 Japan remain generally ignored by Westerners. Many of these publications appealed to special groups, and many were illustrated with style and verve. The bulk and diversity of this material contravenes most stereotypes of social or cultural homogenization in Japan. J.W.D.

LIST OF ILLUSTRATIONS

44. Samurai. Ueno Hikoma. Early Meiji period.

45. Samurai. Ueno Hikoma. Bakumatsu or early Meiji period.

46. Samurai. Ueno Hikoma. Bakumatsu or early Meiji period.

47. Battlement in the Shiroyama area of Kagoshima (Seinan War). Ueno Hikoma. 1877.

48. Solar eclipse (photographed at the Sapporo Meteorological Station). Shiina Sukemasa. April 6, 1894.

49. Ichinomura village (present-day Sapporo). Photographer unknown (possibly Tamoto Kenzō). *c.* 1871.

50. Photographic record of the construction of the Sapporo highway near Akagawa. Photographer unknown (possibly Takebayashi Seiichi). 1872–1873.

51. Ōno village, on the outskirts of Hakodate. Photographer unknown (possibly Tamoto Kenzō). Early Meiji period.

52. Road construction. Photographer unknown. Early Meiji period.

53. Higashihama-machi landing in the port of Hakodate. Photographer unknown (possibly Tamoto Kenzō). Early Meiji period.

54. Hakodate street scene during the reclamation period. Photographer unknown (possibly Tamoto Kenzō). Early Meiji period.

55. Reclamation in Kuttyan. Photographer unknown. 1908–1909.

56. The agricultural experimental station at Nanae, on the outskirts of Hakodate. Photographer unknown (possibly Tamoto Kenzō). 1880.

57. Log bridge over the Toyohira River in Sapporo. Photographer unknown. *c.* 1871.

58. Construction of the Toyohira River bridge in Sapporo. Photographer unknown (possibly Takebayashi Seiichi). February 24, 1875.

59. Test run of the locomotive "Benkeigō" on the Horonai Railroad at Irifunechō trestle, Otaru. Photographer unknown (possibly Sakuma Hanzō). October 24, 1880.

60. The mouth of the Ishikari River. Photographer unknown (possibly Tamoto Kenzō). *c.* 1871.

61. Commemorative photograph of emigrants to Hokkaidō from Yamanashi prefecture. Photographer unknown. 1909.

62. Housing of the farmer-militia *(tondenhei)* at Wanishi village in Muroran county. Photographer unknown. *c.* 1889.

63. Prisoner. Takebayashi Seiichi. Early Meiji period.

64. Prisoner. Takebayashi Seiichi. Early Meiji period.

65. Prisoner. Takebayashi Seiichi. Early Meiji period.

66. Ainu. Photographer unknown (possibly Takebayashi Seiichi). Early Meiji period.

67. River coolies. Photographer unknown. Early Meiji period.

68. Commemorative photograph of the family of the photographer Nagata Tomitarō. Nagata Tomitarō. 1926.

69. Cat of Sakhalin. Photographer unknown. Late Meiji period.

70. Woman and fishermen in Matsumae. Nagata Tomitarō. Late Meiji period.

71. Yard of the Shitakara coal mine in Kushiro. Photographer unknown. 1895.

72. Yūbari coal mine. Photographer unknown. Late Meiji period.

73. Reclaimed land in Kuttyan. Photographer unknown. 1908–1909.

74. Photographic record of the exploration of the Kurile Islands: a field of drifting ice near Shibetoro village on the island of Etorofu. Endō Mutsuo. March 1, 1892.

75. Photographic record of flood damage by the Katsuna River in Otaru. Photographer unknown (possibly Sakuma Hanzō). September 14, 1879.

76. Ainu. Kajima Seizaburō. From *The Ainu of Japan,* published in 1895.

77. *(left)* Lacquer-and-gold cover of a Meiji photo book. Such albums were sold throughout the Meiji period containing tinted albumen prints of famous scenes, beauties, and cultural activities.

    (right) Chiyoko, a geisha of the Nihonbashi district, Tokyo. Photographer unknown. From a mid-Meiji photo book.

78. A merchant. Magic-lantern photograph by unknown photographer (possibly Nakajima Machiyu). Early Meiji period.

79. Buddhist priests. Magic-lantern photograph by unknown photographer (possibly Nakajima Machiyu). Bakumatsu or early Meiji period.

80. A physician. Magic-lantern photograph by unknown photographer (possibly Nakajima Machiyu). Early Meiji period.

81. Girls tending infants. Photographer unknown. Bakumatsu or early Meiji period.

82. "Kago, Travelling Chair" (original title in English). Photographer unknown. Early Meiji period.

83. Street tumblers with lion masks. Photographer unknown. Bakumatsu or early Meiji period.

84. A post-town prostitute. Photographer unknown. Bakumatsu or early Meiji period.

85. "Prisoner" (original title in English): a criminal and a police spy. Photographer unknown. Early Meiji period.

86. Woman in Western dress, child with doll. Kizu Kōkichi. Early Meiji period.

87. Comic entertainer. Photographer unknown. Middle Meiji period.

88. Nihonbashi Bridge in Tokyo in the era of the horse-drawn tram (which first appeared in 1882). Photographer unknown (possibly Shimooka Renjō). Middle Meiji period.

89. The beacon at Kudanzaka in Tokyo (erected in 1870). Uchida Kuichi. Early Meiji period.

90. "View of Main Street, Tokio" (original title in English): Ginza avenue. Photographer unknown. Middle Meiji period.

91. Rokumeikan pavilion (the Western-style hall for social affairs in Tokyo, completed by the government in 1883). Photographer unknown. Middle Meiji period.

92. Kenshunmon gateway at the Kyoto Imperial Palace. Uchida Kuichi. Early Meiji period.

93. Shintomiza Kabuki theater in Tokyo. Photographer unknown. Early Meiji period.

94. "Suruga Tagonoura Bridge, to Fujiyama" (original title in English). Shizuoka prefecture. Photographer unknown. Middle Meiji period, and tinted in original.

95. "Enoshima" (original title in English). Kanagawa prefecture. Photographer unknown. Early Meiji period.

96. Terrace of Kiyomizu Temple in Kyoto. Uchida Kuichi. Early Meiji period.

97. "View of Imaichi, at Nikko Road" (original title in English). Tochigi prefecture. Photographer unknown. Middle Meiji period, and tinted in original.

98. Shinbashi train station in Tokyo. Mitsumura Risō. From a Japanese collection titled "Famous Scenes of Tokyo," published in 1900.

99. Azuma Bridge in Tokyo. Mitsumura Risō. From "Famous Scenes of Tokyo," 1900.

100. "Mitsui-gumi House" in Tokyo (completed in 1872). Uchida Kuichi. Early Meiji period.

101. "Gion-machi, Kioto" (original title in English). Photographer unknown. Early Meiji period.

102. Pagoda of the Yasaka Shrine in Kyoto. Uchida Kuichi. Early Meiji period.

103. "English Club at Kobe" (original title in English). Photographer unknown. Early Meiji period.

104. Sanjūsangendō Temple in Kyoto. Uchida Kuichi. Early Meiji period.

105. Shureinomon gate in Okinawa. Mitsumura Risō. From a Japanese collection titled "Souvenirs of a Trip," published in 1901.

106. Photographic record of the test blasting of a torpedo on the Sumida River, Tokyo. Ezaki Reiji. 1883.

107. Egyptian mummy. Photographer unknown (possibly Yokoyama Matsusaburō). *c.* 1874.

108. "Carved Cat, Nikko" (original title in English): Tōshōgū Temple. Photographer unknown. Early Meiji period, and tinted in original.

109. Construction site in Hokkaidō. Shimizu Tōkoku. Early Meiji period.

110. Head of one of the four guardian deities at Kōfukuji Temple in Nara. Photographed by Ogawa Kazumasa while undergoing repairs. Middle Meiji period.

111. Collage of 1,700 babies. Ezaki Reiji. 1893.

112. Dilapidated interior of Edo Castle. Yokoyama Matsusaburō. Pre-1871.

113. "Home Bathing" (original title in English). Photographer unknown. Middle Meiji period.

114. "Harakiri" (original title in English). Photographer unknown (possibly Ogawa Kazumasa). Middle Meiji period.

115. "Jinrikisha" (original title in English). Photographer unknown (possibly Ogawa Kazumasa). Middle Meiji period.

116. "Girls in Bed Room" (original title in English). Photographer unknown (possibly Ogawa Kazumasa). Middle Meiji period.

117. "Bronze Image (Daibutsu) at Uyeno, Tokio" (original title in English). Photographer unknown (possibly Uchida Kuichi). Middle Meiji period.

118. "Shimoda" (original title in English). Shizuoka prefecture. Photographer unknown (possibly Uchida Kuichi). Middle Meiji period.

119. "Shiraito Waterfall, at Fujiyama" (original title in English). Photographer unknown (possibly Uchida Kuichi). Middle Meiji period.

120. "Scene Sumida River, at Mukojima, Tokio" (original title in English). Photographer unknown (possibly Uchida Kuichi). Middle Meiji period.

121. A courtesan. Oil painting over photograph by unknown photographer. Early Meiji period.

122. Kokiyo, a geisha of the Shinbashi district, Tokyo, portrayed riding on a crane. Photographer unknown. Middle Meiji period.

123. Family commemorative portrait. Kikuchi Tōyō. Taken in New York between 1909 and 1919.

124. Commemorative photograph of officers and soldiers who participated in the army grand maneuvers in Fukui prefecture in 1933. The emperor is in center foreground. G. T. Sun.

125. "Self-portrait." Harry K. Shigeta (Shigeta Kinji). Taken in Chicago in the late 1920s or 1930s.

126. "The Venerable Tagore." Igarashi Yoshichi. Taken in Tokyo, 1929.

127. Commemorative photograph of Shimazu Hisanori, seventh son of Shimazu Tadayoshi, at his Hakamagi ceremony (where boys at the ages of three, five, or seven don the formal divided skirt for males). Platinum print by Shunsho-kan Studio in Kagoshima. 1880.

128. The Meiji emperor. Photographer unknown. Middle Meiji period.

129. The Taishō emperor: commemorative photograph upon receiving the insignia of the Order of the Garter from the King of England. Photographer unknown. 1912.

130. Emperor Hirohito: commemorative photograph of the enthronement ceremony, November 1928. Photographer unknown.

131. Commemorative photograph of a little girl. Tamoto Kenzō. 1887.

132. Commemorative photograph of a little boy. Nagata Tomitarō. 1912.

133. "Young Girl." Ezaki Kiyoshi. 1928.

134. Commemorative photograph of siblings. Fujimoto Otokichi. Late Meiji period.

135. Men wearing mantles. Kajima Seibe-e. Late Meiji period.

136. "Portrait of Teru." Miyauchi Kōtarō. 1901

137. Commemorative photograph of a wedding. Maruki Riyō. 1918.

138. Commemorative photograph of siblings. Hori Masumi. Late Meiji period.

139. Commemorative photograph of a family. Masuda Photograph Studio. 1900.

140. "Portrait Study" (original title in English). Shibata Tsunekichi. 1889.

141. A lady. Photographer unknown. Middle Meiji period.

142. Portrait of Tokugawa Tameko. Maruki Riyō. 1908.

143. A lady. Itani Photograph Studio. Late Meiji period.

144. A lady. Itō Ryūkichi. 1927.

145. Commemorative photograph of siblings. Shibata Tsunekichi. 1912.

146. Commemorative photograph of sisters. Maruki Riyō. 1912.

147. "Portrait of Fujita Yōko." Kikuchi Tōyō. 1928.

148. A young lady. Ariga Toragorō. 1924.

149. A woman. Yasukōchi Jiichirō. 1935.

150. "Child." Ogawa Gesshū. 1928.

151. Vice Admiral Enomoto Takeaki (Buyō). Photographer unknown. 1880–1881.

152. The statesman Itō Hirobumi. Maruki Riyō. Late Meiji period. (This portrait appears on the one-thousand-yen notes in Japanese currency).

153. The parliamentarian Ozaki Yukio. Kobayashi Hiroshi. 1930.

154. Chaliapin. Nakayama Shōichi. 1936.

155. "Portrait of Three Geisha." Photographer unknown. Late Meiji period, and tinted in original.

156. Elderly couple. A portrait of his parents by Ogawa Kazumasa. 1892.

157. Commemorative portrait of actresses in the Imperial Theater, Tokyo. Morikawa Aizō. 1929.

158. Commemorative photograph of the Constitutional Democratic Party (Rikken Minseitō). Photographer unknown. 1929.

159. Commemorative photograph of the faculty and students of the Naval Academy at Tsukiji, Tokyo. Uchida Kuichi. January 1873.

160. Commemorative photograph of Satsuma riflemen departing for the front during the Boshin War. Photographer unknown. 1867–1868.

161. Officers at the siege of Kumamoto Castle during the Seinan War. Tomishige Rihei. 1877.

162. Commemorative photograph of Japanese and Korean dignitaries at the Seoul residence of Itō Hirobumi, the Japanese resident-general in Korea. Itō is seated second from the left. Seated on the left is Tōgō Heihachirō, and on the right, Katsura Tarō. Mitsumura Risō. 1909.

163. Commemorative photograph of women gathered at the Shimazu residence in Kagoshima to celebrate the visit of one of the married daughters of Shimazu Tadayoshi. Sugimoto Photograph Studio. 1902.

164. Commemorative photograph of a gathering in honor of the head of a university. Iizuka Photograph Studio. 1886.

165. Commemorative photograph of a gathering of elementary-school children in Yokohama. Suzuki Shinichi. Late Meiji period.

166. Commemorative photograph of the women's class of the Iwate Teachers School. Nara Photograph Studio. 1914.

167. Commemorative photograph of students in the orchestra and chorus of the Tokyo Music Academy. Miyauchi Kōtarō. Late Meiji period.

168. The emperor (center front) and naval officers and men on the flagship *Nagato.* Admiral Okada Keisuke is seated on the emperor's right. *Mainichi* newspaper. June 3, 1929.

169. Sino-Japanese War: the Third Battalion of farmer-militia *(tondenhei)* of the Temporary Seventh Division on the Aoyama parade ground in Tokyo prior to departure for the Chinese front. Suzuki Shinichi. April 1895.

170. Sino-Japanese War: the battle of the Yellow Sea. Photographer unknown. September 17, 1894.

171. Sino-Japanese War: a battery of mountain artillery shelling near Fankiatun to the west of Port Arthur. Army Land Surveying Section. November 21, 1894.

172. Russo-Japanese War: military bridge at the eastern edge of Siaopehho near Mukden. Hosaka Kōtarō (Army Land Surveying Section). February 26, 1905.

173. Russo-Japanese War: practice firing with a six-inch rapid-fire gun, by the combined fleet of the imperial navy, in preparation for the confrontation with the Russian Baltic fleet. Ichioka Tajirō. From an album published in April 1905.

174. Russo-Japanese War: the Thirty-Fourth Infantry Regiment in battle near Likiatun. Ogura Kenji (Army Land Surveying Section). July 23, 1904.

175. Russo-Japanese War: Russian war dead in trenches midway up the northeastern slope of 203-Meter Hill. Ōtsuka Tokusaburō (Army Land Surveying Section). December 9, 1904.

176. Russo-Japanese War: the First Battalion of the Thirty-Seventh Infantry Regiment walking by an uncompleted Russian military railroad bridge north of Mokiabo. Saitō Jirō (Army Land Surveying Section). March 9, 1905.

177. Russo-Japanese War: the Forty-Ninth Infantry Regiment advancing in Sakhalin. Photographer unknown. July 8, 1905.

178. Russo-Japanese War: wounded soldiers in a hospital in Kaipingting. Hosaka Kōtarō (Army Land Surveying Section). July 20, 1904.

179. Russo-Japanese War: street in Changtu. Morikane Shūgaku (Army Land Surveying Section). April 10, 1905.

180. Russo-Japanese War: explosion in front of the Shungshushan battery on the outskirts of Port Arthur. Ōtsuka Tokusaburō (Army Land Surveying Section). December 30, 1904.

181. Russo-Japanese War: Japanese soldiers killed in the battle of Tashihkiao near Bienhankiang. Ogura Kenji (Army Land Surveying Section). July 25, 1904.

182. Russo-Japanese War: beheading of a spy on the outskirts of Kaiyuan in Manchuria. Photographer unknown. March 20, 1905.

183. Russo-Japanese War: meeting of Russian and Japanese truce delegations on a road north of the Changtu railroad station. Ogura Kenji (Army Land Surveying Section). September 13, 1905.

184. World War I: a storm-tossed landing place at Lung-kou in Shantung. Army Land Surveying Section. 1914.

185. World War I: vendors catering to German prisoners of war at the Ōita depot in Japan (established in December 1914). Photographer unknown. From an album on war prisoners published in 1917.

186. Siberian Expedition: the corpse of Private Yamamoto of the Third Company of the Third Cavalry Battalion, discovered after he had been missing for about a fortnight. Army Land Surveying Section (Fujita). August 16, 1919.

187. Siberian Expedition: Japanese infantry near Nerchinsk. Army Land Surveying Section (Baba and Fujita). May 17, 1919.

188. Siberian Expedition: corpses of partisans massacred by the Japanese army in a battle on April 12, 1920, near Chita. Army Land Surveying Section (Terashima). April 16, 1920.

189. Siberian Expedition: weapons confiscated by the Japanese in a Siberian village. Army Land Surveying Section (Fujita). August 14, 1919.

190. Siberian Expedition: Japanese workers in an engine shed near Chita. Army Land Surveying Section (Fujita). April 23, 1919.

191. Siberian Expedition: trains containing Russian refugees in the Chita railroad yard. Army Land Surveying Section (Baba). July 21, 1920.

192. Siberian Expedition: a reception in Heilungkiang, northern Manchuria, for a delegation from the Japanese House of Representatives. Army Land Surveying Section (Terashima). July 5, 1919.

193. "Bullfight." Nakayama Iwata. Spain, 1926.

194. "Peony." Umesaka Ōri. 1931.

195. "Woman under a Tree." Gum print by Nojima Kōzō. 1915.

196. "White Flower." Tamura Sakae. 1931.

197. "Flowing Quietly in the Ravine." Bromoil by Ogawa Gesshū. 1927.

198. "The Clatter of People and Horses." Yonetani Kōrō. 1926.

199. "After the Rain." Umesaka Ōri. 1933.

200. "Loquat." Bromoil by Nojima Kōzō. 1930.

201. "Snow on Bamboo." Collotype by Takahashi Kinka. 1907.

202. "Moonlit Night by the Lake Shore." Collotype by Fujii Shimei. 1907.

203. "Quiet Temple in the Autumn Woods." Bromoil by Urahara Seiho. 1926.

204. "Estuary." Gum print by Ogawa Gesshū. 1925.

205. "The Shade of Trees." Gum print by Hidaka Chōtarō. 1921.

206. "Moonlight on Snow." Itō Fumikazu. 1922.

207. "Scene of Fura" (in Chiba prefecture). Gum print by Hirao Keiji. 1926.

208. "Scene with Myself." Itō Ryōzō. 1932.

209. "Snow." Yonetani Kōrō. 1922.

210. "Winter." Izumi Toshirō. 1928.

211. "Faint Sunlight." Yamanaka Hekisui. 1922.

212. "Portrait of a Little Girl." Yamamoto Makihiko. 1929.

213. "Portrait of Sisters Standing Outdoors." Takao Yoshirō. 1929.

214. "Person in a Room." Bromide by Matsugi Fujio. 1930.

215. "Scene with Factory." Takayama Toshio. 1930.

216. "Mr. Takada Minayoshi." Tsusaka Jun. 1929.

217. "Young Boy Toying with a Snake." Hagiwara Roshū. 1928.

218. "Backyard." Matsugi Fujio. 1930.

219. "Scene." Bromide by Toyo Kichisaburō. 1930.

220. "Woman in Paris." Fukuhara Shinzō. 1926.

221. "Pond at Shuzenji Temple" (in Shizuoka prefecture). Fukuhara Shinzō. 1926.

222. "Autumn in Okutama" (in Tokyo). Fukuhara Shinzō. 1925.

223. "Nara Scene." Fukuhara Rosō. 1925.

224. "Fifty Subjects in Tokyo (No. 1)." Nishiyama Kiyoshi. 1926.

225. "Bridge." Tsusaka Jun. 1926.

226. "Still Life." Fukuda Katsuji. 1926.

227. "Still Life." Takayama Masataka. 1926.

228. "Lines." Sugimoto Saburō. 1928.

229. "Composition of Lines." Yamazaki Masuzō. 1926.

230. "Study (1)." Matsuo Saigorō. 1926.

231. "Man Holding a Bowl." Fuchigami Hakuyō. 1925.

232. "Portrait of Two." Satō Shin. 1932.

233. "Woman Combing Hair." Gum print by Nojima Kōzō. 1914.

234. "Strength." Tamamura Kihei. 1922.

235. "A Lonely Person." Gum print by Eguchi Nanyō. 1920.

236. "Portrait of a Lady." Chlorobromide by Yasumoto Kōyō. 1938.

237. "People Serving God." Gum print by Ono Ryūtarō. 1915.

238. "Portrait." Gum print by Yoshikawa Tomizō. 1924.

239. "Street Scene." Nakayama Iwata. New York, 1922.

240. "Portrait." Kajiwara Takuma. St. Louis, 1926.

241. "Tamiris in 1927." Suminami Sōichi. New York, 1928.

242. "Portrait of a Dancer." Nakayama Iwata. New York, 1922.

243. "Priest Taking a Stroll." Yamamoto Makihiko. 1927.

244. "Woman." Nojima Kōzō. 1933.

245. "Concept of the Machinery of the Creator." Hanawa Gingo. *c.* 1930.

246. "Fashion." Hirai Terushichi. 1938.

247. "A Dream of the Moon." Hirai Terushichi. 1938.

248. "Balinese Dancers." Dye-transfer print by Kitazumi Genzō. 1942.

249. "A House." Kondō Tatsuo. 1937.

250. "Paper." Kōmura Kiyohiko. 1936.

251. "Ochanomizu Station" (in Tokyo). Watanabe Yoshio. 1933.

252. "Water Flowers." Aida Tamon. 1941.

253. "Sea Bream." Benitani Kichinosuke. 1932.

254. "Crushed Expression." Majima Shōichi. 1940.

255. "Sweat." Narita Shunyō. 1937.

256. "Temptation: the Passion of Steel." Koishi Kiyoshi. 1933.

257. "Hands of Amida, the National Treasure at Kōryūji Temple" (in Kyoto). Domon Ken. 1941.

258. "Composition" (original title in English). Wakayanagi Yoshitarō. 1933.

259. "Chimney." Kōno Tōru. 1940.

260. "Camera: Eye × Steel • Composition." Horino Masao. 1932.

261. "....." Yamakawa Ken-ichirō. 1933.

262. "Merchandise at a Store." Iida Kōjirō. 1931.

263. "Skeleton." Nakamura Kenji. 1934.

264. "Chrysanthemum Wedging." Domon Ken. 1941.

265. "Splash." Yasui Nakaji. 1933.

266. "Swimming." Shibata Ryūji. 1937.

267. "Silhouette." Ueda Shōji. 1936.

268. "So What!" Composite photograph by Hanaya Kanbe-e. 1937.

269. "Piston Fury." Solarization print by Koishi Kiyoshi. 1934.

270. "Delight." Ueda Bizan. 1940.

271. "Feeling of Fatigue." 'Moving montage' by Koishi Kiyoshi. 1936.

272. "Taste of Autumn." Tanaka Shinpei. 1932.

273. "No Title." Matsubara Jūzō. 1935.

274. "Legend of Night" (from a series of photographs titled "Gods"). Hattori Yoshifumi. 1938.

275. "Snake." Kaieda Heiichirō. Late 1920s or early 1930s.

276. "From Nature." Tajima Tsuguo. 1940.

277. "Plastic in a Ghost Image." Shimogō Yōyū. 1939.

278. "Mesembryanthema." Shimogō Yōyū. 1939.

279. "....." Nakayama Iwata. 1932.

280. Untitled. Sakata Minoru. 1940.

281. "Elephant" (from a series of photographs titled "Half the World"). Koishi Kiyoshi. 1939.

282. "Shell Mound" (from a series of photographs titled "Half the World"). Koishi Kiyoshi. 1939.

283. "Butterflies." Nakayama Iwata. 1941.

284. "Uemura Shōen" (painter). Hamaya Hiroshi. 1936.

285. "Takada Tamotsu" (playwright and essayist). Kimura Ihe-e. 1933.

286. "Satō Haruo" (poet and writer). Kimura Ihe-e. 1933.

287. "Go Seigen" (Go master). Katō Kyōhei. 1941.

288. "Fujita Tsuguji (painter). Nakayama Iwata. 1926.

289. "A Master: Yoshida Bungorō" (Bunraku puppeteer). Domon Ken. 1942.

290. "The Late Naoki Sanjūgo" (writer). Yamamura Takao. 1936.

291. "Senda Koreya" (actor and director). Nojima Kōzō. 1932.

292. "No Title." Nojima Kōzō. 1933.

293. "Model F." Nojima Kōzō. 1931.

294. "Woman." Nojima Kōzō. 1931.

295. "Woman." Nojima Kōzō. 1931.

296. "Make-up." Mitsumura Toshihiro. 1934.

297. "Woman." Solarization print by Koishi Kiyoshi. 1936.

298. "Portrait of Two People Holding Artificial Flowers." Tamura Sakae. 1930.

299. "Spring of the Shōwa Era." Matsugi Fujio. 1930.

300. "Dance of Delight on Red Hill." Yasukōchi Jiichirō. 1937.

301. "Wind." Horino Masao. 1936.

302. "Woman." Fukuda Katsuji. 1937.

303. Fashion photograph for a hat. Tamura Shigeru. 1940.

304. "....." Saeki Ryō. 1933.

305. "Nude Woman." Benitani Kichinosuke. 1931.

306. "Woman." Nojima Kōzō. 1931.

307. "Woman from Shanghai." Nakayama Iwata. 1932.

308. "Hosokawa Chikako" (actress). Nojima Kōzō. 1932.

309. "Hair." Kimura Ihe-e. 1935.

310. "Expression of a Woman." Kimura Ihe-e. 1934.

311. "Scene with Clouds." Narita Shunyō. 1938.

312. "The Torii Pass from Kakuma" (in Nagano prefecture). Suzuki Hachirō. 1936.

313. "Train Rushing." Fuchigami Hakuyō. Manchuria, 1930.

314. "In Front of an Eatery." Fuchigami Hakuyō. Manchuria, 1930.

315. "Shoeshine Man." Yoneshiro Zen-emon. Manchuria, late 1920s or early 1930s.

316. "A Shepherd Boy." Sakakibara Shōichi. Manchuria, 1935.

317. "Proceeding on a Wild Plain." Baba Hatchō. Manchuria, 1935.

318. "Man." Okada Nakaharu. Manchuria, 1937.

319. "Beggar." Kitano Kunio. Manchuria, 1939.

320. "Milk." Isshiki Tatsuo. Manchuria, 1938.

321. "Laundering." Okada Nakaharu. Manchuria, 1939.

322. "A Hamlet." Emi Mitsuo. Manchuria, 1938.

323. "Pigs." Shibuya Shōyō. Manchuria, 1939.

324. "Still Life of a Lamp." Baba Hatchō. Manchuria, 1938.

325. "Coal." Nakada Shiyō. Manchuria, 1937.

326. "Setting Sun." Baba Hatchō. Manchuria, 1938.

327. "Locomotive." Tanaka Seibō. Manchuria, 1937.

328. "Three People." Yasui Nakaji. 1941.

329. "Sick Dog." Yasui Nakaji. 1934.

330. "Singing Men." Yasui Nakaji. 1936.

331. "Children Shooing Away Sparrows." Chiba Teisuke. 1942.

332. "Warming at the Fire." Iwase Sadayuki. 1934.

333. "Kadonyū Village" (in Gifu prefecture). Sakata Minoru. 1941.

334. "Fisherman at Hitachi Seashore." Hamaya Hiroshi. 1940.

335. "Old Man." Miki Shigeru. 1944.

336. "A Cantonese." Koishi Kiyoshi. China, 1939.

337. "An Orphanage in Harbin." Hamaya Hiroshi. Manchuria, 1940.

338. "Transient Coolie." Hamaya Hiroshi. Manchuria, 1940.

339. "People." Tanahashi Shisui. China, 1940.

340. "Slow-going." Kuwabara Kineo. Manchuria, 1940.

341. "A Monk of Senzan." Kimura Ihe-e. Manchuria, 1939.

342. "At the Shōwa Steel Works." Nishino Kazuo. Anshan, Manchuria, 1939.

343. "Wind." Mizutani Chikushi. 1935.

344. "Actors." Yasui Nakaji. 1937.

345. "Strolling Musicians." Horino Masao. 1934.

346. "Man Sleeping in a Trash Cart." Iida Kōjirō. 1933.

347. "Poster." Iida Kōjirō. 1931.

348. "Child." Yasui Nakaji. 1935.

349. "Beggar." Horino Masao. 1932.

350. "Laborer at a Calcium Factory in Kuwana." Ōhashi Isao. 1938.

351. "Mother and Child." Kōno Tōru. 1935.

352. "Crewman." Yasui Nakaji. 1930.

353. "Chess." Kimura Ihe-e. 1933.

354. "Western Clothing Store." Kimura Ihe-e. 1933.

355. "....." Kimura Ihe-e. 1932.

356. "Downtown Children" (in Tokyo). Kimura Ihe-e. 1933.

357. "Street Merchant." Kuwabara Kineo. 1942.

358. "Flea Market in Setagaya" (in Tokyo). Kuwabara Kineo. 1936.

359. "Scene at a Fair." Kuwabara Kineo. 1936.

360. "Tākī" (nickname of Mizunoe Takiko, a popular actress who played male roles, depicted here at the Asakusa International Theater in Tokyo). Hamaya Hiroshi. 1939.

361. "Boy Selling Flowers at Ginza" (in Tokyo). Hamaya Hiroshi. 1936.

362. "Backstage at a Cabaret." Horino Masao. 1931.

363–6. From "Looking at a Review: the Tokyo Shōchiku Musical Theater." Watanabe Yoshio. Published in the October 1932 issue of *Fuoto Taimusu* (Photo Times).

367–9. From "The Character of Great Tokyo." Horino Masao. Published in the October 1931 issue of *Chūō Kōron* (Central Review).

370–4. From *Snow Country,* a record of folk customs during the lunar New Year celebrations at Nishiyokoyama village in Kuwatoridani, Niigata prefecture. Hamaya Hiroshi. Photographed between 1940 and 1944, and published in 1956.

370. "Strolling Boys Reciting Chants to Drive Away Pests That Threaten the Crops."

371. "Praying to a Young Tree."

372. "Congratulating a Groom."

373. "Torch Fighting in Honor of the Deity (Sai no kami) Who Guards Against Invasion by Evil Spirits and Disasters."

374. "Retreat in a Community Hall."

375. "Marketplace in Naha" (Okinawa). Kimura Ihe-e. 1937.

376. Newly drafted student conscripts: a send-off rally in the rain at the Meiji Shrine in Tokyo, led by students from Tokyo Imperial University and attended by several tens of thousands of students from seventy-seven schools. *Yomiuri* newspaper. October 21, 1943.

377. Sailors and retainers of the Shōgun on the deck of *Mount Fuji,* a warship built in the United States. Photographer unknown. 1868.

378. Ryōgōku Bridge in Tokyo. Photographer unknown. Early Meiji period.

379. Head of a criminal executed for matricide, exposed at the Hodogaya execution ground (in present-day Yokohama). The placard at the right describes the crime. Photographer unknown. 1872.

380. Exposed head of Etō Shimpei, who was executed after leading the abortive Saga Rebellion. Photographer unknown. April 13, 1874.

381. Death mask (made by Asakura Fumio) of Prime Minister Inukai Tsuyoshi, who was assassinated in the May 15 Incident of 1931. Photographer unknown.

382. A farmhouse buried under volcanic ash on Ōsumi Peninsula, following an eruption of Mount Sakurajima. *Mainichi* newspaper. January 12, 1914.

383. Damage from the Nōbi earthquake of October 28, 1891, in Otai village, Nishikasugai county, Aichi prefecture. Miyashita Kin.

384. The great Kantō earthquake of September 1, 1923: fire in the Hibiya area of Tokyo. Kyōdō Press.

385. The great Kantō earthquake: charred bodies in the area of the former army clothing factory in Honjo, Tokyo, where 38,000 persons burned to death. Photographer unknown.

386. The great Kantō earthquake: women bathing in the puddles amidst the debris at Ginza, Tokyo. *Yomiuri* newspaper.

387. The great Kantō earthquake: charred bodies in front of the Yokohama Shōkin Bank at Nihonbashi, Tokyo. Photographer unknown.

388. Man killed by the eruption of Mount Bandai in Aizu on July 25, 1888. Photographer unknown.

389. Victims of an earthquake in the northern part of Hyōgo prefecture on May 23, 1925. Photographer unknown.

390. Women and children of Ueno village, Aso county, Tochigi prefecture, in the copper-poisoned area surrounding the Ashio copper mine. Photographer unknown. 1887.

391. Construction workers who were physically abused at the Watanabe labor quarters in Taiseiji, Abirashinai, Nakagawa county, Hokkaidō. Photographer unknown. Published in the *Asahikawa* newspaper. 1926.

392. Female miners at the mouth of a coal pit. Photographer unknown. Late Meiji period.

393. Pit workers in Mitsui Company's Miike coal mine, Kumamoto prefecture. Photographer unknown. *c.* 1925.

394. Farmers in Iwate prefecture. Photographer unknown. 1896.

395. Victims of a severe rainstorm flocking to buy cheap white rice offered as a relief measure in Tsukishima, Tokyo. Photographer unknown. October 7, 1917.

396. Children eating white radishes *(daikon)* during a famine caused by crop failure in Kamihei county, Iwate prefecture. *Mainichi* newspaper. November 1934.

397. Farmers suffering from cold-weather damage to their crops in Ninohe county, Iwate prefecture. *Asahi* newspaper. February 5, 1935.

398. Female workers making nets at a factory in Sapporo, Hokkaidō. Photographer unknown. Early Meiji period.

399. Courtesans in the Yoshiwara pleasure quarters, Tokyo. Photographer unknown. *c.* 1905.

400. Crowd at Tokyo station greeting the Duke of Connaught, representative of the British monarch. Sawa Kurō. June 18, 1918.

401. Police guarding Tokyo city hall in preparation for a citizen's demonstration against the merging of gas companies. Photographer unknown. December 1, 1911.

402. Rally protesting a fare hike for Tokyo streetcars, sponsored by the Japan Socialist Party at Hibiya Park. The crowd is gathered on a rise nicknamed "203-Meter Hill" [cf. plate 175]. Photographer unknown. March 15, 1906.

403. Handcuffed prisoners disguised with straw hats being led to a secure place following the great Kantō earthquake. *Mainichi* newspaper. September 1, 1923.

404. Police and protesters struggling in front of the residence of Prime Minister Hara Takashi in Tokyo after a gathering in support of universal male suffrage. Photographer unknown. February 22, 1920.

405. Demonstration led by the Yūaikai labor organization, opposing the government's chosen delegate to the First International Labor Conference. Photographer unknown. October 5, 1919.

406. Protest against the Public Peace Preservation Law at Arimagahara, Shiba district, Tokyo. Photographer unknown. February 7, 1925.

407. Rural response to the first general election under universal male suffrage. The wall writing reads: "Absolutely do not talk about anything related to the election. Let sleeping dogs lie." *Asahi* newspaper. February 1928.

408. A longshoreman being arrested. *Asahi* newspaper. May 31, 1932.

409. A demonstration by Osaka steel-factory workers. *Asahi* newspaper. June 8, 1921.

410. The first May Day demonstration in Otaru city. Photographer unknown. May 1, 1926.

411. Struggle between students and police in front of the former University of Commerce at Hitotsubashi, Kanda district, Tokyo. The students were protesting the abolition of certain academic programs. *Asahi* newspaper. October 7, 1931.

412. Arrest of participants in a protest meeting against the Public Peace Preservation Law. *Asahi* newspaper. March 1925.

413. Devotees of the Tenri religious sect praying in front of their sect headquarters in Tanbaichi (present-day Tenri), Nara prefecture, which was declared off limits by the government following the Tenri Incident of April 3, 1928, in which 385 members of a Tenri study group (including the leader Ōnishi Aijirō) were arrested and charged with lese majesty. *Asahi* newspaper. April 9, 1928.

414. Armed Koreans who were arrested in the Chientao area of Manchuria after the March 1 Movement for Korean independence (the Manzae Incident). Photographer unknown. April 1919.

415. Itō Hirobumi, the first Japanese resident-general in Korea, and Ri Yin, the Korean crown prince. Photographer unknown. *c.* 1907.

416. Persons executed in Korea for participating in the March 1 Movement for Korean independence (the Manzae Incident). Photographer unknown. March 1919.

417–21. The February 26 Incident of 1936, in Tokyo.

417. Troops dispatched to suppress the rebels. Photographer unknown.

418. Navy land-combat unit heading for Nagatachō, where the rebels were assembled. Photographer unknown.

419. Tokyo under martial law. Photographer unknown.

420. Evacuees from the Shiba district returning home after calm had been restored. *Asahi* newspaper. February 29, 1936.

421. Scene in front of the restaurant "Kōraku" in the Akasaka district, which served as headquarters for the rebel army. Photographer unknown.

422. The uniform of commander-in-chief which was given by the Meiji emperor to Viscount Hinonishi. Photographer unknown. 1927.

423. "Akadama Port Wine." Kawaguchi Photograph Studio (Inoue Mokuta and Kataoka Toshirō). Poster, 1922.

424. "Lait Cream." Sawa Reika. Poster, 1935.

425. "Shiseidō Soap." Ibuka Akira. Poster aimed at the Asian continent, 1941.

426. Cover of Shiseidō company magazine *Hanatsubaki*. Ibuka Akira. August 1938.

427. Oriental Can Company advertisement in a propaganda magazine distributed abroad. Kamekura Yūsaku. 1941.

428. Cover of *Front,* a magazine distributed abroad. Tōhōsha company. 1942.

429. Cover of *Front,* a magazine distributed abroad. Tōhōsha company. 1942.

430. "Dai Nippon Beer." Photographer unknown. Taishō period (1912–1926) poster.

431. "Kunji Perfumed Oil." Photographer unknown. 1909.

432. "Daigaku Face Powder." Photographer unknown. 1909.

433. "Hasegawa Cabinet Store." Photographer unknown. 1909.

434. "Milk-White Lotion Lait." Tanimoto Photograph Studio. 1909.

435. "Club Washing Powder." Photographer unknown. 1909.

436. "Misono Face Powder." Photographer unknown. 1909.

437. "Beauty Lotion." Photographer unknown. 1909.

438. "Pearl Perfume." Photographer unknown. 1908.

439. "Pastamusk Soap." Photographer unknown. 1909.

440. "Kaneda Watch Store." Photographer unknown. 1909.

441. "Fuji Bicycle." Koishi Kiyoshi. Winner of an advertising contest for "Ladies and Fuji Bicycle," 1936.

442. "Fukusuke Japanese-style Socks." Nakayama Iwata. Winner of the First International Advertising Photography Exhibition, 1930.

443. "Club Soap." Koishi Kiyoshi. 1931.

444. "Smile Eye-Drops." Koishi Kiyoshi. Third-place winner in the First International Advertising Photography Exhibition, 1930.

445. "Kikkōman Soy Sauce." Ueda Bizan. 1932.

446. "Records." Hori Fusao. 1932.

447. "Salomethyl." Ogawa Taigi. Winner of the Fourth International Advertising Photography Exhibition, 1933.

448. "Morinaga Chocolate." Fukuzawa Tomizō. Third-place winner in the Fourth International Advertising Photography Exhibition, 1933.

449. "Lion Tooth Paste." Takahashi Yoshio. Winner of the Third International Advertising Photography Exhibition, 1932.

450. "Shibaura Motors." Domon Ken. Poster, 1938.

451. "Great Tokyo Architecture Fair." Photographer unknown. Poster, 1935.

452. "Kaō Soap." Kimura Ihe-e. Newspaper advertisement, 1931.

453. "Datsun." Photographer unknown. Advertisement in *Nippon,* a magazine distributed abroad, 1935.

454. "Shinamoto Shoten" (textiles). Takamatsu Jinjirō. Advertisement in a magazine distributed abroad, 1941.

455. "Toyō Bōsuifu" (waterproof cloth). Fujimoto Shihachi. Advertisement in a magazine distributed abroad, 1941.

456. Light-bulb advertisement. Natori Yōnosuke. Advertisement in *Commerce Japan,* a magazine distributed abroad, 1941.

457. Composite photograph (14 x 6 feet) displayed at the Chicago Trade Fair. Photographs by Kimura Ihe-e and Koishi Kiyoshi; composition by Hara Hiroshi. 1938.

458. Composite photographs in a collection titled *Nippon,* designed to introduce Japan abroad. Nihon Kōbō (Japan Atelier). 1934.

459. Cover of *Manshū Gurafu* (Pictorial Manchuria). Photographer unknown. December 1940.

460. Spread in *Manshū Gurafu* (Pictorial Manchuria). Photographer unknown. June 1938.

461. Cover of *Gurafikku* (Graphic). Photographer unknown. July 1938.

462. Spread in *Shashin Shūhō* (Photo Weekly). Koishi Kiyoshi. August 1942.

463. Spread in *Front*. Photographer unknown. 1942.

464. Spread in *Asahi Gurafu* (Asahi Pictorial). Photographer unknown. October 30, 1940.

465. Prime Minister Tōjō Hideki. Kikuchi Sōzaburō. Cover of *Asahi Kamera* (Asahi Camera). February 1942.

466. An officer. Photographer unknown. Published in *Nippon-5,* edited by Natori Yōnosuke. 1932.

467. The emperor at a military review at the Yoyogi Parade Grounds, Tokyo. G. T. Sun. 1936.

468. The army flying school at Akeno, Ibaragi prefecture. Kikuchi Shunkichi. February 1944.

469. Wartime day-care service in Tokyo. Hayashi Tadahiko. 1942.

470. Care packages made by students of the Tokyo Second Public Girls High School to be sent to the front. The packages are arranged to read "To the Imperial Forces." Dōmei Press. July 19, 1937.

471. Labor service in farming by a student of Ichinose National School in Niigata prefecture. Yamada Eiji. *c.* 1942.

472. A female defense corps training with bamboo spears in preparation for the landing of United States forces in southern Kyūshū. Kikuchi Shunkichi. April 1945.

473. Labor service by female students: raking leaves to be used as fertilizer. Katō Kyōhei. 1941.

474. Young factory workers praying before a meal. Hayashi Tadahiko. 1943.

475. Elementary-school children in Tokyo jogging during physical-education class. Kikuchi Shunkichi. *c.* 1940.

476. Tank force exercising at the foot of Mount Fuji (a composite photograph to give the appearance of many tanks). Original photograph by Hamaya Hiroshi; composition by Tōhōsha company staff. Published in *Front*. 1942.

477. *Left:* a battle exercise above the Tokorozawa Airfield, photographed by Hamaya Hiroshi in 1942. *Right:* the same photograph with a falling P-38 fighter painted in, published in 1944 to boost morale. *Mainichi* newspaper. January 26, 1944.

478. "Fight to the Bitter End"—a composite photograph made from originals by Kanamaru Shigene. First displayed as a billboard in 1943.

479. China War: a skull among the weeds on a battlefield at Lotien, central China. Takada Masao. February 23, 1938.

480. China War: special naval combat troops landing against the enemy at Chiu Chiang on the shore of the Yangtze River. Hada Manzō. July 4, 1938.

481. China War: the attack on Canton. Photo by the press section of the South China Expeditionary Army. 1938.

482. China War: the Rape of Nanking. Fudō Kenji. December 1937.

483. China War: corpses of Chinese soldiers in Nanking immediately following the capture of the city. *Mainichi* newspaper. December 13, 1937.

484. China War: the Japanese army entering Ku-shin in the battle for Wuhan. *Asahi* newspaper. September 17, 1938.

485. China War: soldiers taking a brief rest during the Japanese advance through the Tai-hsing range in northern China. Iwamoto Shigeo. May 17, 1941.

486. China War: soldiers marching in the mud. *Asahi* newspaper. Photographer, place, and date unknown.

487. China War: interior of the Tientsin station immediately after the Japanese capture. The photograph is stamped "Censored." *Mainichi* newspaper. July 30, 1937.

488. China War: Chinese in the south being investigated by Japanese soldiers. *Mainichi* newspaper. January 15, 1940.

489. China War: Cheng Pen-hua, a twenty-four-year-old woman soldier captured in central China. *Mainichi* newspaper. April 1938.

490. China War: Chinese citizens apprehended and bound by the Japanese military police after the capture of Canton. Matsuo Kunizō. October 21, 1938.

491. China War: regular Chinese soldiers captured by the Takeshita unit of the navy land-combat forces in central China. The photograph is stamped "Censored." *Mainichi* newspaper. August 23, 1937.

492. China War: dead bodies floating in the water immediately after the fall of Lotien in central China. *Mainichi* newspaper. September 1937.

493. The Manchurian Incident: Sublieutenant Kurihara inspecting his sword after a battle with the Chinese forces in Manchuria. *Asahi* newspaper. March 2, 1932.

494. China War: Chinese residents of Nanchang in central China made homeless by the Japanese attack. Koyanagi Jiichi. March 29, 1939.

495. Pacific War: the attack on Pearl Harbor. Photographer unknown. December 7, 1941.

496. Pacific War: the battle of the Coral Sea. *Yomiuri* newspaper. May 1942.

497. Pacific War: the surrender of General Percival at Singapore. Kageyama Kōyō. February 15, 1942.

498. Pacific War: United States prisoners of war at the battle of Bataan in the Philippines. Miyauchi Jūzō. April 16, 1942.

499. An intellectual soldier from the Shizuoka Regiment who committed suicide with a bayonet during training. Yanagida Fumio. 1938.

500. Student enlistees. Photographer unknown. December 1943.

501. Manchurian youths at a physical examination for prospective conscripts. *Asahi* newspaper. 1941.

502 Female volunteer corps in Kokura preparing for the decisive battle in the homeland. Photographer unknown. 1944.

503. Bombardment of Osaka by B-29s. Yamagami Entarō. March 14, 1945.

504. Burned corpses collected in the streets of Yokohama after a carpet bombing with incendiary bombs. Bessho Yahachirō. May 29, 1945.

505. Charred bodies of a mother and child near Kikukawa Bridge in the Honjo district of Tokyo, following the air raid that turned Tokyo into a city of ashes and death. Ishikawa Kōyō. March 10, 1945.

506. "Heroic Air Commandoes," a suicide unit departing from Kengun Airfield in Kumamoto prefecture to attack air bases in Okinawa, which had been occupied by Allied forces. Unit members are facing in the direction of their native places and bidding farewell to their distant families. Koyanagi Jiichi. May 24, 1945.

507. Girl students seeing off kamikaze pilots at Chiran Airfield with flags and branches of cherry blossoms. Hayakawa Hiroshi. May 1945.

508. Atomic bomb, Hiroshima: applying oil to bomb victims' burns in the streets approximately three hours after the first atomic bomb was dropped. Matsushige Yoshito. August 6, 1945.

509. Atomic bomb, Hiroshima: a bomb victim at the Red Cross hospital four days after the bombing. Photographer unknown. August 10, 1945.

510. Atomic bomb, Nagasaki: scene near Uragami in Nagasaki on the day after the second atomic bomb was dropped. Yamahata Yōsuke. August 10, 1945.

511. Atomic bomb, Nagasaki: bomb victims sharing water from a bottle. Yamahata Yōsuke. August 10, 1945.

512. Atomic bomb, Nagasaki: charred corpse of a young boy, near the epicenter area. Yamahata Yōsuke. August 10, 1945.

513. Atomic bomb, Nagasaki: girl standing in a daze by a charred skull in the epicenter area on the day after the bomb was dropped. Yamahata Yōsuke. August 10, 1945.

514. Children at a home for war orphans in Itabashi, Tokyo. Kikuchi Shunkichi. 1946.